WHEN ALL ELSE FAILS

WHEN ALL ELSE FAILS

MICHAEL PULLEY

ARCHWAY
PUBLISHING

Archway Publishing books may be ordered through booksellers or by contacting:

Archway Publishing
1663 Liberty Drive
Bloomington, IN 47403
www.archwaypublishing.com
844-669-3957

ISBN: 978-1-6657-3813-2 (sc)
ISBN: 978-1-6657-3811-8 (hc)
ISBN: 978-1-6657-3812-5 (e)

Library of Congress Control Number: 2023901861

Print information available on the last page.

Archway Publishing rev. date: 06/07/2023

For Tonya and Alex — siblings, readers

ACKNOWLEDGMENTS

Thanks to the authors who wrote the scores of novels I read over many years, the books that gave me such pleasure and the inspiration to write my own. I am grateful for the college and university professors whose insights into reading novels guided me along the way. Notable thanks to those who lent encouragement as they scanned the manuscript, shepherding and nudging it through many stages: W.D. Blackmon, Jennifer Murvin, Pat Gariety, Greg Holman. Dottie Joslyn, Brian Shawver, Peter Longley, Deborah Cox. I also appreciate help from the literary agent Kevin O'Connor. Thanks to my longtime friend and colleague Richard Turner for his keen editorial eye. And special thanks to Jeani Thomson for her diligent and perceptive proofreading skills. And thanks to family members for their patience, allowing me the time and space to write.

CONTENTS

MOVING IN

CHAPTER 1

When their Lexus hit the first dorm parking lot pothole, Louis Lewis swore softly—an instinctive throwback. His outward swearing had ceased several months ago. While boxes and luggage rattled in the rear, Louis worried about damage to the suspension.

"Everything back there OK?" he asked. Then he hit the second pothole, this time on the other side. "Goddamn it," he said. Now *both* struts were probably fucked.

"Well, hooray for our side," said Arlette, still bouncing slightly. "Did you hear that, Michelle?"

Michelle sat in the back among boxes. "What?"

"Never mind," said Arlette, swallowing her smile.

"Sorry," Louis said. He hoped laughter was in his voice.

He let Arlette's comment go, just as he had so many things coming from his wife's mouth lately. *Help me, Jesus.* The thought twirled several times in his head while he looked for a parking spot not too far from the dorm. Pastor Ummell told him that short, silent invocations to Jesus could be just the ticket. And Louis Lewis was repeating the mantra in rapid blasts as the nerves in his fingertips calmed.

"This spot OK?" Louis said loudly. It would be a long walk carrying things across the lot and then upstairs into the dorm. Probably more stairs once inside.

"Oh, sure," said Arlette. "Perfect. The walk will do us good."

There she went again.

Michelle climbed out and stood by the driver's side. She inserted her head through the open window and kissed him on the cheek.

"Thanks," he said, and knew not to look at Arlette.

~

She knew immediately who the smiling man was. "Let me guess," she said. "You're Webster Boyd."

"Pleased to meet you, ma'am."

Arlette saw Webster Boyd doing what most men did when first meeting her: smiling too much, wanting to say something suave but holding back because he was captured, immobile. But this one was not as completely hamstrung as most. He was shifting into a gear she hated.

"So," said Arlette, deciding to back off and leave the prick alone for now, "you must do lots of things around here."

She wondered if Louis would write the guy a check on the spot. Webster Boyd, Redfern College's Resource Developer (she loved the euphemisms colleges used to describe their fundraisers), had been making financial overtures since Louis's new pastor alerted the Redfern administration that the Lewis family funds were ripe for picking. And even the college president—the pencil-dicked creep— had ingratiated himself to Louis. Louis's recent and sudden conversion to evangelical Christianity had caused any number of God-fearing jackals to circle their St. Louis estate. TV evangelists—all with right-wing political agendas—had made their pitches, appealing to Louis's well-known conservatism. But to Arlette's delight, Louis had risen above the onslaught. She loved her husband's newly found humility, his longing to set for himself a new path, even though he was having a hell of a time bending to his new way of life. The poor man didn't know one thing about what he wanted his life to be, other than something else. Still, she was happy for him, satisfied that he had turned some kind of corner. But she hated so much about it. These people! And somewhere in her depths, she might just hate

Louis too. How he'd handpicked this Christian college for Michelle. And of all things, the place had an outstanding tennis team, his ace in the hole. And then Michelle's acquiescence to her father.

"I do lots of things," said Webster Boyd. "Like moving in the most important assets of this college—our students. This day is always the highlight of the Redfern year."

Oh, he was a peach. He lifted two of Michelle's suitcases, gazing toward the steps leading into Hamilton Hall. But, as Arlette knew, he couldn't help himself. He looked back at Louis first—checking to see if the husband was watching—before giving what Arlette had seen so often from men: the quick glance, eyes meeting briefly, safe from anyone else's noticing. Asshole.

"This is very kind of you," Arlette said, watching him struggle up the steps.

∽

Michelle wasn't fooled when her father suggested she not request a fellow tennis player as a roommate. "Get to know a variety of folks," he said. "College is time for exploring." She knew most tennis players hadn't come to Redfern because of the Christian atmosphere, whatever that meant. They were there to play tennis for David Norman, hoping each year to make the NCAA Division I finals. No one had told Michelle (and certainly not her father) of the team's alienation from the rest of the campus, but on some shared DNA level, Michelle knew she and her father understood. Most of the time, she felt worldly in the same way she had observed her parents operating before her father's astounding, embarrassing conversion. "College is time for exploring" was his way of getting her to swim in his recently acquired pool of spiritual knowledge, a pool she watched him dog-paddle in. Did he know how ridiculous his swimming looked? She didn't mind dipping a toe in every now and then, and at times even found it comforting. She would never, however, look as stupid as he. She wouldn't allow it. There was always tennis.

Her roommate was Clovis Ginch. (Michelle had flinched from

the shock of the name. "Sounds like an infection," Arlette had whispered to her.) The two texted, did Instagram and Facebook, throughout the summer, first getting to know each other in wide strokes (*Clovis:* "I have a happy family ... firmly grounded in our church ... am easy to get to know." *Michelle*: "I'm an only child ... a little freaked about starting college ... looking forward to meeting you.") and then, in late July, more specifically (*Clovis*: "When you see me you'll understand why I wear one-piece bathing suits." *Michelle*: "I'll be busy with the tennis team and all that."). It seemed to Michelle that as summer passed, the distance between them widened. She had no way of knowing what Clovis was actually like—her emails and texts always bore so much happiness that Michelle thought they revealed shallowness; but by August, Michelle worried that Clovis's comments might represent some kind of authentic peace and self-assurance, the kind her father was desperately longing to find and trying to inflict on Michelle and her mother. She feared meeting Clovis.

Webster Boyd stood in the middle of the room, still holding the suitcases. "I guess we know which side of the room is yours," he told Michelle, who hadn't looked the man in the eye. She knew when her father was being worked.

One side of the room was fully arranged: pencils and pens, laptop, and tablet on the desk. Michelle's mother quietly slid Clovis's closet door open and peeked inside.

"I guess you can put those on the bed," Michelle told Webster Boyd.

"Your roommate's already been here," said Louis.

There stood her father, who hadn't carried anything up, making a statement that in his former life would probably have been sarcastic, but in his new life sounded only stupidly obvious. He looked lonely standing in her new room.

BEGINNINGS

Louis Lewis remembered exactly when he realized he was oddly named. Arlette Wainwright had brought it to his attention in the first grade (Louis's mother had held him back from kindergarten because "my boy would show up the others") after a few children had snickered when his name was called on the opening day. Leaning across the aisle, Arlette said, "Why are your names the same?"

Louis said, so all could hear, "My name is Louis Lewis."

Arlette must have been the only one to understand. She whispered, "Different words."

Others continued giggling.

The teacher, Mrs. Askins, tried to shush the class and failed. She must have detected a teachable moment because she slowly wrote on the board "Louis Lewis" so the most literate of the class could understand. At that instant, for some inexplicable reason, Louis decided to change his name. "Call me Ted."

"Your name here," Mrs. Askins pointed to the roster, "is Louis, not Ted."

"It's Ted."

"It's Louis," Mrs. Askins insisted.

"It's Ted," said Arlette, mysteriously coming to Louis's rescue.

A short verbal skirmish ensued between Louis and Mrs. Askins for his naming rights, only to be firmly resolved the next day when Louis's mother—standing a good six inches taller than Mrs. Askins—strode forthrightly into the classroom and pronounced to the first graders that her son was to be called Louis—L-o-u-i-s—and that Ted was a name entirely unsuited for the likes of her son. "And who on earth decided to call him 'Ted'?"

Arlette, in an act of unexplained face-saving on her and Louis's part, pointed to a shabbily dressed, bespectacled boy two rows over—who the day before, by the class's silent acclamation, had been appointed the class dumbbell—and said *he* told everyone to call Louis "Ted." Mrs. Askins, who was spinning helplessly within the force field of the tall Mrs. Lewis, didn't dare dispute the call. Louis was afraid to look at Arlette and the two women in front. His mother pointed to the boy two rows over. "Maybe *you* should carry the moniker. I anoint you 'Ted.'" She derisively made the sign of the cross and walked laughing from the room.

As years rolled on, Louis's sexual development did not keep pace with other boys his age. When his friends spoke knowingly of masturbation, Louis pretended to understand, even though he had no success after many tries. Maybe he was not holding his dick just right, perhaps he had not mastered the correct stroke, or—God forbid—perhaps he was incapable of producing the sought-after result. Yet Louis continued trying and did not worry because he *did* manage to get an erection several times a day; he surmised things would work out eventually. After all, didn't he almost nightly wake with stained sheets? His mother spoke to him of the spots and called the event, in a rare nod to decorum, "wetting the bed." Louis thought she actually believed he was producing urine instead of seminal fluid and was happy not to discuss such things with her until, in a startling encounter, his mother said to the fourteen-year-old, "What's Teddy been doing at night in bed?" She liked to call him "Teddy" at moments of mocking humiliation.

"I don't know," he said.

"You've been wetting the bed with some frequency, Teddy."

Louis had read up on sexual physiology as well as the psychological component. He had turned into an avid reader on the two seemingly unrelated subjects of sex and eighteenth-century ship building and decided, at last, to meet his mother on equal footing. "Nocturnal emissions," he said. "You can stop calling it 'wetting the bed.'"

The two lived in suburban St. Louis, Missouri. Mr. Lewis's death had left them with a large mortgage on a refurbished Victorian house in a gentrified neighborhood just off Forest Park. With no income to make payments, Mrs. Lewis unloaded the house at a sizable profit and moved herself and her son to suburban Webster Groves, where she rented a small, two-bedroom flat and took a job for an apartment management company, quickly working her way up to management, which allowed her to send Louis to DeSmet High School—run by Jesuits who took academic and sexual discipline seriously. He asked why he should attend a Catholic school.

"You need some reason to dismiss religion from your life, and listening to how silly the Jesuits are should do the job. No chance a child of my loins will fall for their bullshit. Besides, it'll get you into a good college." After only one year at DeSmet, the young boy had already sorted out church myth from fact, but was largely puzzled about sex.

"You don't masturbate?" his mother continued. She set her Marlboro in the ashtray. They were in the kitchen, and she was on her first bourbon of the evening.

He might as well come clean. "Mom, I can't masturbate. Nothing happens. I can't reach ejaculation." Here he was, actually speaking to her in a moment of honesty with an underlying plea for help.

"Dear, I know those damn Jesuits won't show you training films on the subject." She rose to refill her glass. The first three drinks of the evening were his favorite time around her. More than three addled her logic and stymied her quick wit, making her more caustic than necessary. "It takes a young lass to get the juices flowing," she said. He had never been forthcoming with his mother about his sexual fantasies because doing so would more than likely have set her off on one of her lectures, the likes of which he was beginning to dread and attempting to avoid (so why had he just fessed up about his masturbation problem? Stupid!). He'd be silent, and if he were lucky, she'd knock back more drinks and start rambling.

When she returned to the kitchen table with a larger-than-normal portion of booze, she lit another Marlboro off the stub burning in the ashtray and appeared to be hunkering down for an extended session.

"You haven't talked, my dear, about your sexuality."

He stared.

"Your bombshell about a deficit in the self-gratification department bears acting upon."

"Please, Mom. I'll work things out."

"Of course you will, dear, but no child as precocious as you should be sexually retarded at your age."

"Exactly what are you suggesting?" He was talking way too much.

"Back up a minute. Don't your wet dreams feel good?"

"Mom!"

"Of course they do, but let me tell you, nocturnal emissions are nothing like the real thing."

Silence and more silence would be his proper reaction here.

"You should be meeting girls. Why did I ever send you to that all-male, sexually repressed factory of a school?"

"We have mixers two or three times a semester." He wasn't going to let her think he couldn't attract girls.

"Next time you're in one of those mix-masters, grab you one and let 'er fly."

Was she really saying what he thought?

"I'm not talking about full-out sexual intercourse, son. Just some careful feeling around. You can take those moments to the sexual bank, and before long, Teddy, you'll be masturbating with the best."

Maybe Arlette Wainwright could help him out.

~

Arlette agreed.

After finishing eighth grade, she attended Ursuline Academy, a Catholic all female college prep school in St. Louis. Her wealthy parents placed her name on a waiting list one week after her birth, then followed proper politically liberal protocol by sending her to a public elementary school, hoping to foster tolerance for a broad social view; yet they reserved high school for the academic rigor at Ursuline Academy, social elitism notwithstanding. Both she and Louis stayed in friendly contact after he moved to Webster Groves—he'd changed schools after the third grade—and the two shared a distant affection and pleasant social interaction on school holidays. Her blonde hair, long thin legs, and perfectly configured breasts caught Louis's attention, making her, in his estimation, unreachable as anything but a friend. He knew nothing about how to act upon what he was seeing and was certain he would be unequipped to pursue such matters. Even while doing homework, he might suddenly look up and ponder in excruciating detail what lay beneath the cashmere sweater and, most importantly, the dark slacks Arlette had worn on their last meeting.

Her agreeing didn't completely surprise Louis because he had planned well, had allowed for several eventualities along the way. They met at a coffee shop in the Central West End; both had come by bus. The two nestled among the self-assured, urbane crowd.

Louis's long, delicate prelude about the institutionalized repression of their respective high schools established the proper tone and provided some laughs—both Jesuit brothers and Ursuline sisters were cut from the same ecclesiastical cloth, all advocating open confession of iniquities, but not willing to foster much open talk about sex except the standard "don't do it!" Louis slid into the crux of the matter:

"Arlette, you're probably more experienced in sex than I am."

"Probably. I've had a session or two with my neighbor's dogs and hamsters."

"Be serious."

"I'm a true virgin Catholic girl and can prove it."

"I'm not asking for that. Fornication is not intercourse." Her direct stare was igniting him. "Exploration," he said. "One friend to another."

"Only a little make-out? Listen, Louis. I can use the practice as much as you. *Servium.*"

"Huh?"

"The Ursuline motto. It's on the crest. *Servium.*"

Where the hell was she going with this?

"Since 1848 here in good old St. Louis, the sisters have been telling us that the Academy motto is our duty."

Her cup clinked gently onto the table, and Louis saw mischief in her eyes.

"It means," she said, 'I will serve.'"

An hour later in Arlette's bedroom, while her parents were gone, she began her tutorial. Louis's eyes watered as he lay on his back watching Arlette undress until she was naked.

"To make this work," she said, "you've got to watch *me* the whole time, not what I'm doing. OK?"

No more than a minute and twenty seconds after Arlette began, Louis took his eyes off her and watched his first ejaculation.

"Was that good?" asked Arlette.

Louis shivered and twitched. "Yeah," he muttered.

Arlette began dressing.

FIRST DAY AT REDFERN

"I suppose you're going to tell me it's better than sex," Arlette said. "You're comparing apples and oranges," said Louis. "Rules of logic don't allow for such comparisons. Sex and an abiding faith in Jesus Christ are hardly comparable."

"So if you were on a desert island," said Arlette, sipping her scotch, "would you rather hump me or go thump your Bible?"

"Phony baloney."

They were on the bed at the Super Eight—Towson, Indiana's only decent motel—discussing the day. Michelle wanted to arrange her room in Hamilton Hall by herself and meet Clovis Ginch alone, without her parents there. Louis and Arlette had offered to take Michelle and Clovis to dinner (Towson's best place was called Steak and Sea and was run by a couple of Greeks who, Louis learned from Webster Boyd, were probably up to no good), but Michelle insisted she wanted to be alone with Clovis on their first night. During dinner at Steak and Sea, Arlette ordered a drink, but Louis nixed the action immediately. "Not here," he said. "You know about the college's policy on drinking."

"We're not at the college," she said.

"Same thing."

Arlette drew a deep breath.

On the way back from dinner, Louis allowed a stop at a seedy liquor store for Arlette to buy a bottle of scotch. After Louis's conversion, he had tolerated Arlette's drinking at home but quashed it in public. There on the bed with the TV volume turned low, her scotch calmed and emboldened her as it always did before later sending her into either acquiescent depression or flailing anger. She never knew which might carry the day and, honestly, had grown tired of trying to understand.

"Sex or Jesus," she said. "Choose you this day whom you will serve."

She was merely being frisky and wouldn't mind having Louis fuck her out of the anger that would surely arrive in the next two drinks or so. Arlette supposed he was faking interest in the stupid TV (a reality show where a man and woman were arguing over something) because his jaw muscle was twitching the way it did when he tried to hold back the honest anger he used to express so clearly. She thought he had no means of cleansing himself these days. His new-found purity carried a big price.

"Sorry," she said. "I'm not playing fair."

"We're here and doing this for Michelle," he said, still watching TV. "Can't we just leave it at that?"

He pointed to the scotch bottle on the table to her right. "Drink up then pass out. You're always kinder the morning after."

She paused briefly, all playfulness gone. "Fuck you, Louis."

He was right. She *was* always better the morning after. But what chance did *he* have of ever getting better?

~

After Michelle's parents left, and after she had put her clothes away, made her bed, rearranged her desk a couple of times, and rifled through Clovis's clothes (she *was* a large girl), Michelle sat on her bed wanting to cry. She and the rest of the tennis team were not officially meeting for a couple of days. Her cell phone lay on the desk. She could call the Super Eight … but, no, she would not do that.

She put her cell phone into her large tennis bag (three rackets, four cans of balls, two pairs of shoes), changed into tennis shorts and shirt, and placed the room key in her shoe. She walked out the door carrying the bag and headed for the courts, hoping she wouldn't see anyone in the hallways. She plunged down the stairs and into the lobby where knots of girls stood talking and laughing. Someone may have said, "Come join us. You must be a freshman," but Michelle couldn't be sure. Maybe the blue Adidas bag slung on her shoulder would let them know she was bound for something else entirely, none of whatever they had to offer. She just would not let herself cry.

She walked down the long stairs, across the parking lot, through a tangle of sidewalks and buildings, and to the courts that welcomed her with their comforting green playing surfaces, high fences, and serene white lines designed to enclose and define the game she cherished. Rows of metal bleachers bordered the courts where people would watch her this year (she was the St. Louis County High School singles champion and the Missouri State runner-up) as she served, returned serve, laced crosscourt backhands, lifted lobs falling just within the back line. Would Clovis watch her?

At the far court (these courts were the envy of other major universities) one person was pounding a ball off the boards and another was watching. "Tough shot," the watching person said. Michelle knew the phrase. It was Coach Norman's favorite expression to describe a good shot. "Tough, tough," he yelled at the person slamming shots off the wall.

When her father arranged for Coach Norman to visit their house on his initial recruiting trip, Michelle reluctantly agreed; after all, what else could she do when her father insisted? Yet, the minute Coach Norman walked in the house, something snapped within her viscerally. Was it the "tennis" in him? His height? The dark hair? Thinking back on it—trying to sort through the startling, perhaps alarming, sensations—she couldn't dismiss the sheer sexuality he exuded. Not that she wanted to ravish him on the spot, but she recognized her bursting sexual energy. Why exactly? All the time he sat and talked, she realized she must have been smiling, her cheeks aching when he left. She wanted to tell Arlette but would have been embarrassed, even mortified and demeaned, to admit such a thing. She wondered if Arlette felt the same.

"Are you sure you want to go there?" Arlette asked after Michelle firmly pronounced her intention.

"Yes, I really do."

"OK."

"Don't you think Coach honestly wanted me to go?"

"Yes."

"I want so to go. And it has nothing to do with Dad this time."

When her family visited Redfern, Michelle thought she noticed Coach Norman's magnetic pull on Arlette, her mother saying little but nodding knowingly when he spoke. Mom liked him, too!

And there he was on the court, handsome as ever, coaching one of his players. Should she approach Coach Norman two days before the official team meeting? The tall boy (should she call males *boys* in college?) was no doubt an accomplished player, maybe even a senior. Would Coach Norman treat her like the no-name freshman she really was, or would he hold her in the same high regard he had in his recruiting visit at their home? That coach was a handsome dude. She put down the blue bag and watched from a safe distance.

"Oh, tough shot," said Coach Norman. "As tough as I've ever seen."

Coach David Norman was pretty sure it was Michelle Lewis. She had her mother's legs, and it was the way her long neck joined up with her shoulders that especially made her look like Arlette. He had recruited plenty of female players and never once entertained impure thoughts for a recruit's mother. Not that he hadn't been hot for plenty of women in his day and—thank you very much—nailed a few. It's just that he had managed to keep things on the up-and-up around recruits, and their mothers.

On his recruiting trip to the Lewis estate, Arlette had had a nip or two; he could smell it on her breath. While he and a few others employed at Redfern sneaked drinks at each other's houses (and even an occasional joint), he was especially attracted to the casual drinking Arlette must have been accustomed to at home. Would that hotshot husband of hers also drink? Probably. How could anyone with his connections and money *not* drink? The college was going after the father/husband's money full bore, and Coach Norman had played along like a good boy, no stranger to working his male charm on women. And he could parley some fundraising success into tennis money since the damned college was nuts over collecting money from any source. "Grubbing" he called it. Landing Michelle was the first step, which wouldn't hurt his program any, even though she would probably be practice fodder for a year or two. Coach had done *his* job. And it might get the college president slightly off his back. The two had never been the best of buddies, but Coach Norman fully understood the head guy might wield ugly authoritarian power if needed. Since money drove the Redfern ship, Norman recognized a captain's overriding power and control. But this attraction to Arlette Lewis was giving him a happy/queasy feeling, the likes of which he hadn't experienced since the last married woman he'd banged. He was hoping to have sworn off that stuff.

The poor kid was just standing there. Without lifting his head high enough for her to see, he saw she was watching him and Abe. Oh, what the hell? He gave her a big wave.

"Michelle Lewis?" he yelled.

She responded too quickly. "Hello, Coach."

"Come join us."

Abe stopped his swings and began picking up balls, glancing at Michelle occasionally as she walked toward them. Not until she arrived did he give her his full attention.

"Michelle," he said, "I'd like you to meet Abe."

Abe wiped his sweaty hands on his shorts and greeted Michelle with a handshake. Coach Norman thought it was a bit too formal.

"Nice meeting you," Abe said.

"You too," stammered Michelle.

"Abe was our number one men's single player last year. You may have heard he took third last season at nationals."

Michelle's bag hung loosely on her shoulder, and Coach watched her body shrink two inches, causing the bag to slide off and thud to the ground. He laughed, glad to see the recruit's body language reacting so impressively to Abe's reputation and status. "Abe's got a promising season ahead. Our whole team does."

Michelle fumbled with her bag.

"Want to hit a few?" said Abe. He was dribbling a ball off the ground with his racket.

"On the wall?" asked Michelle.

"For starters."

"Michelle comes to us from St. Louis," said Coach Norman, sizing up what he was seeing.

"Algeria," said Abe. "Name's Abdul al-Fiasa. They call me Abe here. Much shorter."

Michelle averted her eyes while Abe's bore into her. Coach was always pleased to notice how Abdul's swarthy skin accentuated the paleness of even the most suntanned Caucasian's and lent him a special authority, even mastery, over whomever he encountered. The dark hair on his arms and legs bespoke a dominance, on and off the court, that Norman didn't realize would hold such sway over people. The handsomeness of this North African! And then that French accent. Abe would humble any recruit.

"I'll be over there," said Abe, pointing to the adjoining court, "when you're loose and ready."

"It'll be good practice, unofficially," Coach told Michelle. "Actually I'm not supposed to be with the team yet. You won't squeal to the NCAA will you?" He winked conspiratorially.

"You sure it's OK?"

"I'm leaving. See you in a couple of days. In the meantime, you can see what Redfern tennis is all about."

Michelle was windmilling her arms, beginning stretches.

"By the way, did you have a good trip from St. Louis?" asked Norman. "I imagine you and your parents just arrived."

"Yeah. They're leaving in a couple of days."

"Tell them hello. Unless I see them to say hi myself. I'll be hanging around the courts, unofficially, in case you want to bring them by."

"Yeah, might just do that."

He walked away but watched the courts from a distance. Abe dribbled balls, glancing at Michelle warming up.

Coach David Norman's career as a tennis coach began innocently and accidentally. His MA in art history hardly qualified him to become a nationally established tennis coach, yet his athletic ability and sudden interest in playing tennis led him to become a "sponsor" of a half-assed tennis club at Redfern and then coach of a team first established in the collegiate NAIA ranks. Through his sparkling eyes, personality, and uncanny ties to foreign "Christian" recruiting, his team eventually moved into NCAA Division I. His Redfern coaching success amazed even the most athletically skeptical at the college and pricked up the ears of an administration hoping to cash in on the national recognition. Coach Norman managed to build his own private fraternity of bright, academically talented players who knew how to shut up and ignore what they recognized as the small-mindedness of the college. They were there for tennis.

Born and bred in South Boston, David Norman grew up a non-Catholic, and through both parental precept and personal observation, learned to disdain the "Romans" and their grip on most of Boston. His parents were intelligent and well-read. (An older sister married a bar owner and turned into the kind of "southie" they hoped their son would *not* be.) A small college in the Midwest that harbored anti-Catholic feelings appealed to him, and since Redfern College had no denominational name in its title to sully its legitimacy in others' eyes, his parents sent him on his way to the Towson, Indiana, school. His humble Boston upbringing landed him the ironic nickname of "Back Bay," which he fostered by explaining to the Midwesterners that Back Bay in Boston is the rich, snobby area. The name stuck. After getting a BS in history at Redfern, he earned an MA in art history at Indiana University; then he returned to Redfern to become the first faculty member of a newly formed art department, with a noticeable absence of nude models in the painting and drawing studios. Besides coaching, he taught two art classes to keep his employment looking on the up-and-up.

Leaving Abe and Michelle on the courts, he walked back to his field house office (he had two offices, the other in the academic building), where he had a clear view of his courts so he could watch Abe and Michelle. Shouldn't he have shunned her as he usually did most recruits? Yet ...

The phone startled him. "This is Louis Lewis, Michelle's father. Calling to say we arrived on campus today. Michelle is moved in, and her mother and I are staying in town for a day or two—nice chance to get away for a while—and we're wondering if you and your wife would like to have dinner with us tomorrow night. Our treat. Michelle wants to spend time with her roommate, so her mother and I would be delighted to share a meal with you."

Back Bay reckoned audaciousness and a sense of entitlement must run in the family: Michelle showing up on the courts unannounced, and Papa assuming he had some kind of direct connection to the tennis program. Once having charmed the family, Back Bay needed to cut ties. Still ... He walked the phone to his window. Abe and Michelle had stopped hitting balls. They were sitting next to each other on the bleachers.

"Nice of you to ask," said Back Bay. "Just so happens the wife and I have made other plans for the evening. But so kind of you. Did you have a good trip from St. Louis?"

While Louis Lewis expounded, Back Bay stole some time to think. *Court repairs; three or four new courts would be nice; an endowed tennis scholarship fund; recruiting angles in the St. Louis area. Arlette Lewis.* Back Bay's wife had never been a part of his efforts, except for hosting and cooking meals for the foreign players at holidays, so why bring her into the picture now? *Arlette Lewis.*

"... so many people demand my time, so we thought Towson would be a delightful respite for a couple of days ..."

Leave Webster Boyd out of this. My chance to hustle some money for my own program. And currying more favor with the goddamned president wouldn't hurt. Arlette Lewis.

"... Michelle is excited about playing for you ..."

Those two are still just sitting on the bleachers. Put the kibosh on any budding relationship. Not good for the team.

"... we hope you don't mind her rooming with someone not on the team. It's just that we thought she should get a broad perspective on the excellent Christian atmosphere ..."

"I'd enjoy visiting with you and your wife," said Back Bay. "It will have to be in my field house office late tomorrow afternoon."

"Not for dinner at the Steak and Sea?"

Back Bay scrolled NCAA rules. Nothing illegal he knew of, and if some minor technicality was violated, wouldn't be the first time. "That would be fine," said Back Bay. "I'll rearrange a few things. Probably be just me."

"Arlette and I will be honored. Shall we say tomorrow night at six thirty?"

"I'll be there. And thank you very much," said Back Bay.

Arlette Lewis.

∼

"I probably should go," Abe finally said.

Michelle hadn't even worked up a sweat. She and Abe had spent most of the time sitting and talking.

"Me, too," Michelle said.

Abe said he lived in a dorm on the opposite side of the campus from Hamilton Hall but would walk her to Hamilton.

"I don't know if guys are allowed in our dorm," she said.

"Only in the lobby. This *place*," he said, shaking his head and sweeping his arm campus-wide. "Even my parents in Algeria could visit each other in their dorm rooms. My mother let it slip once that I was conceived there."

"In a dorm?"

"Yes. Before they were married. Of course, they married immediately. No one knew."

Michelle was nearly afraid to look at Abe. Their entire conversation on the bleachers had been about the tennis team. Never once did he mention how *she* might fit in. She had looked him in the eye there, truly interested in what he said, forgetting for short stretches what an overpoweringly striking guy he was. This *guy* was a *man*. Why was he paying her so much attention, going into such detail? And then suddenly she couldn't hear a word he was saying. Those large hands, his white socks just above his ankles, the muscular calves higher up. Higher still, what must be beneath those shorts? For long moments she was circling this man, not understanding where she was.

He had mentioned dorm rooms and conceptions. His parents had fucked him into existence in a dorm, maybe the kind of room where she would spend her first night in college. If she were at another college, would she fuck a man like Abe in her room on the first night?

He walked with her up the long stairs into Hamilton Hall. The groups of girls were still clustered there in the lobby, but this time Michelle thought they looked at her more closely. Why did they stop their yammering? Were they that interested in her? Were they accusing her of something? But it was Abe. They were looking at Abdul al-Fiasa, the white of his shorts contrasting with his nut brown skin. He touched her shoulder.

"Glad we got to meet," he said. The French accent seemed to echo around the lobby.

Didn't he notice how quiet the lobby became? Was he used to such a reaction?

"See you," she said, attempting nonchalance.

"I live in McKensey Hall," he said. "Look me up."

He was gone. Michelle didn't know how long she stood there. She turned quickly and climbed the stairs to her room.

As she removed her shoe outside the door to retrieve her key, she thought she heard someone stirring inside. She slowly twisted the knob on the unlocked door and stood startled at what was before her.

"You must be Michelle."

Before Michelle could put down her shoe, she was engulfed in Clovis Ginch, whose arms were cinched around the thin Michelle, nearly lifting her off the floor. Clovis's large breasts mashed into Michelle's white tennis shirt. Their mouths nearly touched, yet Michelle had to lift her head slightly to see all of Clovis. She was even taller than the five foot eight Michelle. And Clovis's breath. *What* had she been eating?

"Welcome to our new world!" gushed Clovis, still hugging Michelle. As she released her, Michelle's shoe fell to the floor, the key tinkling on the terrazzo surface. Clovis held her at arm's length, like a grandmother inspecting a growing child she hadn't seen in months. "Let's look at you. You're so pretty!"

"Clovis," is all Michelle could manage.

"You got one shoe on and one shoe off," said Clovis, pointing to the shoe on the floor.

"My tennis bag is out in the hall," said Michelle. "I'll get it."

"No such thing," said Clovis. "*I'll* carry it in for you."

Clovis, wearing a mid-calf dress that Michelle recognized from her earlier closet inspection, darted through the door. Quick on her feet for such a big one.

"Oooh," said Clovis, slamming the door. "Adidas. Nice."

"Thanks."

"Must have been practicing with the tennis team already. Here." She handed the bag to Michelle. "You know where you want to put this. Your side of the room is arranged so cool. Snacks." She pointed to a large bag of chips on her desk. "Care for some? Barbeque flavored."

"No, thanks."

"It's so nice to finally meet you." Clovis cocked her head, looking at the chips. "It really is."

Michelle thought Clovis was starting to cry. "Are you OK?" asked Michelle.

"Yeah, yeah, of course. It's just that I've been waiting so long to see you. Tears of joy."

Michelle walked to Clovis and put her hand on her shoulder. What else could she do?

They compared schedules and discovered they had a class together (Advanced English Composition), causing Clovis, again, to cry, and Michelle, again, to console her.

"These really *are* tears of joy," said Clovis.

Michelle knew they were not.

Clovis appeared to be a smart girl, taking classes students could enter only with high placement scores or advanced prerequisites in high school.

"Where did you go to high school?" Michelle asked.

"Wadsworth Christian Academy. In Ohio."

"I see."

"You?"

"Ursuline Academy. St. Louis. My mom went there, too.'

"A Christian school?" asked Clovis.

"You could say that. College prep."

"So was it Christian?"

"Yeah. Catholic to the gills. All-girls school."

"Wow." Clovis reached for the chips, but only crumbs remained. She emptied them into her mouth from the bag. "Why did you come to Redfern?"

"Tennis and my dad. He thinks Redfern will be good for me. Also, I think the college president might be after Dad's money." Should she have said that?

"Does the admissions office know you're Catholic?"

"I'm not, really. But I guess you could say I lean that way. The people here probably thought Ursuline Academy was like Wadsworth Christian Academy."

Clovis slapped the desk and laughed. "Were you taught by nuns?"

"Yup."

"Nuns weren't allowed within a hundred yards of Wadsworth." She winked at Michelle. "That's a joke, of course." She pulled another bag of chips from a drawer.

Clovis seemed to be a good sport. "There's something else about my dad," said Michelle. "He's a believer, like you." She pointed to a well-worn Bible on Clovis's desk. "A new convert who reads from the Bible all the time. He's a good father, and I love him. But my mom and I don't really understand all of what he says he believes."

Had she said too much?

Clovis grabbed her Bible and walked to Michelle, chips in the other hand. "Before you know it," said Clovis, "you'll be searching the scriptures like your dad. Redfern is just the place for you."

"I hope so," said Michelle.

"Here," said Clovis, handing the chips to Michelle. "Let's have a snack before we begin."

"Begin what?"

"Searching the scriptures. For the truth."

Michelle opened the new bag. It was nacho flavored.

GOOD FOR THOUSANDS OF DINNERS

The morning of the second day (after a late night discussion with Clovis about religion) Michelle phoned the Super Eight, waking her mother, who had morphed into a cheery and clear-headed human after a night of drinking. (She and Louis engaged in frenzied and tense sex the night before; the memory didn't occur to her until well into her conversation with Michelle.) Louis was out getting coffee and rolls.

"Your father has invited Coach Norman to dinner tonight. Better than the president, who's been riding him for a meeting."

"God, Mom, why can't Dad leave things alone?"

"You're asking him to change? Come now, sweet thing."

"I'm asking him to leave me alone."

"He should be back soon. Want to try to change his mind?"

"No."

"That's my baby. Give in like the rest of us."

Arlette, still naked from the night's sex, was talking on her cell phone and tidying up the bed. She laughed aloud and fell backward on the bed, phone still at her ear.

"What's wrong?" asked Michelle.

"You'll never guess what I'm doing. I'm making the bed."

"In a motel?"

"Is there a chance I'm losing my mind?"

"Mom, stop."

"Making the bed or losing my mind?"

Silence. Arlette thought Michelle might be pondering the choices.

"Michelle?" asked Arlette. "You still there?"

"Why don't I bring Clovis to dinner?"

"I almost forgot about her. You two getting on all right?"

"She's a little weird, Mom."

"Is she there now?"

"No. She went to breakfast. I'm not hungry. Classes don't begin for two days, but we've got mixers, chapel services, barbeques, intramurals, stuff like that. I've got to get Clovis out of this room, or she'll hang here forever."

"Are you presiding over her?"

"She's a lot like Dad. I kind of like her."

"Is that a reason to like someone?"

When Michelle thought her mother was attacking her father unduly, she bristled inwardly but rarely went on the attack herself. Instead, the anger lay huddled in her gut and rose achingly to her throat. Often she couldn't speak, the ball of anger plugging up the words.

"Clovis makes some sense," said Michelle.

"Everyone makes *some* sense, dear."

"About the Bible and stuff."

Just where the hell was this kid going? The child was succumbing right before Arlette's eyes. Where was that scotch? Did she drink it all last night?

"Dear, go play some tennis. Clear your head."

"All I'm saying, Mom, is that even though Clovis is strange, she makes some sense. Can we drop it?"

"Love to."

"So tell Dad I'll be bringing Clovis to dinner tonight. Pick us up?"

"I'll call you back about the time—when His Majesty decides. But I can already tell you he won't like this. Might want to prepare yourself."

Michelle ended the call before picking up the campus directory. She wasn't sure how to spell Abe's last name. The listing for McKensey Hall should work.

~

The Lexus pulled into the Hamilton Hall parking lot at precisely 5:58 p.m. because Louis had said he would pick up Michelle and Clovis at six o'clock, no later, to give himself enough time to be at Steak and Sea by six fifteen so he could locate a table for five (the place did not take reservations) by six thirty, the time he had told Coach Norman to meet there. Timing was always of the essence. "You and Clovis be ready outside the dorm by the stairs," he told Michelle.

Earlier at the motel, Arlette told Louis, "Don't expect much from Clovis Ginch."

"Why's that?"

"Michelle says she's weird."

At moments like these, Louis trusted Arlette—her direct view of things and even her sharp tongue. He saw much of his former self in her. Often he would run his past behaviors though his mind, even picture how he'd looked to others—stand outside himself in those former times, noticing his expressions back when he was the consummate asshole. His mannerisms—not just his comments—must have revealed much to others. But was he *all* bad in those days? Trying to figure it out was tiring. Of late, he had been dwelling on the positives of his preconversion self—an effort to cull the wheat from the chaff—to establish some kind of matrix at which he could glance quickly and see what of the positive he could place into the present, taking the best of his past and eliminating the bad. He was a rational man. Order in all things. He wanted to improve—and would. Being a better man motivated him. An all new drive! He would listen to Arlette because he owed her so much, this woman who would, in time, come to appreciate her new-and-improved Louis.

The parking lot was more crowded than the day before. He reached for Arlette's hand, squeezing it slightly. "I'm happy for Michelle," he said. Arlette squeezed back. Even in her silence she was standing firm as a wife and mother. "Thanks you, Jesus," Louis whispered to himself.

"What?"

"Just happy," said Louis.

Arlette withdrew her hand.

Lots of people were standing on the stairs, most not moving. Some kind of rally? Then he saw a large canopy just beyond the stairs, smoke circling it and drifting into the crowd.

"Looks like a cook out," said Arlette. "How fun."

Students standing in the parking lot blocked Louis's movement. He honked.

"Jesus Christ," said Arlette. "Why'd you do that? Can't you see they've blocked off the lot?"

He wasn't sure why he honked. People turned to look, smiling kids holding paper plates. Some waved inward into the gathering, apparently a friendly gesture for Louis and Arlette to join in the fun. Music blasted from speakers on tripods.

"Please don't curse," said Louis. He wished he were at the Steak and Sea.

"Now what?"

"We find Michelle and Clovis."

"Wouldn't you think they'd rather stay here?"

"We're going to the Steak and Sea." Louis looked at his watch.

"Heard you honking," said a familiar voice to Louis's left.

Michelle leaned in through the lowered window. "Hi, Dad and Mom." She kissed Louis on the cheek. "It's a Hamilton Hall mixer. Clovis and I met tons of people. But we saved our appetites for dinner with you."

"Where's Clovis?" asked Arlette.

"Over there with Abe."

"Who's Abe?" asked Louis.

"A new friend. Can he come to dinner with us, too?"

Louis thought of the table for five. Another person would foul up the original plan.

"Of course he can, sweetie," said Arlette.

A few people were flowing in behind the Lexus. "How do we get out of here?" asked Louis.

"Back up and kill one or two," said Arlette. "That should send a clear message."

Michelle was smiling, the happiest Louis had seen her in several days. "Maybe you can honk your way out," Michelle said.

He looked at his watch again.

"I'll get Clovis and Abe," said Michelle. "We'll meet you on the street side of the dorm. Love you."

She was gone.

Arlette reached for Louis's hand as he turned his head after shifting into reverse. "Let's have a good time tonight, dear," she said.

"If I can ever get out of the parking lot."

People moved out of the way as he backed up. He shouldn't let such minor annoyances trouble him so. Who was this Abe? "You think Michelle has already found a boyfriend?" he asked.

"Jumping to conclusions, Father?"

"No, damn it. I'm not."

The street side of the dorm was free of students, only shrubs and a manicured lawn. The brick front of the dorm and well-ordered landscaping calmed Louis. He looked at the short stairs leading into an entryway with "Hamilton Hall" etched into the lintel. At least the wait would be more peaceful out here.

Michelle emerged first. Then a large girl followed. The two walked down the stairs. Maybe this Abe character had decided to stay. Louis could at least hope.

"Dad and Mom, this is Clovis. My roommate."

Greetings all around. Not exactly what Louis thought Michelle's first roommate would look like.

"Climb in," said Arlette.

"Don't leave yet, Dad. Abe's not here. He's coming."

In the next instant, Louis watched a tall man walk down the stairs and toward the car. A Black man was getting in Louis's car!

"This is Abe," said Michelle.

"Very nice of you to join us," said Arlette, too quickly to suit Louis.

"Yes," said Louis. The two shook hands, Louis's nearly lost in Abe's.

"Thanks for inviting me," said Abe, in some kind of accent.

Well, thought Louis, we *didn't* invite you.

~

Here was the only decent restaurant in town, and it didn't take reservations, so, of course, the Lewis party had to wait … and wait. Instead of passing the time in the bar—which he and Arlette had always enjoyed in a previous life—the group huddled outside around a metal bench. Arlette was keeping the conversation moving with the girls. Louis and Abe stood looking into the women's happy group. Clovis was a talker and fit right in. A good portion of her hung over the end of the bench.

The wait wasn't helping a thing. And where was Coach Norman? Louis never considered the team might have Black players, let alone his daughter immediately buddying up with one, and here Louis was standing with him, trying to figure how to make the all-important preemptive strike to establish dominance. Fortunately on the drive over with the kid in the back, Louis had been out of range of any first engagement, but Coach's late arrival was forcing the issue. Louis hated sports and particularly jocks (tennis and Michelle, of course, were notable exceptions). Even in his dating years with Arlette, he had abided her sports talk only to a point and shifted the subject whenever possible. In marriage, however, he could pretty much direct any conversation he wanted.

"We would have loved to take you and Clovis to a top-notch restaurant, but I guess this is all Towson has to offer."

"Seems a good place to me," said Abe. "I've never been here. I usually eat dorm food."

Good start. "If you're ever in St. Louis, look us up. You name it. Greek, Italian, French, whatever. We'll show you some restaurants."

The kid didn't look exactly Black. The mouth. And his hair didn't kink like your usual Black guy.

"I appreciate being here," said Abe.

Louis was happy to have come in strong initially. A little flattery couldn't hurt. "I imagine with your height, you're powerful on the court, especially with your serve. A high, sweeping reverse kick?" Louis had schooled himself in tennis enough to know what was what.

"My serve always needs work. I'm messing around with two or three different ones."

There was another thing about this boy. He didn't talk Black. And that accent indicated some kind of breeding Louis wasn't acquainted with.

"Where did you play your high school tennis?"

"Algiers. I'm from Algeria."

"In North Africa," said Louis, maintaining himself.

"Correct."

Would Redfern actually recruit a Muslim? Maybe he was a convert to Christianity. Then again, maybe he *was* a Muslim.

"My name is Abdul al-Fiasa. They call me Abe here. Shorter."

Images of the World Trade Center towers collapsing flashed in Louis's head. An Arab at Redfern? Michelle with an Arab?

"I played tennis at an American high school in Algiers and wanted to attend college in America. Coach Norman has lots of contacts. I heard about Redfern, and here I am."

"I see."

"My parents, they work hard, but money isn't easy there. When they heard about Coach Norman, who wants me to come, they wanted me to go. He came all the way to Algeria. They want me to have the opportunities they didn't. They like him very much."

Who could believe all that? Something not right there. "You speak English very well," said Louis.

"Thank you. Do you speak any French?"

"French?"

"That's my native tongue."

The boy was boring into Louis. Was that an insulting smirk? Who could tell what was on an Algerian's mind?

"No," said Louis. "Only English."

Where was Coach Norman?

Louis glanced at the door of the Steak and Sea where people stood waiting to enter. When he looked back, Abdul al-Fiasa's dark eyes tunneled straight into his before looking up. "Here comes Coach Norman, Mr. Lewis," said Abe.

A smiling Back Bay walked toward them.

～

Back Bay pushed his way through the crowd blocking the door. He didn't see the Lewises anywhere. They probably were not in the bar, but he checked there anyway. Outside, he caught a glimpse of who he thought was Louis Lewis (he didn't see Arlette) standing by ... was that Abe?

"Good to see you," said Back Bay, shaking hands. Louis looked like he'd just taken a bite out of a shit sandwich.

"You're finally here," said Louis.

What was wrong with this guy? "Maybe I'm a bit late."

"We're waiting for our table," Louis said, blankly.

"What brings *you* out?" Back Bay asked Abe.

"Michelle does," Abe said, pointing to a bench. There were Michelle and Arlette, both smiling up at him.

"Hello," said Michelle. "Hope it's OK that I came along."

"Certainly," he finally said. He and Arlette's eyes locked full on. "Good to see you, Mrs. Lewis."

"And you," she said.

Back Bay looked quickly at Louis before latching back on to Arlette; she was still with him. She said, "And this is Clovis Ginch, Michelle's roommate."

So this was who old man Lewis was so adamant about Michelle rooming with, keeping her off the tennis wing of McKensey Hall. "Glad you could join us." What was this family trying to pull by bringing all these people?

The burden of conversation appeared to lie with Back Bay. Louis was staring off while Arlette, Michelle, Abe, and the fat girl were looking at him. Seize the opportunity.

He swept his arm toward the crowd. "Pretty packed tonight. Good place to eat. I come here often."

"What's good here?" asked Arlette.

As Back Bay expounded, Arlette's smile never waned, nor did she seem to lack interest in the minutiae of the Steak and Sea menu. Louis was still staring off (actually, Back Bay noticed, more at Abe), and Michelle and Clovis had started a conversation. Drawing Louis in seemed proper at this point, but when he began, the hostess shouted, "Lewis, party of six."

"Come on," said Louis, as though he were a pissed-off camp counselor.

The five followed like obedient children. Arlette lagged to the rear with Back Bay, and they entered Steak and Sea together, well behind the other four.

Good table. Back Bay sat opposite Arlette and Louis. "Order whatever you want," said Louis, suddenly transformed into the gregarious and just-shy-of-asshole guy that Back Bay had remembered. What had been up with his silence outside? There wasn't a snowball's chance Back Bay could work Louis now, or even Arlette for that matter. Louis appeared to be making a point of engaging everyone in the conversation, especially Abe—maybe Abe too much.

Then Louis homed in on Back Bay's recruiting. "How did you find him?"

Everyone listened carefully, even Clovis, as Back Bay went over how he'd discovered Abe; how Abe's parents wanted their son to come to America, were thrilled for the opportunities here. About Abe's excellent command of English. How Back Bay had talked by phone with Abe's coaches, and their initial reluctance to trust an American recruiter. Many phone conversations. Back Bay's trip to Algeria. And then Abe's arrival on campus. His immediate dominance; his fine academic record.

Was he laying it on too much, as though he were trying to hide something about Abe's past—or present? One thing was sure. Abe's Islamic devotion would *never* reveal itself. Only Back Bay knew, and that was only after he had seen the lad—hiding behind an abandoned maintenance building at dusk—repeatedly bowing toward Mecca, praying. The next day, Back Bay confronted Abe, who mourned by hiding his face and admitting he had falsified his Redfern application by listing his religion as Christian and naming an actual Algiers Christian temple as his "home church." That day, the two of them made a pact never to reveal Abdul al-Fiasa's deep religious constancy and his shame in admitting fidelity to Christianity. The Qur'an lay at the bottom of a drawer in Back Bay's field-house office, covered by old files. He read from it often, as often as he ever had the Bible.

"So," continued Louis, "a Christian college like Redfern is a fine place for an Algerian to end up. Right?"

Louis's happy enthusiasm in interrogating Abe made Back Bay want to stick a fork in Louis's neck.

"Yes it is," said Abe. "I'm happy to be here."

"The Christian life is by far the best," said Louis. Now he was looking squarely at Abe and expecting a response. Arlette and Michelle were looking at the tablecloth, but Clovis, with wide eyes, was looking straight at Abe.

Then Louis's cell phone went off.

"Yes?"

All at the table held silence as though Abe might be phoning in his response to Louis.

Louis blanched. His free hand fell onto the table.

"What?" said Arlette.

"We're coming home," he said into the phone, ending the call.

"Daddy?" said Michelle, a plea for news.

"Our church in St. Louis has been blown up."

"Blown up?" said Arlette.

"Some people were injured. No one killed."

"Jesus God," said Arlette.

Clovis spoke next. "Let's pray."

"Oh, no need," said Arlette, dismissing Clovis with a wave of the hand. "It's too fucking late now."

Clovis lifted her eyebrows, apparently too bewildered to speak. Michelle, Abe, and Back Bay looked at each other. Arlette led the nearly catatonic Louis toward the door.

"Wait," she said, as she reached into Louis's back pocket and pulled out his wallet. She tossed a stack of bills at Back Bay. "Pay with this. He's good for thousands of dinners like this."

The money landed at Back Bay's feet.

REMEMBRANCE OF THINGS PAST

Louis's mother had always encouraged him to make money and be damned competitive about it. He got a fine start at DeSmet High School by excelling in debate and winning local, state, and national competitions. The Jesuits loved the way he combined calm rationality with a full-steam-ahead spirit. He lay waste his competitors; the bloodier the battlefield the better. Destroying as competitive sport.

His mother never attended his debate tournaments but leaped into the fray only after the fact, when at their kitchen table Louis would recount his incisive blows into his opponents' logical fallacies, how he would impale their logic with his swift and sure rejoinders, leaving them helpless. His mother laughed to hear how her son could humiliate the best.

But with his mother, he could not muster the aggression he imparted on the debate circuit. Going toe-to-toe with her, he might as well have been the "Teddy" of old—simpering, looking for praise yet feeling unworthy when getting it.

"Give 'em hell," she would say.

The money chase came easily. First, in college (St. Louis University, the Jesuits again) he sold life insurance policies to classmates, and in a scheme that he kept silent from his insurance higher-ups, he recruited fellow students to hawk policies, which was overtly illegal, but all profited handsomely. To this venture his mother shouted, "Bravo!" No need to stay in college. What good would it do?

Onward. District manager. No more peddling policies. He *managed*. Money flowed, and he offered much of it to his mother, but she declined. "Just let me watch," she said, as she poured a drink and lit another Marlboro. Louis loved a happy mom. She was laughing more, a sure sign of well-being.

After insurance success, enter the season of real estate adventures. He bought up small tracts of land in south St. Louis beside bungalows where generations of German descendants had grown beets and kohlrabi in their gardens. They were amazed at how they could sell their next-door plots and have cute little houses built there. Louis always guaranteed the sellers' protection from unwanted renters, namely north St. Louis Black folks who would "break" the neighborhood faster than you could say "urban renewal." After a few years of small potatoes development, he began buying up dilapidated houses, razing them and building convenience stores, then small strip malls with stylish fronts and run-of-the-mill businesses.

Marriage came. Arlette climbed on board as his development business pushed into west St. Louis County where Louis formed a cadre of investors—all carefully selected to be beneath his financial worth yet hungry to make much more—that bankrolled the bulldozing of much earth where high-rise office buildings later sprouted. Then he developed large complexes full of stores, condos, entertainment venues, and restaurants, with plenty of fountains and green plants. Moving further west into St. Charles County, a golf course materialized. Arlette stood up front with Louis as he made and formed relationships with contractors. She was a sight to behold, and Louis loved trotting her out where she wheedled and dazzled—her charm sparkled like freshly minted coins.

Louis needed her, and, he could certainly tell, she needed him. He liked to say they created a synergy. Never once did Arlette ask about the financial underpinnings or seek to know from whence came the capital.

He loved the freedom of making the money decisions (oh, he gave her free rein on architectural choices and amenities), but at times, actually wondered if their empire would stand firmer with *her* mind in the money, too. No, it would not, his heart told him. And so did his mother.

His mother insisted on knowing Louis's business. "Down to the last jot and tittle," she said, quoting from the Bible, a book she claimed to know nothing about. In their times alone, which were many, Louis explained the complicated workings of real estate development.

Somewhere within him, he understood his motivations for power, but those dark incentives revealed themselves only occasionally when he wanted to please his mother, the same person who often shamed him. Yet he was certain, most of the time, she loved him; but when he doubted, she would be right there reinforcing his desire for control. He'd happily double down on his stirrings to overpower whatever people or circumstances stood in his way. His few and transitory lucid moments of self-awareness usually frightened him, and then he would return to the cycle his mother established so cleanly and clearly.

"Tell me about all the Byzantine affairs," she would say. "Warts and all."

And he always did, usually wondering why he was implicating himself to his mother.

"Screw the man every chance you get," she would say.

He always told her just how dirty he was getting. "Ha," she might say. He did love to hear her laugh.

≈

They were barely out of Towson before Arlette started in on him. He supposed he deserved it.

"The explosion has something to do with the Fleur de Lis development, doesn't it?" she said.

"The church explosion?"

"Cut the crap. Why didn't you keep me apprised?"

"Arlette, people were hurt. The church building is partially destroyed." They had just hit the interstate, and he was up to ninety miles per hour.

"A church doesn't just blow up for no reason," she said.

"What are you saying?"

"That you've kept most of the Fleur de Lis deal hidden from me. Why didn't you consult with me on the layouts? That's not like you. I let it go, thinking you were giving me a rest for some damned reason. You didn't want me to know who you were dealing with, did you?"

"I've always been up front with you."

She craned to look at the speedometer. "Jesus, Louis. Slow down."

"Sorry." He figured he'd better slow down *and* ignore the swearing.

"It's that group in Milwaukee, isn't it?" she asked.

"You and everyone know they're a major partner. The *Post-Dispatch* ran a story on them, for God's sake."

"That's not what I mean. Why are they coming after you?"

"Maybe I can reason with them."

Arlette turned to the window. No doubt she would sit there, ignoring Louis, until he finally told her the story. How his gut ached! "You hungry?" he asked.

She was still watching Indiana fly by. "What I want is for you to start talking."

Louis knew her too well. Her voice was settled, not on the edge or twitchy anymore. He owed it to her. But to be honest, he wanted to tell his mother first, to see her delight, to hear that elderly cackle she could still produce as she lay dying in the nursing home. But Arlette had called his hand.

He pointed to a billboard. "There's a Shoney's at the next exit. Let's get started there," he said.

"Whatever."

~

She knew about his second golf course development out in St. Charles County with several dozen mansions set on acre-and-a half lots meandering beside the fairways. The kind of place to host PGA tournaments.

Now he would tell her what she *didn't* know. One Friday afternoon he was having a few drinks at Benito's on The Hill, an Italian neighborhood, before going up to Forest Park where he would meet Arlette to watch Michelle play in a tennis tournament. Did she remember the evening? About two years ago?

She did. Michelle's first big tournament win.

Louis was throwing around his country club idea at Benito's. There was even an off-duty cop at the table, along with a few other guys who usually hung around Benito's before the evening dinner crowd arrived. He knew all the people, but hadn't done business with any of them. These guys always talked about how they had socked money away in investments—securities, solid rentals, safe land speculations—no big projects like Louis had become so famous for. These were south St. Louis guys who had done well in neighborhood renovations and hit pretty big. They had backed and built lofts and renovated brownstones, the kinds that had young folks moving back into the south side, down around the warehouse district and river wharfs. These guys were pretty conservative in their business dealings. Italians mostly. Some with grandparents still speaking Italian at home; the south side was full of them, especially on The Hill.

So, on that Friday afternoon, Louis pulled out his laptop and showed them on Google Earth the plot that he was pretty sure could be developed. He had already spoken with a couple of banks. But this was such a big deal the banks weren't certain they could stake just Louis alone on this one. He told the guys at the table that it pissed him off when the banks didn't offer a loan immediately. He kept moving the cursor back and forth on the St. Charles County map as everyone crowded around. Then four men walked in, and all the others came to attention, even the off-duty cop. Louis thought, *What the hell?* Turns out they were big shots from Milwaukee in the fresh-produce business, but from the way everyone acted, you'd think they *owned* Milwaukee. The cop looked kind of funny standing there, like he knew who they were but didn't want to say anything. One of them said, "So what have we here?" pointing to Louis's laptop. Louis started laying it on about his big plans, and when he mentioned the PGA tournament idea, they suddenly listening more seriously. Lots of questions.

The guy who appeared to be the big cheese said, "Let's drive out there. Can't see nothing from a fucking computer anyway. What the hell good is that?"

From The Hill on a Friday afternoon, driving northwest and then crossing the river over that jammed bridge into St. Charles would be a joke. Forget it. It could take hours, and besides, Louis had to be in Forest Park to watch Michelle play tennis. What did these fruit peddlers know about St. Louis, and especially about Louis's business plans? Louis probably said something similar to them—in a kinder fashion—before one of the Milwaukee guys reached over and pushed down the lid on the laptop. Then he looked at no one in particular and said, "What time does Benito's open tomorrow?"

"For breakfast?" one of the St. Louis guys joked. Everyone knew Benito's didn't open for breakfast.

"Get Benito in here," said the laptop closer.

A St. Louis guy went out and came back in with Benito.

"Benny, we want to have a small meeting right here," and he tapped his forefinger twice on the table, "tomorrow morning at nine o'clock. Bring in some of that nice bread from over at Amberghetti's. We're gonna go over some plans, then we're heading out to …" He looked at Louis. "What's the place?"

"St. Charles."

"That's it."

He told Louis to bring with him all the paperwork the banks had vetoed.

"I'm not sure I want to do that. Privileged information," said Louis.

The room got quiet and Benito walked out.

"We might be able to make this deal of yours go," said Milwaukee Big Cheese.

"Just who exactly are you?"

"John Smith. And these are my pals. Dick Smith, Joe Smith, and Sam Smith."

"What the hell?"

"Look, I'm just messin' with you. We all got names." He gave Louis their names, all foreign sounding. "We don't even know *your* name."

"Louis Lewis."

Milwaukee Big Cheese laughed. "Louis Lewis from St. Louis. Come on, yeah. What's the name?"

"That's it. Honest."

The next morning Louis was at Benito's and showed the men the bank papers. In a caravan of three cars, they made the Saturday morning trip across the river to the St. Charles County site where the Milwaukee guys promised that within a week they would have a Milwaukee bank contact Louis. Surely then a St. Louis bank would go along with the Milwaukee bank, wouldn't it? Two weeks later the financing was set, and Louis contacted the media. A new suburban development would be the envy of the Midwest. A joint venture with Louis and an investment group from Milwaukee. It was to be called Fleur de Lis.

~

Back on the interstate there was still much to tell. "I didn't know if I misread the contracts or if the Milwaukee bank slipped one by me."

"Hold on a minute," said Arlette. "You've never gone into a project with a group like that. Why this time?"

"I needed the backing. I saw this project as our crown jewel."

"*Our?*"

"You and me."

"If I was so goddamned important," Arlette said, "why'd you exclude me?"

"Not sure."

"Because you were afraid of those guys from the start, and telling me about them might cause you to pull out."

Louis held tightly to the steering wheel. "Anyway," said Louis, "there was a huge balloon payment coming due that I must not have noticed."

"Not noticed?"

"It was in there. And here's the catch. The payment was to be made directly to the investment group, not the Milwaukee bank that supposedly made the loan."

"So was the bank calling the shots or the group?"

"I found out through my guys on The Hill that the Milwaukee barons control lots of Milwaukee, including a bank or two." For the first time since getting in the car, Louis looked at Arlette. "I'm in debt to an underworld syndicate," he said.

"This sounds too hokey." Arlette blew out an exasperated breath. "Did you make the balloon payment?"

"I refused and told those guys I wouldn't pay *them*, only the bank."

"Nice work, Louis. So they bomb your church."

"It's been several months that they've been hounding me. The guys at Benito's kept telling me to make the payment, and they said they could hold off any bad stuff for a while but that the Milwaukee outfit wouldn't wait long. Finally the Benito's crowd stopped talking to me."

"But you haven't been drinking with them since you found Jesus. Right?"

"I still go in there and order soda. I always make a point to pass on to them my Christian influence. It's my obligation."

"Let me get this straight," said Arlette, who went silent for a moment. "You get in with guys who you knew were bad, and then you agree to share the development of Fleur de Lis with them, and then you don't read the fine print—or else you let them fuck you over from the start. And then you really piss them off by not making payments, and then you rile them up more by spouting your Jesus nonsense. Have I got this right?"

"I guess you could put it that way."

"Then you decided to stand firm on your so-called convictions until they bombed your church."

"I don't exactly like the way you phrased all that."

"Why the hell didn't you pay them?"

"Arlette, that balloon payment was incredible."

"Sell off something. Some of your other holdings."

"That's another problem. Most of my other stuff I put up as collateral on Fleur de Lis."

If they were anywhere other than in a car, Louis could have diverted the flow of the conversation: walked out, any number of things. But he was trapped all the way to St. Louis. He couldn't even lie his way out. He'd already said too much.

"So that wonderful Milwaukee bank," said Arlette, "could call in your—I mean *our*—holdings?"

"I've got some hedges against that."

"Please don't bother telling me now."

For several miles she was quiet. He looked over to see if she were asleep. She was crying.

"I'm sorry," said Louis.

"I don't suppose you've thought about what those bastards' next move might be if you don't play their game."

"Why are you crying?"

"I'm crying for myself and Michelle. They could come after the two of us."

Louis had not thought of that. But surely ...

Arlette was wiping tears. "How do you and Jesus plan on protecting us?"

"Please don't talk like that."

$\sim$

Arlette decided to shut up and let him silently stew the way he always did when faced with something insurmountable; at least that was what he *once* did. Now, who the hell knew what went through that mind of his? Maybe he didn't stew any longer; maybe the calming voice of Jesus soothed him. She looked at him, sitting nearly frozen while steering the car. How could he drive that way? Maybe her crack about what he and Jesus had planned for protecting her and Michelle was unfair. In the old days if she got sassy—about anything—he would have shot back with a controlled fury that she had seen wilt even the most indomitable, not just her. But she now had the prerogative to say almost anything, with impunity. It didn't feel right to her. Why must she flail him so?

Truth be known, she liked Louis's new humility, even the child-like—no, it was *childish*—naiveté. All of it reminded her of their first years of struggle and the happiness before he launched himself into the money-grubbing fray, barely avoiding becoming criminal. And now, after he had been born-again and dedicated his life to calm and quiet, he suddenly *was* in the criminal world. How ironic. Who is this God that Louis prayed to so fervently?

She wanted to reach over and pat his shoulders with both hands, to rub out the fear that must be lodged there. But she couldn't. Too much to think about. With all this time in the car, she would try to put their lives into perspective. To this point, she had thought through things only in dribs and drabs.

"I'm going to sleep," she told him. Faking sleep might be much like faking orgasm.

"OK, honey. It's a long drive."

She remembered when he first hinted at the change, the time when he cried in front of her and Michelle. Could this have been when the Milwaukee group entered the scene? He had come home early one evening (Wait. It *was* after he met the Milwaukee group, because the three of them were still excited over Michelle's big tournament win in Forest Park.). He overdid the hugs to both of them. She and Michelle thought the embraces represented residual elation over her win, but during the evening he would, for no apparent reason, offer more hugs. Arlette remembered she and Michelle looking at each other rather stupefied but not thinking much about it, until at dinner he began the crying, his head nearly falling into his plate.

"Maybe I need to slow down at work," he said. "All the pressure."

She and Michelle thought it was the work; the two talked about it later. It made sense. Because of the stress at work, he had come home early—and crashed. A normal physiological and psychological response. Arlette remembered that evening in bed. She and Louis cried after a rare simultaneous orgasm, and they fell asleep still in the position they copulated in. She awakened first (she had been on top, falling asleep with her head on his chest) and tried to coax him from the middle of the bed to his side. He usually didn't talk in his sleep, but he mumbled nonsense as he finally rolled over. Arlette wished she could remember what he'd said.

The next day, he left early and came back in the middle of the afternoon, still distressed but trying to hide it. This must have been the day he looked over the St. Charles site with the Milwaukee group. More hugs. Arlette remembered him sitting glazed in front of the TV, not reacting to what he saw, not flipping channels—just sitting. She and Michelle made an occasional overture to engage him in conversation, but he only intermittently smiled at them; he was lost, and they didn't know where. And then some damned evangelist's show appeared on the screen, and before she and Michelle knew it, he was sitting upright, not slumped as he had been, and progressively becoming interested in what was before him. Arlette remembered being pleased that he was perking up, but also amused by the source of his change.

"Louis, what are you watching?"

"Watch this with me," he said.

She sat by him on the couch. A handsome young man with black, wavy hair was holding a Bible and moving from one side of a large stage to another, speaking calmly to an arena full of people (the camera would now and then pan the crowd). Arlette remembered being drawn to the man's captivating looks, which emitted a sexual edge she found frightening because she resented all he stood for. Yet, he seemed to be making some sense—he spoke not with evangelistic bombast but with calming self-help psychological jargon: "We must develop a special inner space free from outside babble ... co-opt the nature of those we know are truly at peace ... happiness comes from leaving what we *think* is real and being led to what we *know* is real ... we trouble *ourselves* more than others trouble us ... give yourself permission to be happy and content." For a moment, she might have forgotten he was a Bible thumper, another huckster selling himself to an audience for the vast amounts of money that would roll in. But that striking face paired with the slender body outfitted in such a finely tailored suit! She felt her heart thwack for a brief moment as she saw only the physical beauty of the man. She reached for Louis's hand to steady herself from the evangelist's magnetism.

Louis must have thought she was as immersed in the young man's message as he, for he squeezed Arlette's hand and held the grip. She wondered if Louis would cry again as he had the day before, but when she looked at him, his face was alive.

Now the man on TV was reading from the Bible. He flipped pages while the television audience heard the onion skins rustle, a whisper from God. "The earth is the Lord's and the fullness thereof, the world, and they that dwell therein." Louis squeezed Arlette's hand harder, and she tried to pull away, but he would have no part of it. The young man read: "Who shall ascend into the hill of the Lord? Or who shall stand in his holy place? He that hath clean hands, and a pure heart; who hath not lifted up his soul unto vanity, nor sworn deceitfully. He shall receive the blessing from the Lord, and righteousness from the God of his salvation."

Michelle walked through the room, passing between the TV and the couch where Arlette and Louis were locked. Arlette hoped she would not glance at them, but she did.

"What are you two watching?"

Arlette was speechless.

"Dad, you're smiling."

"Come unto me all ye that labor and are heavy-laden, and I will give you rest," read the evangelist.

The man closed the Bible and was now holding a book up to the camera. On the jacket was his picture. The title was *Wealth with Jesus*.

"I can send you this very important book for only half of what it cost me to print it." The preacher stated the cost. "All you need to do is ask."

Louis released Arlette's hand. He grabbed a pen from his pocket, and seeing no paper handy, he wrote the email address that appeared on the screen in the palm of his hand.

∽

Restroom break. Ten minutes later they were back in the car. She immediately closed her eyes.

"I've been thinking some things over," said Louis.

"That's good." She kept her eyes closed.

"I thought about how I should deal with the Milwaukee group. I can't go into a counseling session with Pastor Ummell like I always have. He's helped me in the past, but this explosion is too close to him."

"In those earlier sessions, did you tell him about the group?" asked Arlette.

"No."

"Good."

"How about you and I visit a real therapist? A psychologist."

Arlette opened her eyes and looked straight at Louis, incredulously. "Why *we*?"

"Let me finish," snapped Louis.

There was a taste of the old Louis: the interruption and curt response.

"Sorry," she said.

"We need to seek help elsewhere. This whole mess is as much about *us* as it is anything."

"Are you saying *I'm* to blame," said Arlette, "for stupid business decisions, for the explosion—"

"Wait just a minute—"

"No, *you* wait." Arlette stiffened, then relaxed. She needed to rein this in. "Sorry, Louis."

"Can't we begin by seeking help together?"

That might be fair enough. "If that's what you want," she said. Was he up to something again—like the first time he insisted she and Michelle go with him to visit with Pastor Ummell?

She closed her eyes and thought about that time.

Louis had done his research. He actually called the young man he had seen on TV; his monster church was in San Diego. Louis sent him money. Lots of it, Arlette assumed. Then Louis asked the TV evangelist to recommend a local church in St. Louis where he might attend, one that was in sync with all that the young man espoused.

That's when Pastor Ummell and Crestview Evangelical Temple came into the picture.

Neither she nor Michelle were about to read *Wealth with Jesus.* They had heard enough about it from Louis already. But after a girl-to-girl confab, they agreed to go with Louis to meet the pastor because of the change they had seen in Louis after he had attended several services there by himself and announced he had met Jesus.

"Dad's really sweet now," said Michelle.

"He is," said Arlette.

The women agreed to meet the pastor in his wood-paneled office, opulently appointed and smelling of air freshener.

"So these are the lovely ladies you've been talking about," said Pastor Ummell, clasping Louis on the shoulder.

Louis beamed.

Ummell wore a double-breasted suit with a red tie. Arlette scrutinized the large ring on his right hand.

"Please make yourselves comfortable," he said, pointing to a leather love seat for Arlette and Michelle, a wing chair for Louis.

He sat behind a polished desk. "I'll tell Joyce, my secretary, to bring us beverages." Ummell picked up his phone and gave Joyce the order. "We're delighted Louis has chosen us for his church home."

Is this the way things will go? Putting us on the spot with leading statements?

"He seems to like the church," said Arlette.

"There's much to like here. You may have noticed we have multiple facilities that can minister to the needs of the entire family. Banquet rooms supported by a full-service kitchen, three chapels independent of our large worship auditorium, a fitness center, a complete range of recreational activities. He looked at Michelle. "I understand you're quite the tennis player."

"I like to play."

"We even have an indoor tennis court."

"You do?" said Michelle.

"In fact," said Ummell, "I've arranged for two of our youth to show you around. When Joyce brings in the beverages, I'll ask her to ..."

In walked Joyce, tray in hand.

"Joyce, would you please introduce Michelle here to Darlene and Jacob? They might like to show Michelle around while I chat with Louis and his lovely wife."

Seconds after Joyce served the drinks and left the office, two sharply dressed young people walked in.

"Oh my God!" said Michelle.

"Do you know these folks?" Ummell asked Michelle.

"We were in tennis camp together last summer!" said Michelle. "I didn't know you two went to this church."

"Wanna check it out?" asked Darlene.

"Back in a bit," said Jacob.

They were gone.

"The Lord works in mysterious ways," said Ummell.

So that's how they're going to play, thought Arlette.

"That will be all, Joyce," said Ummell. Joyce left, pulling the door closed behind her.

"So, Arlette," said Ummell. "Louis tells me you and Michelle are in need of a church home."

"Is that so?" she said, eyes on Louis.

She should tone things down. After all, she had no defenses, and Michelle had already been sucked in.

"Louis is very happy here," she said.

Soon Ummell was laying it on, selling Jesus as a product. Louis nodded and radiated joy as Ummell talked to the silent Arlette.

Now, what had Arlette gained by scrolling her memory? Maybe only some solitude during the long drive back to St. Louis. But the remembrance of things past affirmed her resolve that never again would Louis force her into something she didn't want. She had attended Crestview Evangelical Temple with Louis and Michelle out of sheer delight for Louis's changed demeanor, a high price to pay for the half-baked theology he spouted. Even the times when she nestled in the calm that his beliefs brought him, she always knew twinges of the old Louis would burst forth, resulting in the oddest mixture. Could she continue living with such a patchwork of human behavior?

Within fifty miles of St. Louis, she and Louis had let the monotony of the drive lull them into innocuous conversation that Arlette guessed represented a steadying attitude they needed to face the trauma of the Crestview explosion. She would work to soften her hard edges.

And maybe the visit to the psychologist would be the best thing. What did she have to lose?

CABBAGES AND KINGS

Michelle realized she could never be together with both Clovis and Abe. She guessed the two represented different worlds she had suddenly been thrown into, and since her parents had gone back to St. Louis, she alone could manage those worlds. Then there was the world of classes, which would plunge her into other situations with possibly more acquaintances. Who knew what might come of that? And there was the world of the dining hall where everyone on the small campus ate three times a day—really twice, since most didn't eat breakfast. Lunch was hectic with people dashing in and out between classes, but it was dinner that brought everyone together for long stays at the table and even longer lounging around after. Clovis seemed to be the expert on offering advice about such things.

"You have to be careful not to waste too much time after dinner when you should be studying."

They were into only their second day of classes, but Michelle felt as though she had been in the routine forever. Already she saw alliances shaking out into the three chambers of college life: dorm, class, dining hall. Then there was tennis, which cross-pollinated the others. (Michelle came up with the "cross pollination" analogy on her own.

She mentioned it to Clovis, who didn't find it as clever as she should. Clovis seemed not to hear any references Michelle made to tennis.)

Things were settling in, especially after learning from her parents that her church friends, Darlene and Jacob, had not been injured in the explosion; she didn't know any of the unfortunate ones, so even though she tried to work up concern—even guilt—for the injured, she didn't find herself spending much time thinking about them or the church. St. Louis was distant.

Abe occupied her thoughts when she wasn't studying or in class. On the first day of classes, she had run into him on a crowded sidewalk outside the science building. He wasn't hard to pick out. He actually took her by the arm and pulled her onto the grass. She was so stunned that the only thing she remembered about their conversation was his reminding her of the first tennis meeting that afternoon. When he left and she reentered the stream on the sidewalk, two girls she didn't know asked how she knew him.

"Tennis," she said.

"You're tennis?" one girl asked, making Michelle wonder if tennis players at Redfern took on the appearance of rackets or balls.

"Just starting."

They walked away.

At the first tennis meeting, Back Bay introduced Michelle, along with four other freshmen recruits, to the rest of the team. Everyone was nice. Abe wasn't there.

"Where's Abe?" someone asked.

"Late," said Back Bay, not looking up from his clipboard. "He'll pay."

Abe trotted across the court to the bleachers. Several people laughed and hooted.

"Sit down Mr. Abdul al-Fiasa," said Back Bay. "Feel like extra sprints today?"

"Sorry," said Abe.

He squeezed in next to Michelle, making the person next to her move over. Back Bay lifted his eyes momentarily. "Maybe you need to be treated like a freshman if you're going to sit by one."

"Who's your new friend?" someone asked.

All were snickering. Back Bay even waited for Abe's response. "Michelle. From St. Louis. We know each other already."

"Don't arrive fashionably late anymore," said Back Bay, "or all your friends will run extra sprints."

Michelle watched the ends of Back Bay's mouth curl slightly. Abe pressed his leg into hers.

~

In the first week, Michelle's acquaintances she made in the classroom stayed there. She saw some of them in the dining hall, but nothing grew. She was flattered when guys would sit by her at lunch and try to strike something up. One even told her she was beautiful, and five minutes later told her that the Lord revealed to him in a vision they should minister together in some obscure place. (She was told kooks like that were common on campus. In the first chapel service—they were held twice weekly, required—after the semester-opening pomp of the faculty in full academic regalia, she listened to a couple of campus leaders lay the church vocation pitch on pretty thick. So Mr. Future Foreign Missionary at lunch didn't surprise her much.)

Generally, Clovis was a good roommate, but after Michelle's mother's outburst at the Steak and Sea when she responded to Clovis's "Let us pray" with "It's too fucking late now," Michelle worked at damage control for a solid hour.

"I'm not used to hearing that kind of language and especially not from a parent," said Clovis. "If anyone at our Christian high school had said anything like that ..."

Even after the feather-smoothing and convincing Clovis that her parents (and herself) were upstanding citizens and Christians, Michelle felt obligated to contain Clovis's ire and establish herself to be as outwardly Christian as possible. Michelle found the task surprisingly comforting while confined to their dorm room. Clovis was easy to talk with, and after the first day of classes, Michelle located the Bible her father had packed for her and asked Clovis what she should read for an uplift. Michelle loved the look of pure joy Clovis gave her, and she welcomed Clovis into a secret chamber of her heart that Michelle never knew existed. She had found a place for the odd girl. The dorm room for Michelle was a retreat from her other worlds into a remarkable sanctum that she found comforting.

Still, Clovis was a peculiar one. The first time she and Michelle walked to the dining hall for dinner, Clovis filled her tray and disappeared before Michelle could locate her. When Michelle found her, she was at a full table. Clovis just waved, smiled, and continued shoveling food. Michelle was left to find her own table where Abe and a few others joined her immediately. When Michelle would look at Clovis's table occasionally, Clovis was looking back, smiling, never appearing to be engaging with anyone at her table. In ten minutes, Clovis was standing beside Michelle.

"I'm going to the room now," she told Michelle.

"This is Clovis, my roommate." Michelle swept her arm into the round table.

A few said hello, but Clovis walked away before most could even look up.

"I guess she's not on the tennis team," someone said, causing most at the table to suppress laughs by smiling down at their plates.

To Michelle's relief, Abe did not laugh, but, instead, caught each person with a stare which calmed things without a word. No one mentioned Clovis again.

Each evening at dinner, Clovis sat across the room, watching Michelle and her friends. As the days went along, Michelle's dining-room friends increased, while Michelle noticed Clovis sitting with fewer people each day. But Clovis always positioned herself to watch Michelle's table; both girls would wave and smile across the room.

～

The world of Redfern tennis took an odd turn. At the first tennis meeting after Back Bay Norman had gently upbraided Abe for being late, the coach said he would be gone for a few days.

"I'm leaving this team on its own to conduct practice sessions according to the schedule I've worked up." He pulled several sheets of paper from his clipboard. "Everything is laid out in detail with the number of minutes assigned for each activity."

He walked to Abe and handed him the paper. "Our late-arriving friend here is in charge of making sure everything is carried out according to these plans."

Michelle felt Abe's leg rub against hers as he rose to grab the plans. Something she had never felt stirred within her as she watched Abe's backside.

"Be on time," Back Bay said to Abe, "and see to it everyone else is."

The team laughed.

Coming back to her side, Michelle found herself looking directly into his crotch. She hadn't intended that. Had he noticed? Michelle thought quickly about her earlier stirring. He slid in beside her again. Abe was in charge of the team's practices, and she wanted him to be in charge of her. She was in love with Abe's control, pure and simple. What exactly did that mean?

"Coach," someone behind Michelle said, "where are you going?"

"An important gathering … meeting. Two or three days, tops," he said, looking away. "I'll have the athletic director drop by every once in a while to see things are running smoothly." Now he was looking at Abe. "Keep things under control."

Abe smiled and held up the pages. Michelle was aware of another stirring. This time it was a tingle, and she felt its exact location.

Back Bay went over the season's schedule, focusing on the many long road matches and emphasizing the need for team members to study. "You're here not just for your athletic ability but for strong academics, too."

Michelle's dorm room flashed into her head. She was lucky to have Clovis and a quiet room. Even their suite mates seemed docile. Michelle could study all she wanted.

"This team has always formed lasting friendships," Back Bay said. "It's important we stick together. Those on the team in past seasons know what I'm talking about, so for the new ones among us, let me just say that some students at this college don't always understand us. For whatever reason. In so many ways, we stand outside this student body. And we should."

He let the moment hang. Michelle thought of Clovis.

"The new ones can talk to the upperclassmen on that issue."

More silence.

"But petty bickering that comes from too close ties," Back Bay continued, "can harm the whole team."

Why was he looking at Michelle and Abe?

"Enough said," said Back Bay.

Michelle felt Abe applying pressure to her leg.

The meeting lasted about forty minutes with Back Bay doing the talking, very little coming from the team. The coach dismissed them. Michelle was still attracted to his strong sexual aura and assumed all the females were, too. But then there was Abe sitting by her. Oh my! When she rose to leave, her bottom ached from the sitting on the hard bleachers. She watched Abe rub his.

"Meet you in the dining hall," Abe said.

"OK."

"Save a place if you get there before me."

That accent of his! Did she smell a spicy, exotic aroma on his breath? Something caught in the back of her throat.

"Will you save a place?" he asked.

Michelle was certain she said she would.

At dinner that evening, Michelle joined Abe and some of the tennis team—along with a few others the team accepted.

"Has Coach ever gone away like this?" Michelle asked.

"Never," said Abe.

Michelle watched him, wondering if his short answer was the beginning to more or if he had finished. She had no way of reading him, this twenty-year-old who was not only handsome but alluringly mysterious. His dark fingers—North African, actually Arab—contrasted so sharply with his white fingernails, which appeared to be manicured. She had never paid much attention to guys' fingernails. (Surely they don't spend time on their nails.) She remembered his legs, covered with a thin dusting of black curly hair. And the hair on his head—she wanted to feel it, test its texture ...

Someone had apparently spoken. All were watching.

"What?" she asked.

Abe was smiling at her. Those white teeth! "Maybe he trains me for being the coach," he said.

While others at the table laughed, Michelle righted herself. "You *would* be a good coach." Was that the right thing to say?

"If he was ever on time," someone said, taking the pressure off Michelle's statement.

His speech mannerisms: "Maybe he *trains* me for being the coach." What's the word for him? *Endearing* popped into Michelle's head, a word she'd heard her mother use to describe Michelle's qualities. Could Michelle and Abe *both* be endearing? If so, then ...

"He sleeps too much," someone else said.

"But not with me," a girl across the table said, and mimicked rubbing tears from her eyes.

How could such a dark man actually blush? But he was. Michelle watched, in wonderment, as the table converged, happily, on Abe's sexual experience. Should she smile like the others? Why was she the only one not finding such delight in his embarrassment? Did someone just call him "the Algerian Mule"? But wait. It wasn't serious. What's the word? "Ironic"—they didn't really mean it. She listened carefully, regarding the nuances, body language, and subtle comical jabs. He was speechless while they mercilessly ribbed him as only athletes can do to one another. She knew the routine. And as she scrutinized the shadings and colorings of their volleys, she understood. He was "the innocent" among them. Oh my God. How could this hunk of Algerian flesh be so inexperienced? Certainly not a virgin. Even Michelle was not a virgin, yet she still had much to learn—and there at the round dining-hall table she wanted to learn from Abdul al-Fiasa. Could they teach each other?

Did someone just say *blonde*?

"Ah, ha," a female team member said, pointing to Michelle, whose ears rang and whose face suddenly ignited. Eyes and smiles were on Michelle.

"A good old American blush," someone said, pointing to her.

Abe and Michelle were looking at each other. He grinned. How could she help but grin also? She looked around the table. She was the only blonde.

Abe said he would walk her to Hamilton Hall. She wondered if people always looked at each other the way others looked at her and Abe. They strolled here and there, back and forth through the campus. The evening was warm, windless. They eventually sat on a stone bench in full view of three buildings, two of which were dorms. Were people watching? She didn't look to see because she didn't care. They talked of many things. "Of cabbages and kings," she said.

"What?"

"It's from *Through the Looking Glass*. Did your parents read it to you?"

"No."

Michelle wondered what Algerian parents read to their children. "My mother read it to me. I memorized that part of it for some reason."

"Memorize it to me," said Abe.

His language was not only charming but delightfully funny. Should she correct his minor slips? No. If she tried to speak French—she'd had two years in high school—would she want him correcting her?

She recited the part she remembered: "'The time has come,' the Walrus said, / 'To talk of many things: / Of shoes and ships and sealing wax, / Of cabbages and kings.'"

She spoke the lines with such delight that she wanted to hug him—was it because she enjoyed remembering the lines or because she was actually teaching Abe something new? "We've talked about a lot of things tonight," she said.

"Why cabbages and kings?"

"My mother said that the Walrus and the Carpenter didn't have much in common, and what they talked about didn't have much in common either. Like shoes and ships and sealing wax. Like cabbages and kings. Nothing seems to be connected."

"What should we speak about?" asked Abe.

"Blonde hair and black hair?"

"I know what you choose to speak of. It's why I chose you."

"I'm a freshman. You're a senior, the number one ranked player. Did you choose me for my hair?"

"May I touch it?"

She looked up quickly at the dorms. "Haven't you touched blonde hair?"

"No."

"Touch," she said.

She did the most amazing thing. As he touched her hair, she put her hand on his head and not only touched his hair, but rubbed it. No, she caressed it, actually made love to it.

When Michelle returned to her room, Clovis greeted her coldly. "You look different," Clovis said.

"I do?"

Michelle went straight to her desk, opened a book, pulled down a notebook from a shelf, riffled through a syllabus—anything to mask what she knew Clovis had so perceptively noticed about her. Michelle's hand that had fondled Abe's hair alternatively burned and tingled.

"How was dinner?" Michelle asked. Jeez, that was the kind of question adults use to make small talk. She glanced at Clovis, who was looking straight at her.

"Several of us saw you," said Clovis.

Why wouldn't people have seen them? "Gets pretty crowded in the dining hall," said Michelle. She avoided returning Clovis's stare.

"On the bench outside."

What right did she have to say that? "Abe and I were talking about tennis and stuff."

"Abe isn't his real name."

"I know."

"He's an Arab," said Clovis.

"Abdul al-Fiasa. He's from Algeria. He told me he attended an American school in Algiers."

Michelle wanted to tell Clovis all he had told her. About his parents. How they cried when he left them to come to Redfern. How they made their one trip to America last year to see him play in the NCAA tennis tournament. "At great expense," Abe had said. Instead Michelle went for the abstract, the truest and most emotionally honest admission she could muster.

"He's really nice, Clovis."

"He seemed to keep you very entertained."

Michelle drew a long breath.

"I've heard some things."

Was she jealous? Michelle should be angry, should be lashing out at the desperate, isolated girl. There she sat, overweight and decked out in that frumpy long dress, probably ready to pull a jumbo bag of chips out of the drawer. What was Michelle to do? She couldn't be mad at her.

"Clovis, I don't know what you're trying to say. Just tell me."

"Oh, Michelle." Clovis walked the short distance to Michelle's desk and hugged her. The girl was actually crying on Michelle's shoulder.

"You're the best friend I have," said Clovis. "I don't want you doing the wrong thing."

Michelle tried scooting her chair back to allow more room, but Clovis's weight wouldn't allow it. Her breasts mashed against Michelle's shoulder.

"You're a friend," said Michelle. "Tell me why you're crying."

"For what might happen to you. I don't want to lose you."

Clovis straightened up. Her face was the reddest Michelle had ever seen. "Sorry," said Clovis. She wiped some tears and was back in her chair.

"Why would you lose me?" asked Michelle.

"Sometimes I think you might find another roommate."

"I like being here. Really."

"Good."

Michelle pulled out Clovis's food drawer and sure enough a bag of unopened pretzels was there. When did she find time to buy all those snacks? "Let's munch," said Michelle. "It'll help." She ripped open the bag with her teeth and emptied the pretzels on Clovis's desk. They both ate. "Better?" asked Michelle.

"Sort of. But I'm still worried about Abe."

"Worried that I'll kick you out and have *him* move in?"

Clovis gently punched Michelle's shoulder. "Nooo."

"Then what?"

"You don't know?"

Michelle waited while Clovis raked off a pile of pretzels into her hand. Eating and chewing slowly, she whispered, "They say he's a Muslim."

"Who says?"

"Everyone."

Watching the worried girl eating pretzels by the handful struck Michelle as more funny than sad. Obviously Clovis wanted her to be alarmed, yet what was so surprising about an Algerian being Muslim? And exactly what did Clovis and "everyone" know about Abe? Why were people butting in like this? Michelle had Clovis deep in the back court; coming fast to the net was both an offensive and defensive tactic.

"What's so awful about being Muslim?" Wait. Michelle was admitting he was when she had no idea.

"Michelle! A Muslim!"

Michelle would slam a hard crosscourt shot. "I mean, really, Clovis. Who is *everyone*, and why is everyone so sure he's a Muslim? And even if he is, so what?"

"Muslims are infidels. It's in the Bible."

Now Clovis had charged the net, and they were facing each other, both from a position of power. What exactly was an infidel? "Show me," said Michelle.

In lunging for her Bible, Clovis knocked a few pretzels to the floor. She was flipping pages like a madwoman, but Michelle could tell she might be too full of fury to ever find what she was looking for. Maybe Michelle had called her bluff.

"Clovis, you can prove anything you want with the Bible." Her mother had taught her well. "Sixty-six books written hundreds of years apart by bunches of different people. What sense does it make?"

Michelle thought Clovis might choke. "Are you questioning the Bible?"

Why had Michelle let the conversation get so out of hand? "No. Let's get back to Abe. He's the point here."

Clovis's face was redder than before, and her fingers were shaking as she continued rustling pages.

"Let's not get mad at each other," said Michelle. She reached for Clovis's shaking hand. "We like each other too much."

Clovis was crying again. "Don't leave me for him."

"I said I wouldn't. You'll always be a friend."

Michelle held both of Clovis's hands.

"I'm a Christian, and he's not," said Clovis.

No sense in plowing *that* ground again. Michelle moved her hands to Clovis's broad shoulders and looked at the mess of pretzels on the desk.

WHAT'S AN INFIDEL?

CHAPTER 7

"My God, Michelle. It's one forty-five in the morning."

"Sorry. I need to talk."

"Where are you?"

"In the bathroom with the cell phone. Clovis is asleep. I didn't want to wake her."

"This better be good. Wait a minute, honey. Let me call you back."

Arlette gently slid from beneath the covers, careful not to disturb Louis. She listened for his snores and walked quietly from the bedroom through the dark house to the kitchen, where she turned on a counter light. A soft glow lit the kitchen. She put ice in a glass, poured a bit of scotch then dialed Michelle. "OK, honey. I'm back," said Arlette.

"What's an 'infidel'?" asked Michelle.

Arlette choked slightly on her first sip. "You're calling to ask me *that*?"

"Just tell me."

Had the girl been reading her thoughts? "It's a person who isn't faithful to another. Like infidelity in marriage."

"That doesn't make sense."

Arlette supposed she was right. No one should be unfaithful to a husband, but … "Who's an infidel, dear?"

"Clovis said Abe is."

"Abe the tennis player you brought to dinner the other night?"

"Yes."

"How would she know?"

"Clovis said Abe is a Muslim, and all Muslims are infidels."

Arlette pictured large groups of Muslims fucking each other. "Michelle, I'm not following you."

"Clovis said it's in the Bible that Muslims are infidels. She looked but couldn't find the place. She said Muslims aren't going to heaven."

If Arlette weren't holding the phone in one hand and a drink in the other, she would have slapped herself on the forehead. "Oh, honey, in that sense it means something different." She took a more acceptable drink of her scotch. "It's what people of one religion call others who don't believe the way they do." Arlette scrolled back to history lessons. "During the Crusades I think that Christians called Muslims infidels."

"Mom, I thought it might be something like that."

"Tell me what this is all about."

"Clovis said everyone knows Abe's a Muslim. It's like they hate him."

Was their daughter already getting serious with this guy? Arlette envisioned Michelle bringing Abe to St. Louis for Christmas, and Louis putting him through hell. "Why is this bothering you so?" Arlette asked.

"I'm not sure I like this place."

Of course she didn't like the place. Who would except people like Louis and Clovis? She had to admit, though, that Back Bay Norman seemed to be a regular guy. "Sweetheart, you just got there. Three days isn't long enough to decide."

"I knooow."

She could almost see Michelle's face, her way of conceding she was wrong. Arlette wished she were there. She had wondered how long it would take for Michelle to become homesick.

"Do you and Abe have something going?" asked Arlette.

"He's really nice."

"How nice is 'nice'?"

"We talked for a long time today, and he didn't mention being Muslim."

"Forget Muslim, OK?"

Arlette knew these sidetracks well and had gone down them with Michelle many times right there at the kitchen table, always when Louis was gone. She hoped she could carry this out on the phone.

"Abe's nice," said Michelle.

"He seemed nice when we met him."

"Oh, he really is."

"After talking with him today," asked Arlette, "did you find yourself thinking about him? Getting excited?"

"We touched each other's hair. Did you notice his hair when you met him?"

"He's a handsome man."

"Oh, he really is."

"Tell me more about this hair thing."

Arlette wanted to hold Michelle tightly and say, "I know, sweetheart. I know." Was the scotch already starting to kick in, and why was she so near tears?

"We like each other's hair," said Michelle. "It's so different."

And forbidden. Abe is an outcast at that damned college, and, baby girl, no wonder you want him. Back Bay Norman's hair might not be exactly like Abe's, but ...

"He seems to understand everything I say," said Michelle. "He's not like ..."

Other men, thought Arlette. She let Michelle talk on. Neither was Coach Norman. Since he and that fundraiser had arrived, Arlette's thoughts kept returning to him when he was off with Louis talking with people at the church. She couldn't say it was his hair exactly that was so enticing, but he carried himself differently and never once tried to engage in church talk. He acted like he really wanted to help ...

"Mom?"

"Yes?"

"What do you think?"

"About what?

"About what I just said."

Shit. "Tell me again."

"That Abe and I really like each other."

"I think you should go slowly. Focus more on studies and tennis."

Why the hell was the same thing happening to both her and Michelle?

"I'm wide awake," said Michelle, "thinking about Abe, and can't sleep."

Join the club.

"And I don't want him to be an infidel," said Michelle.

"He's no infidel. I'm sure Clovis and those people at the school are sweet and well-intentioned, but accept or reject him on your own terms, dear."

"Thanks, Mom."

Arlette had apparently helped her daughter, but what about herself? She told Michelle Coach Norman had been a big help at Crestview, with Michelle saying the team didn't know where he had gone.

Arlette walked to the scotch bottle and poured more.

"Are you drinking?" asked Michelle "I hear ice cubes."

"He's been helpful," said Arlette. "You're lucky to have such a good guy as a coach. Are you practicing while he's gone?'

"Yeah. He left Abe in charge. Everyone on the team likes Abe."

"But not everyone else on campus likes him."

"Coach says we're different," said Michelle. "But Clovis is nice. Sometimes she just needs some help."

"I can see she would."

"OK. Goodnight, Mom."

Arlette shrieked when she bumped into Louis after she turned off the kitchen light. "My God, Louis, you scared the crap out of me!"

"Who's an infidel?" he asked.

"How long were you listening?"

"I heard you say that somebody was no infidel."

"I was talking to Michelle."

Arlette was still shaking from being startled. How much should she tell Louis? "The word 'infidel' came up in conversation with Clovis. Michelle wasn't sure what it meant."

Arlette realized both she and Michelle were caught in something outside Louis's realm of understanding—maybe even realm of consciousness. He knew nothing of women's need to talk—free of men listening—or of the occasional raw physical attraction women have toward other men. He should not be allowed to participate. Some things were best left hidden.

"They were talking," Arlette said, "about someone on campus that certain people think is not a Christian. Clovis used the word 'infidel,' and Michelle didn't know what it meant."

"Is that why she called?"

"I think she's getting a little homesick."

"Oh," said Louis, looking relieved.

Was it fair to mislead someone as gullible as Louis?

"I heard you say Coach Norman was a big help at the church," said Louis. "You haven't said much about him. I didn't know where you stood with him."

"I stand with him just fine," said Arlette. "Want me to fix you a sandwich as long as you're up?" She was already bending into the refrigerator before he could answer. Then it occurred to her she was presenting herself rearward to him in her short nightie. And there it came. His hand, right in there.

"I'd rather have something else," he said.

So would she. But at the moment Louis would do.

～

Maybe it was a poor choice of wording when Back Bay told Webster Boyd that he could "piggyback" on Boyd's effort to get money out of Louis Lewis for the college. Back Bay had never liked Boyd, and for years had managed to avoid him and the college's hidden but well-established commitment to unearthing money, scouring where the smell of cash might lie hidden, untouched, always foraging. Webster Boyd, the front man. But this chance to make the trip to St. Louis with Boyd to help with the church explosion gave Back Bay a prime opportunity to procure some tennis money. Arlette Lewis was also an interesting sidelight.

"His daughter is on the tennis team," Back Bay told Boyd. "I could piggyback on the ground work you've already laid."

Boyd bore into him through those thick glasses. "I raise money for the entire college, sir. Not just the athletic department."

"Well, I ...," began a surprised Back Bay.

"And for your information, I've established a sterling reputation, not only at Redfern but nationally, for impeccable fundraising. I did it on my own, and no one, thank you very much, will ever *piggyback* on what I've done."

Apparently Boyd didn't know about Back Bay's meeting with the college president: when the president had learned he was recruiting Michelle Lewis and that Louis Lewis's wealth was free for the picking, the president had almost ordered Back Bay to get him a meeting with Lewis. Back Bay would have to admit he did a commendable job of calming Boyd down—even with a bit of groveling here and there—but, still, their flight from Indianapolis to St. Louis was somewhat cool. At the airport, though, Back Bay made a point to get to the car-rental counter first and put the car in his name and accept the keys. He would drive to the church, knowing the person behind the wheel always has a subtle power advantage, and if that person kept talking and directing the conversation, then the control-tone would be set. It worked. By the time they reached Crestview Evangelical Temple, Webster Boyd was like a disruptive child gone meek, sitting in his car seat having learned his lesson.

"What's the preacher's name?" Back Bay asked Boyd as they ap-proached the church.

"Ummell. Can't remember his first name. His church has given money to the college, but never much. I don't expect anything out of the church now."

"How about Humble?" asked Back Bay.

"What?"

"For a first name. Humble Ummell."

Back Bay actually had the fundraiser laughing. "You'll see how humble when you meet him."

Back Bay and Boyd had already discussed the fancy footwork

needed in this venture. They should show all due concern for the plight of the church—for example, the college president had sent a team of students to help with cleanup—but subtly their mission was to curry favor with Louis Lewis in the hopes of extracting money. The problem, however, was that Lewis surely would be dishing plenty of money to the church in helping get it back on its feet. Not an easy assignment.

Back Bay would let Webster Boyd paddle his own boat. Any tennis money might best be forthcoming through Lewis's wife, who could very well be Back Bay's pipeline: a mother's concern for her daughter's well-being on the tennis team.

Wheeling into the church parking lot, they could not see any damage to the building. Louis and Arlette were standing under an overhang talking with another man. A large dump truck full of rubble thundered from behind the building, lifting dust from the asphalt, causing the Lewises and the man to shield their eyes. Back Bay and Boyd exited their rental car and headed for the overhang at the same time that another noisy truck entered their side of the building; the racket had died and the dust had settled by the time they reached the three. Back Bay stepped back to let Boyd walk swiftly to Louis, making the first contact.

"I'm sorry to greet you in such sad circumstances," said Boyd.

The two were still in the clinches and talking when Back Bay approached Arlette. He'd forgotten just how appealing she was. Dressed for physical work, she wore jeans with a loose shirt, blue bandanna holding her hair back, no makeup.

"We're here to help," he said.

"Nice of you to come."

They shook hands rather formally, yet Back Bay held the grip for what he hoped would be a noticeably longer time than necessary. Arlette stayed with him until he released.

"I'm sure there's plenty to be done," said Back Bay.

"Just being here says a lot."

Michelle was a younger version of Arlette. Abdul al-Fiasa flashed into Back Bay's mind.

"You look dressed for work," Back Bay said.

"We're cleaning inside. I'll show you."

He looked at Louis and Boyd who were now engaged with the other man. Shouldn't he at least greet them, find out who the other guy was? "First, let me say hello to your husband and the other gentleman."

"He's the preacher here," Arlette said, her shoulders slumping.

"A moment." He held up one finger to her and walked to the men.

They opened ranks, letting him enter. Back Bay could see Webster Boyd was holding forth superbly.

"Louis," said Boyd, "of course you know Coach David Norman."

Louis's face was drawn and sad. Louis clasped Back Bay's hand with both of his. "This means a great deal," said Louis.

My God, the man could wilt at any moment.

"Whatever we can do," said Back Bay.

"And," said Boyd, "this is Pastor Ummell."

Maybe the guy *didn't* have a first name. Ummell was wearing what looked to be a tailored suit that fit his lean frame precisely and handsomely. He smelled of too much cologne. Back Bay hated the son of a bitch instantly.

"A coach?" said Ummell.

"Tennis. Michelle plays on our team."

Ummell threw his head back. "Of course. I've heard so many good things about you."

No you haven't, you lying sack of shit.

"Whatever we can do," Back Bay said.

"The Lewises are working hard, along with many others," said Ummell.

But not you, you prima donna.

"What can we do?" Back Bay asked.

"I'm putting you in the care of the Lewises."

"We're honored you came," said Louis.

"Thank you," said Webster Boyd.

Back Bay looked over at Arlette. She was gone.

~

"We can check into the hotel later," said Webster Boyd. "Would you mind bringing our suitcases from the car?"

The dipshit was already ordering Back Bay around. He watched Boyd walk into the building with the two men. Where had Arlette gone?

Back Bay and Boyd headed for a church restroom to change into clothing more suitable for work. "Now," said Back Bay in the restroom as they changed, "what's the program here? Do we just work our butts off, or do we have a plan?"

"I plan to follow the Lewises' lead and wait for the right moments."

"No planned time to make pitches?"

"Not under these circumstances. I've done these things for years and know how to improvise. On the surface, we're here to help."

"Just how many church explosions have you cleaned up after?"

With Boyd stripped to his underwear—gut hanging out—Back Bay was emboldened; he had done twice-daily sets of stomach crunches for years.

Boyd turned his back.

Look at the size of that ass.

Boyd was pulling on jeans. Back Bay was already in a pair of tennis shorts.

"Back Bay, a word of warning. We've got to work together on this. We're here for the good of the college."

"Sure."

Back Bay grabbed his suitcase and headed for the door. "See you later, Webster."

Boyd was still struggling with his jeans.

Back Bay walked the empty hallways toward the noise of large machines operating; the smell of dust and grit became stronger, and then he entered a large area enclosed by a massive blue tarp, apparently the only barrier between the room and the outside. Louis, Ummell, and Arlette were talking and gesturing, the noise of machinery outside coming through the tarp. How could they hear each other? Arlette's blonde hair coned out from the back of her blue bandanna. When he reached the group, he wanted to touch her. Instead, he tapped Ummell on the shoulder.

"This must be the place," said Back Bay, barely loud enough to be heard above the din.

Ummell shouted, "God was with us. No one was in the room. Such a blessing."

Back Bay nodded.

"And just to imagine," Ummell continued, "this was our gym and recreational facility, where both children and adults spend lots of time. God chose to spare those precious lives."

"Let's get to work," shouted Arlette while Pastor Ummell shook his head in gratitude for God's goodness. "You two can talk. Coach Norman came here to work. There's rubble to sift through."

She pointed to a far part of the bombed-out room where a pyramid of ceiling-high debris was stacked, apparently shoved there with large equipment. She tossed a pair of work gloves to Back Bay. As he followed her, Webster Boyd entered the room in his dad jeans. Back Bay thought he saw Arlette rolling her eyes.

For such a slender lady, Arlette worked strongly. They each had a wheelbarrow to load rubble into, and there was a larger trailer-like affair where they put anything that might be worth saving: balls, locker doors, tennis shoes, badminton rackets, shower fixtures. This would take lots of time.

They worked alone. Why weren't the others helping? Back Bay thought about the trouble Boyd would have bending over in his jeans, and Louis was probably too upset to force manual labor on himself. Back Bay and Arlette talked sparingly. A few times they caught each other sneaking peeks. Arlette smiled each time. She must have set up this work detail herself. They worked about forty-five minutes.

"Let's take a break," she said. "We'd better see what the others are doing."

As they walked out of the room, Back Bay asked, "Do you play tennis?"

"Yes. I try to keep my game up, but I admit to slipping over the years."

"Did you ever play competitively?"

"In high school, but I wasn't good enough to make the team at St. Louis University even though tennis wasn't a very big sport there."

Self-deprecating. Charming.

"You look to be in good shape," said Back Bay. "Maybe you should take it up again more seriously."

"I just might, now that I'm not attending so many of Michelle's matches here."

"You're not planning on watching her play at Redfern?"

"That's a long way to travel."

"Short plane ride from St. Louis to Indianapolis."

"I suppose you're right."

Ummell, Louis, and Webster Boyd had joined up with three or four others—none of them in work clothes—in a hallway close to the parking lot. Ummell was holding forth: "... and the fire department said it was ..." He acknowledged Back Bay and Arlette. "I was telling these folks about the explosion."

"Go right ahead," said Arlette. "Coach Norman might like to know, too."

"Anyway," continued Ummell, "the fire department speculated the explosion was intentionally set."

A woman standing there clucked in astonishment.

"That's right," said Ummell.

"But we don't know for *certain* it was a bombing," said Louis.

Arlette crossed her arms.

"Oh," said Ummell, with a ministerial degree of certainty, "a bomb squad actually investigated. It was a bombing all right."

"Why on earth?" said the clucking woman.

"Lord only knows," said Ummell.

"Gas lines were directly over the ceiling," said Louis. "A possible leak could have ignited an explosion ..."

Arlette nudged Back Bay and whispered, "Let's get back to work."

Back Bay loved the woman's spunk, but wouldn't leaving together be a bit obvious? As they walked away, Louis was still holding out for gas leaks, and Ummell was sticking with the bomb squad's findings.

"We'll join you in a minute," Webster Boyd said, tossing his head in the direction of Back Bay and Arlette.

"Fat chance," Arlette said to Back Bay.

Walking away, Back Bay looked over his shoulder. Pastor Ummell was giving him and Arlette a long stare.

This time they worked slowly and talked more, adjusting somewhat to the noisy trucks outside the blue tarp. The woman had some pluck and didn't mind saying what was on her mind. What was that word his old coach used to use? "Moxie." She was full of it.

Apparently she had noticed Michelle's attraction to Abe and wanted to talk about it. She asked him what kind of guy he was. How old is he? Is he honorable? "Word has it he's a Muslim," she said.

Where the hell did *that* come from? Surely Abe hadn't been spreading it around after keeping it secret with Back Bay for three years.

"Where did you hear that?" he asked.

"Michelle said everyone on campus knows."

To deny it could mean the truth would come out later, and Arlette could accuse him of holding out. To admit it would be betraying the confidence Abe had entrusted with Back Bay.

"On his freshman application," said Back Bay, "he listed his religion as Christian."

"Is he a Muslim?"

The woman was relentless. "Yes."

"Good."

He could feel any power or control he had ever expected to hold over her slipping away. She was too puzzling.

"Michelle's not used to repressive environments like Redfern," said Arlette. She was rapidly tossing rubble into her wheelbarrow and raising her voice as she did. "She needs to learn about the real world."

She was also smart and articulate.

"Her poor roommate is diluted with evangelical Christian propaganda," said Arlette. "Michelle needs to experience something else while she's there. She's there because of her father. I guess you know that."

"I figured. But the tennis players aren't like the average Redfern student. I work on that."

"I guess you have to." She stopped throwing debris and looked at him. "I like that about you." She started removing her gloves. "Does your wife fit in with the Redfern crowd?"

"She tries to keep up appearances."

"Does she succeed?"

"I suppose."

She lobbed her gloves into the wheelbarrow. "My husband is as deluded as Michelle's roommate. But he comes at it honestly. He's trying hard to quit being the son of a bitch he always was and, I fear, is slowly becoming another kind of person."

"What kind is that?"

"The kind who doesn't know his wife anymore."

Arlette's dispirited face nearly buckled Back Bay right there. He came close to embracing her—this woman he thought he might hoodwink into being the pipeline from the Lewis money to the Redfern tennis program. This pleading woman. But was she pleading for Back Bay's affection or for a lost husband?

Anyway, here came the group across the large room—Ummell had them in tow.

"We've decided to knock off," said Webster Boyd, apparently the crew boss. He was all smiles.

"Bastards," whispered Arlette.

That night in the hotel room, Webster Boyd told Back Bay the whole story of how not only Louis Lewis had ponied up some money—all pledged, of course, but Webster knew he was good for it—but how two of the others had also jumped on the bandwagon.

"The trip," Boyd said, "is already a success. Let's get the biggest steak we can find in St. Louis." Boyd was giddy.

All Back Bay wanted was a stiff drink. "Any chance we could celebrate with a drink or two?"

Webster Boyd whirled on Back Bay. "I don't know why not, my man. Redfern's a long way away."

Thank God for small favors.

"Oh, and by the way," said Boyd. "We're spending the next two nights at the Lewis estate. Louis's good wife insisted."

THE GREATEST OF THESE

CHAPTER 8

Louis's mother's nursing home was nestled beautifully among elms and oaks in Kirkwood, an established St. Louis suburb. At 1:56 a.m. he pulled and rattled on the Kirkwood nursing home's locked door. He pushed an emergency bell and waited. Outside was pleasant, quiet. He listened to the breeze in the tall trees. The whine of the freeway seemed miles away. The wicker chairs and love seats on the large front porch looked inviting. If he couldn't get in, maybe he would park himself in one and rest until morning.

Helen opened the door. "Mr. Lewis. What on earth?"

He knew all the nurses and attendants and kept on their good side by covering their palms with an occasional fifty—or a hundred, depending on how cruel his mother had been to them. He thought of the place as a prison without razor wire. Always he came at lunch or dinner and brought KFC for himself and his mother. The attendants would arrange a private lounge that they would push her to in a wheelchair. He always left the rest of the KFC bucket and side dishes for the staff, making him think of Jesus feeding the five thousand.

"Good evening, Helen. I didn't know you worked nights."

"Mr. Lewis, I work whenever they tell me. This place can be a trial sometimes."

The staff always hinted for his tips. He extended his hand. Helen shook it and immediately pocketed the bill without looking.

"We're not allowed to let visitors in at this time," Helen said meekly.

Damned if she would hold him up for more money. "Helen, what's it going to hurt?" He gently touched her on the arm then turned her slowly around. They walked down the hall.

His mother's room was dark, but a dim night light was enough for Louis to see her in bed. He touched her forehead and leaned down to kiss her on the cheek. She smelled of hand lotion. The room never smelled of urine. She was to be turned every two hours during the day and changed three times, a request he had given the entire staff. Money in palms made it a standing order.

"Mother?"

She looked at him. Had she been awake?

"Louis," she said.

"I've come to see you. To talk."

She was curled up in a ball. An arm emerged from the white sheet. "Bend down here," she said.

When he did, she stroked the back of his head. "Must be the middle of the night," she said. "What's happened?"

"They've bombed my church."

"Of course they have."

"Did you hear about it?"

"I've known all along something would happen."

"No one was killed."

"Then they didn't do it right."

For years he had spoken with his mother about everything, even the Milwaukee group's most recent shenanigans. Not that she had ever offered any earth-shattering advice. Their conversations had merely turned into a habit, usually over the KFC. He wished they could eat now. She was still stroking the back of his head.

"Mother, I think it was a first warning. Next time might be different."

"Probably will be."

What worries did she have here in this safe place? She reminded him of an old house cat that spends its life sleeping all day. It wasn't fair. "You encouraged me, Mother, to stand up to the group." He removed her hand from his head and laid it on the sheet.

"So?" she asked.

His stomach knotted the way it had all his life somewhere into every conversation with her. Why couldn't he just hate her and be done with it?

"I think I'll negotiate with them," he said.

"Did you bring anything to eat?"

"It's two in the morning, Mother. KFC is closed."

"I wouldn't know about those things."

Of course she wouldn't. Curled up like a cat all day.

"What else is wrong?" she asked. "Coming here like this with no food."

"Arlette and I are going to see a psychologist. Marriage counselor."

"What good would that do?"

"In a way I was wondering that myself."

"Then why the hell are you telling me?"

Louis's mind was jumping. "I'm worried about Michelle. She may be interested in a foreigner. Arab. He's too old for her."

"What time does KFC open?"

"I'm having second thoughts about sending her to Redfern."

"I would hope so."

"And then there's Arlette. She and Michelle love me. They're sweet and want the best for me, but …"

"Why don't you let them know who's boss?"

Since discovering Jesus, he never had an answer for that one. Maybe if he gave her the right answer, she'd stop asking. Louis lifted his mother's hand from the sheet and replaced it on the back of his head. She pulled it back onto the bed.

"What else, Louis?"

"It's getting pretty late."

Maybe she would touch his face the way she sometimes did before he left. He waited.

"What do you plan to do about Arlette?" she asked.

"What do you mean?"

"You better be figuring out what I mean."

Those kinds of statements usually meant something special, but Louis was damned if he knew what *that* meant.

"Next time remember the KFC. Might be a good idea to come at lunch or dinner."

"Goodbye, Mother."

He bent over and kissed her cheek.

"Arlette and Jesus," she said into his ear. "Watch out for both."

As he was pulling away from the kiss, she touched his face.

∼

Within three days, Louis had gained some perspective: Webster Boyd and Coach Norman had arrived, the psychologist's appointment had been set, the cleanup at church was progressing, Arlette was loving and kind (*something* had certainly come over her), and from what he was hearing from Arlette, Michelle was adjusting to college—a touch of homesickness notwithstanding. He hoped the Abe situation would resolve itself.

Yet, exactly how he would confront the Milwaukee people gnawed at him. Only Arlette and his mother knew about it. They were not about to tell anyone, at least his mother wouldn't, and Arlette was his wife, after all. She held his confidence. He felt better about her than he had in several weeks. She had prepared a wonderful meal for Webster Boyd and Coach Norman and a delightful breakfast the next morning. His large pledge to Redfern seemed to make everyone happy. But it was only a pledge. He'd figure a way to actually come up with the money. Which brought him back to the Milwaukee group since so many of his holdings were attached to the loan. He would think of something.

Coach Norman sure was a good worker. The way he and Arlette had put their backs into cleaning freed up himself and others to handle much of the administrative work associated with the massive rebuilding. Pastor Ummell was counting on Louis's expertise. Dozens of things to do.

Every time he tried to find Coach Norman, however, he never seemed to be around; but the coach always left word with the church secretary, Joyce, that he had gone to buy cleanup supplies. He and Arlette were giving Home Depot and Lowe's plenty of business.

Louis wondered why he was looking forward to seeing the psychologist—seeking secular guidance went against his grain. He had left it to Arlette to find the therapist.

The office was downtown, the twenty-eighth floor of an impressive high-rise. Nice digs. Louis guessed the man was used to seeing wealthy clients. Plush chairs, cut flowers on a marble-top table. He and Arlette sat in adjacent chairs, the therapist across from them. A clock sat on a table next to the therapist's chair so that, Louis guessed, he and Arlette could tell how much time was left in the session. Louis liked the symmetry and order of the place, and the therapist was cordial, not cold as he had imagined he would be.

The man said, since therapy was expensive, he wouldn't take up much time with opening details, but they were important. First, personal histories. Louis talked and the doctor wrote. Louis found himself taking pride in listing all the St. Louis developments he had been a part of. The man nodded at each mention and seemed to be more impressed as Louis rattled them off. Louis began the list from the first and lowliest and worked up to the most recent and most striking. He concluded with the St. Charles County project. The doctor stopped writing and put down his notepad, looking first at Louis then Arlette. "OK," he said. "Enough of the preliminaries."

Louis began. "I suppose you see people like us all the time. We're having marital problems which could stem from the fact we're not communicating as we should. We have a fine daughter, beautiful home, security. But things aren't right."

"And you, Arlette?" asked the doctor.

"Louis pretty much said it."

"Arlette," said the doctor, "why did you come along with your husband to this therapy?"

"Excuse me?"

"We've been here less than ten minutes, and your husband has done all the talking. You heard him fill in your history for you, and you heard him tell me that your marriage has problems. And you tacitly agreed with his vague assessment. Now, Arlette, tell me why you came to this session."

"We need help."

The doctor leaned slightly forward in his chair. "Every marriage has problems. *People* in marriages cause problems. Marriages don't have anything but people."

Louis's head buzzed. He reached for Arlette's hand on her armrest, but she withdrew it. She was actually smiling.

"And so that we're clear on this, you don't *have* a daughter, as Louis said. Nor do you *have* a beautiful home or security. Your daughter is a person free of your marriage and yourselves. What your marriage *has* is the two of you, and my guess is each of you individually is the problem."

Louis's soft chair turned rock hard. Is this how therapy worked?

"By saying that your marriage *has* a problem, you are avoiding the fact that *you* are the problem. Let's begin with you, Arlette." The doctor leaned back into his chair.

What exactly did he want from her?

"So you want us to talk about ourselves, not particular circumstances?" she asked.

"You can talk about circumstances, but it's how you react to them that's important."

Louis guessed this made sense.

Arlette said, "I'm not reacting well to Louis throwing us into danger by getting involved with the mob."

What was that woman doing? The therapist sat there acting like every client talked of such things. The man didn't blink!

"How are you reacting to that?" the doctor asked Arlette.

"Wait," said Louis.

"Arlette is speaking," the doctor said.

"At times," said Arlette, "I resent the control he takes over our family by making ill-informed decisions and generally foisting his will on us. This underworld fiasco is the worst. At other times, I appreciate how he has provided for us and looks out for our well-being."

She looked at Louis but spoke to the doctor. "I've always been ambivalent about Louis."

Why was Louis choking up?

"Louis," said the doctor, "you appear troubled that Arlette mentioned the mob."

"To say the least," said Louis.

"Why are you troubled?"

"Would you want your wife telling others how you've messed up?"

"Let's avoid hypotheticals."

"I'm more troubled that she said she was ambivalent about me."

"Arlette," said the therapist, looking at her, expecting a response.

"Isn't love-hate a common feeling in relationships?" she asked.

"Indeed. Louis?" said the man, expecting something.

"'Love should always abide,'" said Louis. "'Love one another.' 'For the greatest of these is love.' I'm quoting the Bible."

The man just sat there.

"Sir," said Louis, "I'm a changed man since I found Jesus. He expects us to always love one another. He didn't say to love-hate one another."

"Do you always love everything Arlette does?" asked the therapist.

"Of course not. But I always love her."

"That's a vague notion, free from troubling circumstances that arise in life. People reveal themselves based on how they react to situations, not on held beliefs. Arlette said she is troubled by the mob. Arlette, do you hate what's happening with it?"

"Yes, I do."

"That appears to be an honestly held feeling of Arlette's. Like it or not, such hate can manifest itself into a person's feelings for another."

"I'll stick to the Bible," said Louis.

Now he knew exactly why Arlette had chosen this guy. Pastor Ummell had spoken of secular humanists.

Arlette reached for Louis's armrest and patted it. He couldn't resist. He put his hand on hers. And when he did, the most humiliating thing happened. He started crying. Not wimpy sobs, but the full-out bawling of a man losing control. Why oh why?

"Here, Louis," said Arlette, calmly. She put a box of tissues in his lap.

As he wiped his eyes and nose, Arlette's hand rubbed the back of his head until the crying had mercifully ended.

STILL IN TRAINING

CHAPTER 9

"About halfway through the session your dad started crying."

Michelle shifted her cell phone to the other ear and felt sweat running down her leg. She needed to be in the shower instead of talking with her mother. Abe had just put the team through a long, tough practice, and, besides, the weather had turned incredibly hot. For some reason Clovis had left the temperature in their room too high—very odd because the girl was always too warm—and Michelle hadn't yet cranked up the air-conditioning because her cell had been ringing when she'd walked in. While her mother talked, she tried to figure out the thermostat; Clovis always handled that.

"It was sad and also kind of funny," her mother said.

"How was it funny?" Michelle pictured her dad crying, and nothing about that seemed funny.

"He tried to steer things his direction, and the therapist was too much for him. I guess 'funny' isn't the right word. Pathetic is more like it."

Michelle turned the gauge to fifty degrees, then heard a click and the low roar of the air-conditioning.

"The therapist is good. By the time we left, he had our family figured out, and as much as it hurts, I think he's right."

"I thought you went there for you and Dad."

"Sweetheart, we're all in this together. We're trying to get some help."

"What's so bad about our family?"

"He says we're destructive."

"Does this guy have a name?" Michelle was still sweating and couldn't feel the AC yet.

"No need to get defensive, Michelle."

"Well ..."

"His name is Dr. Ramsey."

"Mom, maybe you and Dad are the ones having the problems and are just dragging me in."

"If you don't want to hear this, then—"

"Go ahead. How are we destructive?"

In the last couple of days, Michelle and Abe had talked and talked about their families, and she found herself telling him more than she had revealed to anyone: her father's wealth and compulsive drive, his recent conversion to evangelical Christianity, his pathetic attempts at change. Even how the college president was circling—his eyes on her dad's money. She said her mother was bright and maybe on the verge of drinking too much. When she told Abe that she loved her parents a lot, it was as though she had permission to distance herself from them; somehow she could speak critically of them more freely and justifiably. This phone conversation with her mother was starting to annoy her.

"Dr. Ramsey said some people can't handle their own freedom and want to flee it."

"Freedom?"

"Making your own decisions. All of us have that right. Some people try to avoid their own freedom by destroying it. Are you following?"

"I guess."

"He said that your father and I are both victims of authoritarianism. He said that I have submitted to the power of your dad's authority, and by doing that, I've destroyed my freedom to be myself. And by your dad being the authority, he has destroyed his own identity and, thus, his own freedom."

Michelle wished Abe could hear this.

"We each are destroying ourselves," her mother said.

"It makes sense."

Michelle pictured Abe sitting in their living room in St. Louis on Christmas break. Her mother would be saying something beautifully profound, and her father would be listening, nodding. *And, Abe, this is the way we can be some day!*

"Michelle? Are you still there?"

"Sure."

"He also said you could be involved in all this."

"Can this wait?"

"Don't be angry."

"Maybe I have a right to be."

"Just let me tell you what he said."

"Whatever."

"He said we may be a symbiotic family."

"Was this guy trying to impress you?"

"He knew we were both educated, dear."

"Maybe someday I will be, too."

"Listen to what he told us. Symbiosis is the relationship two organisms have that cannot live without each other. Some members of a symbiotic family get overpowered by other members of the family and can't realize their own freedom."

She and Abe would never overpower each other.

"I didn't say this to your dad and the doctor," her mother continued, "but maybe that's what happened when your dad sent you off to Redfern. He swallowed you up in his own beliefs and overpowered you. He destroyed your own freedom. Know what I mean?"

"But I really like Redfern, Mom. Especially Clovis and Abe. They're both good friends and both so different. I'm glad I'm here. Dad did me a favor." Michelle didn't like her mother's long pause. "Mom?"

"I'm only saying what I think."

"I know."

Now the room was cooler, but the back of Michelle's shirt still clung to her. She stood up and walked around the room.

"Mom, Abe told me he was Muslim. It's true."

Another pause. "So he's been hiding it."

"Had to. Some people around here would freak out about it."

"But apparently, according to Clovis, *everyone* knew."

"I didn't tell Abe that."

"Why not? Is he too weak to take it?"

"Why are you being this way?"

Michelle wished she were with Abe and in his arms, like last night on the bench when they'd spoken of trying to find a place to make love. He'd said he would work it out.

"Do me a favor," said Michelle. "Don't be talking about me in any more sessions with your friend the doctor. Leave me out of it."

Michelle heard ice cubes rattling.

"I'm sorry if I made you angry," said her mother.

"Don't let Dad make you drink. He may be swallowing *you* up."

Michelle was sorry she'd said it.

"I guess," said her mother, "we've talked long enough."

Keys rattled outside the door. "Clovis is coming in, and I need to get in the shower. Talk with you later."

Clovis burst in the room. "Whew," she said, "it's like an oven in here."

"But cooler than before. I adjusted the thermostat."

Michelle couldn't remember if she'd told her mother goodbye or not.

～

Back Bay's return to campus gave Abe more time to spend with Michelle. Abe had taken his interim coaching duties seriously, and Michelle had noticed that, in the times they spent off the court, he seemed to be preoccupied.

She looked forward to those long times after dinner and before the evening study time in her room. People appeared not to notice her and Abe so much as they sat talking and laughing on the bench. They did not show displays of affection, but Michelle was certain people thought of them as a couple. Once, a student Michelle didn't know saw her in the library studying alone and asked, "Where's Abe?"

With Back Bay coming to campus and resuming the coaching duties, Abe was giving her his full attention. God, she loved that. Even when she had boldly asked him about the rumor that he was Muslim, he did not appear shocked. Instead, he admitted—rather proudly she thought—he was indeed Muslim, and, thus, they began a long and exhilarating discussion about religion in general. They didn't dwell on particular religious differences but, rather, on religion's function in people's lives, a thrilling exchange with a man she was to discover had a natural curiosity for intellectual pursuits. Afterward, while climbing the stairs to her room, she found herself sexually excited thinking of the past hour and a half with Abdul al-Fiasa, talking of serious matters. By the time she reached her room, her mouth was dry, and when she said hello to Clovis, her voice squeaked oddly. She immediately went to the bathroom and took a long shower where she stimulated herself, brought on by nothing more than an open exchange with Abe on religion. My God, how could that be? When her orgasm arrived, she placed a hand on her mouth to muffle any sound. What would Clovis think? Did Clovis masturbate in the shower? It didn't matter. Michelle was still limp as she toweled off, and her studying that night was relaxed and productive. Look what that man had done.

The first practice after Back Bay's return (he wasn't as tough on them as Abe) when she had just finished showering (no *long* shower that time), her mother called. Clovis was at her desk. Michelle was eager to get to the dining hall.

"Are you still angry about what I told you?" asked her mother.

"I haven't even thought about it." Would that in some strange way disappoint her mother? "No, I'm not mad."

"Good."

"Is that why you called?" Michelle wanted to move the conversation along.

"Yes and no. There are some things I need to tell you."

Ice cubes rattled. No chance to make this short.

"I don't have anyone but you to talk with about this," her mother said. "I've thought this over a lot in the last day. You're stronger than I am in many ways, especially since our last conversation when you stood up to me. I'm hoping you'll understand and accept what I'm about to tell you. I think you will."

Michelle didn't like the feel of this.

Her mother continued. "You seemed to appreciate what I was saying about how our family might be destroying each of our freedoms. You did, didn't you?"

"I guess so. Mom, what is it?"

More ice cube rattling. "Oh, honey, this is so hard for me to say."

"Then don't say it."

"I cheated on your dad."

Michelle had been reaching across the bed for her purse. Her knees buckled, and she fell face down across the bed, knocking the phone from her ear.

Clovis twitched. "Are you OK?" She lumbered from her chair.

"I dropped the phone," said Michelle.

Clovis hoisted Michelle back into her chair. "Where's the phone?" asked Clovis.

Michelle discovered it was still in her hand.

"What happened?" asked Clovis.

"Tell you later." Michelle brought the phone to her ear.

Back in her chair, Clovis lifted her hands and mouthed, "What?"

"I'm talking with Mom."

"What happened?" asked her mother.

"I tripped with the phone in my hand."

"I heard you tell Clovis you would tell her later. Are you going to tell her what I said?"

"Maybe you should tell *me* what you just said."

Clovis was bending intently toward Michelle, who waved her off.

"I said," said her mother, "I cheated on your father, had an affair, slept with a man. I had to tell someone. Michelle, you're my best friend in this. The only one who would understand."

Michelle shifted the cell phone to the other ear. The laptop on her desk appeared to be spinning, and she couldn't make it stop.

"Say something, Michelle."

Still nothing. She heard her mother start to cry. "Please talk, Michelle."

Michelle placed her hand on the laptop to steady it—and herself. "First off, stop crying," said Michelle. "Take a fucking drink, for God's sake."

Clovis touched Michelle's shoulder and looked at her wide-eyed. Michelle had no time for Clovis's feelings. "Mom, I can only listen if you get yourself under control."

Sniffing and nose blowing on the other end. For some weird reason, Michelle wanted to shove Clovis from her chair. She had no right to be in on this.

"I told myself I wouldn't cry," said her mother. "I'm sorry."

"Maybe you *should* be sorry. What do you want me to say?"

"Just listen to me. That's all."

And listen Michelle did. All the way through dinner and Clovis's return and until the pounding on the door, when someone said Abe had tried to call wanting to see her. Why wasn't she answering her cell phone? That's when she finally stopped listening to her mother. Both women had done their share of crying during that time, and once, looking over at Clovis, Michelle saw her crying too. Of course, Michelle realized, even listening to only one side of the conversation, Clovis knew what was up. Before heading out of the room to find Abe, Clovis hugged Michelle and said she was sorry.

"For what?"

"For your parents. And you."

"Thanks."

"Are you going to see Abe now?"

"Yeah."

"Be careful."

"What do you mean by that?"

Clovis wouldn't say anything more, which caused Michelle to slam the door as she left.

Abe sat on the stone bench wearing khaki shorts and a black polo shirt, the first time Michelle had seen him wear it. His skin and sable hair combined with the blackness of the shirt in such alluring and varying shades that she nearly wept. He rose from the bench, walking briskly to her. She was *feeling* him long before they touched.

She needed to tell him about her mother and Coach Norman, but her first words to him astonished her. "Did you find a place?"

The September sky was already darkening. How long had she been on the phone? Michelle achingly refrained from embracing him there at the stone bench where many people strolled in the evening, always throwing furtive glances at the distinctive couple—one white, the other swarthy; one Christian, one Muslim.

Abe touched both her shoulders, holding her at his long arms' length. "Not the best. Found a place."

"Let's go there," she said.

"Your head is going in many directions."

Michelle felt people circling them and staring, but when she looked no one was there. The entire area was theirs.

"Do me here," she said. "Right now."

He snickered and removed his hands from her shoulders. "Why did you not come to the dining hall?"

Michelle hardly heard what he said. Instead she boldly looked at his khaki shorts for a sign. And there it was. She snickered because that dusky face was blushing.

"This way," he said.

With each step they seemed to walk a little faster.

He told her to wait on the tennis court bleachers for ten minutes before entering the dressing room door that he would leave unlocked.

"I kept the extra key from when Back Bay was gone," he told her. "I will keep it longer, until he asks. Hoping he will forget."

After tennis practice, the courts were open for all students. Coin-operated lights allowed night play, and several people had turned them on. Michelle watched as awkward students slapped at balls, some nearly falling down when swinging. For a few seconds, she actually concentrated on how she would coach such awful swings, showing correct footwork, racket placement ...

How long had she waited? As she rose to leave, she felt the readiness between her legs. She walked slowly. Some people spoke and waved. "Time to study," she told one couple. Abe had told her the outside door to the men's dressing room was always locked and rarely used. Fortunately it was at the back of the field house. Her hand was shaking as she turned the knob.

Abe waited inside and, taking her hand, walked with her through a darkened locker room into a small training room. He had turned on a desk lamp in one corner, illuminating metal shelves full of bottles and rolls of tape. A padded training table sat in the center of the room.

"I brought sheets," he said, pointing to the table. He hadn't yet put them on. "I'll do it," he said, snapping open a sheet.

His back to her, Michelle began quickly undressing. When naked, she felt the cool of the room on her skin. She rubbed her erect nipples and shivered. Walking to Abe, who was trying to tuck the sheet into a table ill-equipped for sheet-tucking, she moved her hands around his hips until reaching his fly. He stopped the bed-making. She squeezed him gently, feeling the bulge.

"Let me do this," she said, his back still to her. "Don't turn around."

When the khaki shorts and boxers were pooled at his feet, she told him to step out of them. He did as told, but in an instant, Abe turned and lifted her onto the training table. He was fumbling with his shorts on the floor, reaching into a pocket. She didn't look as he tore open something that must have been a condom. She heard a snapping sound. He was suddenly on top of her, kissing her gently.

This alone is enough, she thought.

After entering her ("Oh, Jesus," she said, throbbing), it must have been only a short while before she was aware of the training-room door opening. Abe must have been too busy to notice. When she looked at the doorway, Back Bay Norman stood there.

Was this true?

"Abe." She panted and tapped him on the back. "Abe."

Now Abe was looking into the doorway. Michelle felt him go limp.

THE LIGHTS
CHAPTER 10

For two days after Coach Norman left, Arlette would not allow herself to cry, and she certainly could not tell anyone. Their tryst had been full of passion, and David Norman—she refused to call him Back Bay—was caring and considerate throughout the whole process. "Process" was the right word for what they did. Everything about it satisfied any assumptions she might have held about having a fling with a handsome man. It began and ended on all the proper notes—and then it was over. But not completely.

She still replayed select moments. The fucking was a fine experience—perhaps the best she had known—but other more subtle memories remained: caressing his body and exploring in near obsessive detail; the way he combed her hair with his fingers; the gentle temple rubs he gave her as he slowly thrust in and out.

"This can't be your first affair," she said after regaining a measure of composure during their first of four encounters.

"Nope," he said, too off-handedly for Arlette's liking. "It's not. You?"

"My first."

Their first time had been at Crestview Evangelical Temple itself. Going out for supplies at Lowe's had provided them with a surprising detour that caught her off guard. The church's choir-robe room was quiet. Wearing her jeans and work shirt that day, she hadn't worn the best underwear. That morning, she had thrown on panties that might have belonged to a woman twice her age. When he removed her jeans, the thought of him seeing those frumpy things shamed her.

The next day, their encounter took place in wholly different environs—her bedroom after Louis and Webster Boyd had dashed out to the church. She and Coach Norman said they would follow after they picked up supplies at Lowe's. Sleek and dainty panties this time—so much so that the coach asked for a model's runway walk before the real show. She was embarrassed, giggly, and happy to finally take them off. This time in their lovemaking, she assumed more dominance, and in doing so, had more exploratory adventures. The man's body was stunning.

Yet, she was surprised to learn—after he had left town—that he was only a man. What more could she say? The astounding thought occurred that she could possibly have other trim and delightful bodies with only minimal effort. She could work it. And when she did, how would Coach Norman stack up? And what would she have gained?

Her afterglow crashed miserably within hours of his leaving. Oh, she tried to resurrect the soft and tender moments with him, but an emptiness hurled her somewhere else, leaving her groveling, almost as though she might crawl to Louis in supplication. Is this what happens with affairs? What was Coach Norman thinking about all this?

Her call to Michelle seemed to be the right move, especially after the therapy session; she and her daughter could commiserate about Louis's faults—the *family* faults, really. She supposed it was a way for her to gain some kind of equilibrium. Michelle's reaction knocked Arlette loopy, and the next day left her shaky and alone. The girl was gaining strength, and Arlette was stuck with no one, not even the man who provided moments of amazing pleasure. Even if he were there, Arlette might be so wracked with guilt she couldn't carry through.

When she told Michelle about sleeping with David, she was glad she did. Something cleansing about it. Maybe Arlette was beginning to nurture Michelle into becoming her one true friend amid this mess that had the family reeling. It was time the girl began facing some hard facts. Arlette had to believe that, or otherwise she might explode.

∾

The sight was so shocking that he was frozen in the doorway—that long dark body on top of the white girl. Back Bay was dizzy. Then the girl began whispering, "Abe, Abe." Who in the hell is she? No mistaking the guy.

Several years before, he had walked in on a fellow coach banging some chick in a locker room. He had her bent over the table—one just like the one he was looking at—and the chick didn't see Back Bay, only his buddy, the coach. Back Bay gave him a smile and a sly little wave, then left the room.

"I'll treat this like it never happened," he later told his buddy. And that was that. No one was any worse for the wear.

Back Bay watched Abe roll off the girl. She turned her back to the doorway. Back Bay thought he smelled more than the usual locker room funk.

"I'll talk to both of you when you leave," he said. There was only one way out of the training room. He closed the door and gave them their privacy.

She had to be Michelle Lewis, and if she was, did he report what he saw to Arlette? In fact, should he even try to contact Arlette again? When he'd left St. Louis, Arlette had been becoming too clingy for his taste, and he'd resolved to drop her as a possible pipeline to her husband's money. Something wasn't right about the vibes she'd been sending out. He should have realized that most first timers would place too much weight on such intimacy. Time to back off. The woman, though, was sweet beyond measure.

Those kids were staying in there a long time. He could hear their muffled talk. Did they think they could outwait him? Finally, Abe emerged first and closed the door behind him. "She doesn't want to see you," Abe said.

"Not good, Abe."

The lad was looking Back Bay straight in the eye, showing none of the meekness he should. The boy should be fawning and licking Back Bay's boots. Didn't he know Back Bay could have him expelled, tossed out of Redfern in disgrace? Maybe even sent back to Algeria, for Christ's sake! But of course Back Bay wouldn't do anything like that. They were almost like equals. Abe would be this year's NCAA Division I national champ, with any luck at all. No, the kid was safe here. Still, Back Bay had hoped for something less bold after being caught fucking in the training room.

"I guess you still have the locker room key I gave you," said Back Bay.

Abe held it up. "And I'll keep it," he said.

"What?"

"I plan to use it again for the same purpose."

Surely the kid was playing some kind of game. How long could he keep it up?

"Who's the girl?" asked Back Bay.

"Someone you know."

"I figured as much."

"And you have been knowing her mother very much too."

Nothing much popped into Back Bay's head. It was like he had been hit by a sudden electrical shock with the full impact waiting to strike later. Then the jolt. They knew about him and Arlette. What was that family up to?

"Abe, what are you saying?"

"You fucked Michelle's mother. And, yes, she fucked you, too. Both of you are guilty of a terrible thing. Now you see Michelle and me. But we are not married to another person."

Back Bay knew match point when he saw it.

He walked away then stopped and turned. "Each time you leave," said Back Bay, "remember to turn out the lights."

~

After Back Bay left, Michelle and Abe sat fully clothed on the training table talking things over. Abe's long arms had encircled her until she stopped quaking, and he could eventually get her to see the humor of the situation. Would marriage be like this, with Abe gently holding her until she was released from fright and back to normal? She could only hope. She made him tell her several times the exact scene with Coach Norman. Sometimes in retelling, he would remember something else. She wanted to know exactly what was said. Would Coach Norman hold this against them?

"He can't," said Abe. "He knows we know about him. And didn't he let me keep this key?" He held it up before Michelle. "Insurance. Think what this means to us. We play tennis, and he stays away. Simple."

"Should we come here every night?"

"Every night you say." Abe laughed and kissed her nose. "Every night?" he asked.

"Yes, and more tonight," she said.

~

She and Abe didn't discuss whether Michelle should tell her mother. But since Clovis already knew about her mother and Coach Norman, Michelle wanted her roommate to know everything.

"I hope everything went OK," said Clovis when Michelle returned to the room.

"Yes and no. It was weird."

Clovis must have been nervous. Michelle saw two empty bags of chips wadded in the trash can.

"Were you worried?" asked Michelle.

"The first time with a man can often be confusing."

"So you think we had sex?"

"Having sex when you're upset can be dangerous."

The girl never ceased to surprise Michelle. This was like talking to an adult. "You seem to know what you're talking about," said Michelle.

"I do."

Clovis pulled open a drawer and removed a package of cookies. Oreos. Double Stuf. "Want some?" said Clovis.

Michelle took three.

"You've had sex?" asked Michelle.

"Yeah. Strange isn't it?"

Michelle reached for a fourth cookie.

"Who would have guessed, me sleeping with someone."

"I'm surprised," said Michelle. "I thought maybe you were against that."

"That's not why you're surprised. All people have to do is look at me and assume no man would ever want me."

Michelle chewed on her Oreo which gave her time to consider how to backtrack. Jeez, how she loved Clovis at this moment—making herself so vulnerable.

"You can tell me what happened tonight," said Clovis, grinning. "We got a full package of cookies."

Michelle burst from her chair and hugged Clovis's wide shoulders. As Michelle cried, Clovis stayed firm in her chair, patting her back until the crying ceased. And then she told Clovis everything about Coach Norman finding them, and how she and Abe had stayed and talked until he had soothed her back to normal, and they had put things in perspective.

"Sounds like he has the key to your heart," said Clovis.

She wished Clovis could be with her forever.

"I can read minds," said Clovis. "You're going to call and tell your mom." She pointed to Michelle's cell phone.

"But Abe and I promised not to tell."

"You told *me*."

"You're different."

"You got *that* right."

"Please listen while I talk," said Michelle.

Clovis answered by biting into an Oreo.

～

Exactly how does a born-again Christian deal with a bunch of scoundrels? Louis told the therapist and Arlette he would try to negotiate his way out of the mess he had gotten himself into, but Louis knew from experience that real negotiations take place only from a position of power. And he had none. In fact, the Milwaukee group had asserted such power that all he could do was give in and let them take all the collateral he had so stupidly put up. Where would that leave him then? Arlette was used to her way of life, with all the clothes, cars, club memberships, and soirees at their estate—the estate itself, for God's sake. Michelle's tuition would need to be paid—he had enough for one year—and then what? Community college? Reneging on his pledges to Crestview and Redfern would be humiliating. Of course, unloading the house and the land it sat on would bring ready cash ... ah, shit. That was part of the collateral, too.

He'd forgotten about his mother. Eight grand a month he paid the Kirkwood nursing home, not to mention the fucking tips to the employees. Why were words like *fucking* popping into his thoughts so readily?

Jesus seemed to be the one thing Louis could cling to, but he knew so little about Him. Pastor Ummell kept Louis and the Crestview congregation updated on what Jesus would expect them to believe about important issues like abortion, gay marriages, creation, and a host of other topics. On that stuff, Lewis was just fine. He hadn't had to change his thinking on any of that. But what would Jesus want when Louis's world was starting to come apart? When he felt trapped?

Several times a day, Louis thought he might vomit, and his head usually ached. Sometimes he hugged Arlette so hard, hoping to get a sudden splash of peace, but all she usually said was, "Louis, that hurts." Often he found himself repeating the mantra Pastor Ummell had advised, "Help me, Jesus. Help me, Jesus." Sure enough, saying it brought comfort from time to time, but other times, when driving in heavy traffic with his gut aching from worry, he had to concentrate to keep from crashing, and the mantra fell away.

Once, while driving on I-270, he passed a pickup that had on the back windshield "Read the Red" with a cross emblazoned within the lettering. When Louis asked Pastor Ummell what it meant, he said that in some Bibles, Jesus's words were printed in red.

"Always focus on Jesus's words," Pastor told him, and clapped him on the back.

Louis went right out and bought such a Bible and then sat down that night and read the red, all of it. Puzzling stuff. The next Sunday at church, Louis asked Pastor if every word of the Bible was true. Louis thought the man might implode. "Who have you been listening to?" asked the outraged pastor.

"Just doing some reading."

"Every word is literally true."

That night, just to be certain, Louis reread the red and was more stymied than ever. Jesus was sure full of contradictions, and Louis saw no clear way to reconcile the inconsistencies. Why hadn't the Jesuits at DeSmet High School pointed out all these problems? Who knew all that stuff was in there? Did Arlette know about the contradictions? Did Michelle? How about his mother? Was that why the three took such a dim view of his decision to be born-again?

Both nights after staying up late reading the red, he sneaked into Arlette's scotch, hoping for an increased measure of calmness to sort through what he had read. In thinking it over, he began from the premise that because he was born-again he was going to heaven instead of hell—that was pretty black and white. Yet it was those unsettling words of Jesus that had him flummoxed. Where in there was the solution to how he should handle the Milwaukee group, the double-crossing bastards? From what he could figure, the Pharisees and Sadducees were scheming scoundrels trying to trip up Jesus at every turn, but Jesus would calmly say something back to them that sounded profound (but that Louis thought was equally tricky), and the rascals would walk away either astonished at the wisdom or scratching their heads in wonder. If Louis did that to the Milwaukee group, it would mean certain crucifixion.

He had to go easy on the scotch since he needed a clear head. Too much booze would addle him, as it did Arlette.

All his life, he had heard about Jesus and His turn-the-other-cheek, go-the-extra-mile advice. It always sounded like a surefire way to get your balls cut off in the business world. But there it was, smack in the red: "Do not resist one who is evil. But if any one strikes you on the right cheek, turn to him the other also … and if any one forces you to go one mile, go with him two miles." Should he let the Milwaukee sons of bitches have everything they wanted and then give them more?

Honestly, though, Louis hadn't been on his toes in that deal and hadn't thought it out well, so maybe God was punishing him for not being shrewd enough.

And then there was the part where Jesus told His disciples to follow Him and "take no gold or silver or copper in your belts." Leave all your money behind and follow Jesus? Well, if things kept going the way they were, that sure as hell might happen!

How about the time some guy told Jesus he had followed all the commandments and asked what else he should do? "If you would be perfect, go, sell what you possess and give to the poor, and you will have treasure in heaven; and come, follow me." Is that what Arlette and Michelle would want? To become poor? They might skin him alive.

This one, "Do not lay up for yourselves treasures on earth, where moth and rust consume and where thieves break through and steal." So, Louis reckoned, his problem must have been making all that money in the first place so the Milwaukee pricks could steal it.

All of those things made Jesus look like a humble, peace-loving guy—which Louis aspired to be, regardless of how much money he had to lose.

But then Jesus pulled some stunts that contradicted His nice guy image; He could be downright pompous. One of His disciples said he would follow Jesus, but, first, the guy had to bury his father. "Follow me, and leave the dead to bury the dead." What? Ignore burying your father?

Once a woman came to Jesus with expensive oil and poured it on His head, and the disciples asked why she should waste it when they could sell it and give it to the poor. "She has done a beautiful thing to me. For you always have the poor with you, but you will not always have me." Rather arrogant.

Louis was dizzy, and he didn't think it was from the scotch.

One day Jesus was hungry as he walked along with his disciples. He saw a fig tree that had no fruit, only leaves. "'May no fruit ever come from you again.' And the fig tree withered at once." Poor tree—wrong place at the wrong time. Why would Jesus get pissed off and kill a tree just because He was hungry?

Speaking of pissed off, how about the time Jesus entered the temple and overturned the tables of the money changers and started whipping them?

Then the topper. Louis nearly fell over when he read this one. "Do not think I have come to bring peace on earth; I have not come to bring peace, but a sword ... and a man's foes will be those of his own household." Fight your family?

Who knew Jesus said all that? Why hadn't Pastor Ummell filled him in? Jesus must have had a split personality or a touch of manic depression—humble and gracious one minute, arrogant the next. Maybe He took the Messiah business too far.

Louis supposed he was glad to know exactly what Jesus said. After reading and rereading the red, Louis was comforted mostly; he could practice slash-and-burn techniques ("I have not come to bring peace, but a sword"), then when the occasion was right, he could feel good about losing his wealth and following Jesus.

Interesting guy, that Jesus. A complicated one.

～

The call came through from Webster Boyd at Redfern College as Louis sat in his office trying to figure how to approach the Milwaukee group. Did Boyd want Louis's money already? It had only been three days since he made the pledge.

"From one friend to another," said Boyd.

Money always made friends. "Glad to hear from you," said Louis.

"I only share this with you because I'm concerned about you personally. This has nothing to do with your commitments to Redfern. This goes beyond business."

"Is Michelle in some kind of trouble?" Probably something about that tall, Arab kid.

"No, no," said Boyd.

"By the way, is that tennis player named Abe a Muslim?"

"Well, Louis, I don't know ..."

"Because if he is, the whole Redfern community needs to know."

"That's not why I called ..."

"Not just because my daughter invited him to have dinner with us when we were there or because she needn't be seeing someone of his religious belief, if indeed he is a Muslim. But because, if he is a Muslim, he could be a threat to our whole Christian belief system, let alone the integrity of Redfern's admissions standards, not to mention the terrorist possibilities."

"Louis, I doubt there's a need to be alarmed."

The thought of casting out the money changers from Redfern College was sparking Louis's imagination. "The whole thing might be something to look into," said Louis.

"I suppose I could ..."

But Jesus would probably want humility coupled with righteous indignation. "Forgive me, Webster. This isn't why you called. I'll get off my high horse."

"Again, Louis, as a friend I'm telling you this." Long silence. "Your wife is seeing another man."

Louis felt almost no reaction, nothing like he felt when hearing the church was bombed. And why was that? Had he been expecting the news?

"You called to tell me *that*?"

"Did you know?"

What could Louis say? Of course he didn't know. "Is that any of your business?" asked Louis.

"I don't want to see you hurt by anyone at Redfern."

"Slow down, partner." Louis grabbed a heavy, glass paperweight from his desk, one Arlette gave him, and walked to a window. "Before we go any further, tell me why you thought you needed to tell me this, if it's true." A raw hatred for Webster Boyd was building in Louis.

"Pastor Ummell and I have discussed this at length and ..."

"What does he have to do with this?"

"I told him after I watched your wife slip into a small room at Crestview Temple with another man, then watched them emerge some time later. I told Pastor Ummell because I needed to confide in someone. This whole situation is most unfortunate on several fronts. We felt you should be the one to handle it. Not us."

Louis rolled the paperweight in his hand. "So you two think I should handle a situation that I have no evidence of knowing is true. You're accusing my wife of something that might not have actually happened. This is bordering on slander, my friend."

"It's all true. The man she was with confessed."

Louis found himself marching around his office wanting to fling the paperweight through the damned window. He let Webster Boyd talk, telling him how Coach Back Bay Norman had slept with Arlette, confessing under pressure in front of Boyd and Ummell. Boyd said he knew that if word of the liaison was made public at Redfern, Coach Norman stood to be fired. Did Louis want the college to take action against Norman? Webster Boyd was certain that Louis didn't want the incident to be made public, and Louis could trust Boyd's discretion. Any action or lack of it was entirely up to Louis. He told Louis all this from their relationship as friends, of course. Boyd said he and Ummell would be praying for Louis and Arlette.

By the time he hung up, Louis was weak. He burned with hatred for Webster Boyd but felt an intense love for Arlette. (Why was her indiscretion giving him a hard-on?) About Coach Norman, Louis was neutral. Why waste emotion on a man who was guilty of nothing more than recognizing and enjoying the charms of his lovely Arlette? Louis could turn the other cheek to that man.

But he hated finks like Webster Boyd. He imagined bashing in his face with the paperweight, and if he had any strength left, doing the same to Pastor Ummell. Drive them both straight from the temple. Louis guessed he was *really* starting to see red.

A TEST EVERY DAY

Coach Norman knew himself to be cautious and diplomatic about the way he conducted himself in the world. Growing up in South Boston, he had observed plenty of his buddies trying to be wise guys, attempting through sheer brio to carve themselves niches and push their way through the neighborhood, then taking their acts to school, usually getting bloodied and becoming hopelessly weak. They could never see themselves as pathetic losers, mainly because, Back Bay learned later, they didn't know how to hold back, not give it all at once. Most people in his neighborhood were dealt losing hands, yet through no shrewdness of his own—but probably out of fear—Back Bay learned that he who hesitates often learns more. Waiting can keep a guy out of trouble. Plan the move carefully.

He was being blackmailed by two kids—his own players—and held hostage. It was like Abe and Michelle were two haughty southies sneering at him and ready to pounce. He might even need to alter his coaching style with them, pussyfoot and let himself be their toady.

Back Bay couldn't forget the larger ramifications either—his wife finding out or the college administration tossing him out if Webster Boyd ratted on him. And the Lewis family must be one tight outfit. The only way Michelle could have found out was if Arlette had told her. Jesus, what kind of mother tells her daughter something like that?

When the call came in, Back Bay had already determined he had nowhere to turn and should lie low for a while. He was in his field-house office going over some of last year's stats before he started planning the day's practice schedule. He answered without looking at the caller ID.

"This is Louis Lewis in St. Louis."

Not since he'd last been chased down an alley in South Boston did David Norman feel such fear. "Hello, Mr. Lewis."

"I've got a couple of things on my mind, Coach."

"Good to hear from you."

"I've always been your biggest fan."

"Thank you. Everything OK at the church?"

"I imagine the church will take care of itself. This is personal."

Why did he even answer the fucking phone? "Anything I can do?"

"You and my wife have already done enough. So if you're thinking of bluffing your way through this, forget it."

He was chased down a blind alley. "I'm sorry for everything."

"The oddest thing has come over me. Care to hear what it is?"

Was the question rhetorical?

"Well?" asked Lewis.

"What is it?"

"I still like you."

"And I like you, too." God. How stupid.

"I'm not going to have you publicly drawn and quartered," said Lewis. "Arlette didn't tell me about the two of you. And to be honest, I'm not sure if I'll even let her know that I know. Sound fair enough?"

"Certainly," said Back Bay.

"Arlette is a beautiful woman, and I can't blame men for wanting her. In some ways I guess I'm flattered, if that makes any sense."

"It does." Shut up for God's sake.

"Which doesn't give you or her the right to betray me in the way you two have."

"I understand."

Blackmail coming, no doubt.

"I've decided that I can fight only on one front at a time," said Lewis. "I have no desire to bring Arlette into the battle that I might have chosen to wage against you two. I have other battles to fight. All I know is that it feels good to forgive you. Which is more than I can say for a couple of other people you and I know."

"Oh?"

"I got wind about you and Arlette through Pastor Ummell and Webster Boyd. I'm not sure if they told me because they want me to do something for them or because they're just a couple of assholes. I don't trust either of those guys. Judging from the way you carry yourself, I'm guessing you don't care much for them either."

"That's right."

"I gathered as much. But here's the strangest thing. I think I might have some kind of alliance with you."

Back Bay thought he detected a slight catch in Lewis's throat.

"I don't know," continued Lewis, weakly, "but I believe I can trust you to level with me."

"About what?"

"It's really about Michelle's welfare. I imagine she's seeing that Arab tennis player. Am I right?"

Back Bay shifted in his chair. Lewis *was* blackmailing him.

"They appear to be friends," said Back Bay.

"The guy, Abe is his name I think, seems to be nice enough. But I'm concerned about his affiliations. Is he Muslim?"

"Yes, he is."

"Now that opens up lots of questions. Why would you recruit a Muslim at a Christian college? Two, why would the admissions office allow such a thing?"

"On his application he put Christian. He doesn't push his beliefs on others. We both keep it a secret, which doesn't seem to harm anyone."

"You're wrong there. If he and Michelle get too close, we've got problems. First thing you know, they'll be raising little terrorists."

Just when Back Bay had begun to fear Lewis's clearheadedness, he started talking like a fool.

"Understand what I mean?" asked Lewis.

"Abe is a gentle soul, Mr. Lewis. In no way is he a terrorist."

"I'm counting on you to control those two," said Lewis. "If I hear of anything happening between them, then I'll consider our alliance broken."

Alliance?

"What do you mean by 'anything happening'?"

Back Bay had a sudden vision of the padded training table with Abe mounted firmly on Michelle.

"I know you can't control what they do behind your back," said Lewis. "But don't encourage them in your presence."

"Tennis is my focus, and that's what goes on when I'm around my players."

Back Bay flashed to Michelle's legs in the air—nearly perpendicular to the table—as Abe served up his Algerian best.

"Thanks for being so honest with me, Coach. I'm glad we see things eye to eye."

After hanging up, Back Bay sat for only a moment before he hurled the papers from his desk and watched them flutter to the floor.

~

"He actually called you?" asked Arlette, with far too much hatred in her voice for Back Bay's liking. "What the hell for?"

Back Bay had hoped to tell her under calmer circumstances, but he let it fly, everything Louis told him—Webster Boyd, Ummell, and the whole shitty mess, including the "alliance" Louis had so proudly said he'd formed with Back Bay, whatever the hell that meant.

"Superb," said Arlette. "Now you two are chums."

If he'd known she would be this way, he wouldn't have called. "I thought you'd like to know," he said.

"Half the time he's out of his mind," said Arlette. "The other half he's a sweet man. What more can I say?"

Maybe she was calming a bit.

"In my conversation with him," said Back Bay, "at one point he was forgiving me, and the next madder than hell."

"Why did we think we could have sex in the choir-robe room and get away with it? You say Ummell saw us?"

"No, Webster Boyd saw us then told Ummell."

"And you confessed to those two assholes?"

"They had me dead to rights."

"Now Louis knows," she said, softly.

"And I've since learned that you must have told Michelle about us."

After a brief silence, "*She* said that?"

"In a way."

All the earlier fight appeared to have left Arlette. "In what way?"

"I caught Michelle and Abe having sex in the locker room."

"I think I might throw up."

Silence.

"Are you OK?" he asked.

"No."

"They blackmailed me with the knowledge they had of you and me having sex. I assumed Michelle found out about us from you."

"I tell her most everything, something I obviously can't do with my husband."

"They've got me in a corner. Redfern could fire my ass."

"Why hasn't Webster Boyd spread it around?"

"My guess is he thinks I've got something on him, which I don't, so he's afraid I'd tell on him."

"That whole college sounds like a big clusterfuck."

Back Bay laughed in one sharp burst, which must have resounded in Arlette's ear.

"Well, Abe's a handsome guy," said Arlette, a bit of hope in her tone. "I hope Michelle's enjoying herself."

"I'm turning my head and letting them do whatever they want."

Back Bay heard what sounded like a long sigh. "Please say you didn't tell Louis about Abe and Michelle."

"I didn't. But he assumes they've got something going. He made me promise I wouldn't encourage them."

"Sexually-charged kids don't need much encouragement." Her resignation came through.

"What do we do?" asked Back Bay.

"For me," said Arlette, "I pour my first drink of the day."

"Wish I could join you."

"I'll sit in St. Louis," said Arlette. "You'll sit in Towson, Indiana, and we'll wait for my husband to make his next stupid move."

Back Bay looked at the papers still scattered on his office floor.

$\sim$

Michelle turned off her cell phone, not wanting to hear anything outside Redfern College. Things were just the way she wanted; Redfern was her world now, but she had carved a much smaller niche within that world—Abe and Clovis. She attended her classes, and even with the narrow Christian focus that most professors put on topics, she found her courses stimulating and more rigorous than she would have thought, making her evenings with Clovis in the dorm closed off and secure.

The thought of her mother having sex with Coach Norman was ceasing to disgust her in small increments, especially as she was learning the delights of what true sexual passion mixed with a fervent emotional longing for a man could offer. The locker room was always hers and Abe's for at least an hour each evening. Sometimes, in a class, she would remember some particular move she or Abe had made the night before.

Michelle found Clovis becoming sweeter, less judgmental, and since Clovis had told Michelle that she'd had sex, a certain veil had lifted between them. Finally one evening, Michelle said, "Abe is so slow and caring when we make love." She was surprised at how naturally and suddenly that popped out.

Clovis sat at her desk, her head hovering over a book, hair covering her face. She almost never studied on the bed the way Michelle did. "He doesn't ever get in a hurry?" asked Clovis.

"When he gets excited, he goes faster. I try to make him relax."

"I didn't know a man could be calmed down when he gets up a head of steam."

"There's a point when I notice he *can't* stop," said Michelle.

"I like that part. It means the deal is about over."

"You're too funny," said Michelle.

Clovis put both hands to her ears, hair still hiding her face. "I'm glad you're enjoying sex with Abe," she told Michelle, quietly.

"Afterwards it makes me feel light and springy, like I want to get up and do good things. Come back here and study. I like our room, don't you?"

"Love it," said Clovis.

The next time Michelle looked up, Clovis was in the same position. "Got a test tomorrow?" asked Michelle.

"I have one every day," said Clovis, then quickly turned a page of her book.

BRINGING DOWN THE TEMPLE
CHAPTER 12

Louis didn't care much for psychologists and lawyers, but saw them as expendables who only occasionally did good things. His thoughts about them didn't change much after reading the red, except now he compared them to the Pharisees and Sadducees who lurked behind hedges, popping out every once in a while, trying to clog up Jesus's doings and generally being pests. Jesus even showed them up in front of His disciples, who must have gotten a good laugh over the way He one-upped them. Louis wondered why the Bible didn't record more of those funny times. There appeared to be lots of "gotcha" left out of the Bible.

"Gotcha" was on Louis's mind, now that he knew more about Jesus and had set his sights on getting out of his messes, especially the one with the Milwaukee group. His lawyer would be the key to that, but with the psychologist, Louis would just have fun, pure and simple. He had to admit Arlette was persistent about the two of them seeing the psychologist, but he supposed that wasn't so bad.

Like last time, there were no preliminaries at the session.

"Did the two of you discuss the notion we raised about your family's destructive tendencies?"

Louis and Arlette glanced at each other.

"Not really," said Arlette.

"And why is that?" asked the psychologist, looking at Louis.

"Pretty busy," said Louis.

"It's only been three days."

"I'm not completely sure our family is that destructive," said Louis.

"Being too busy," said the psychologist, "can itself be destructive. Arlette?"

"The last time you said something about authoritarianism destroying us," said Arlette. "By Louis wanting to control, he destroyed his freedom to look outside himself and see others. And that Michelle and I destroyed our freedom by not asserting ourselves against Louis's authoritarianism. Isn't that what you said?"

"Basically," said the psychologist.

"OK," said Arlette.

She rubbed the side of her forehead the way she always did when lost in thought.

"Louis?" asked the psychologist.

"What?"

"Is that the way you remember our last session?"

"Seems like," said Louis, "you're putting most of the blame on me."

"How's that?"

"If I weren't so bossy, we wouldn't have to be going through all this."

"Going through all of what?"

"These needless assumptions you're drawing about my faults."

"One person's faults are no greater than another's. There are no bad guys in this situation."

Louis watched Arlette's hand leave her forehead and rest comfortably in her lap.

"What did you not understand in our last session?" asked the psychologist.

"Oh, I understood how I'm the source of our family's problems. I feel like I'm being set up here."

He looked at Arlette. Her hand still lay in her lap.

"Can we talk about people's faults?" asked Louis.

"We can make that side trip for a moment before we get back to the nature of our destructiveness," said the psychologist.

"Good," said Louis. "In a marriage, what would you say is the biggest fault a person can make?"

"We're not talking about the biggest of anything."

"What about adultery?" asked Louis.

Louis felt his face burn, but he wasn't going to look at Arlette just yet. Now we're talking faults!

"What about it?" asked the psychologist.

"Committing adultery would have to rank right up there in marriage faults."

"Where are you taking this?"

"Perhaps Arlette should answer that," said Louis.

Louis's stomach ached with what he guessed was excitement. He had the peculiar feeling he had just struck his wife with a blunt object.

"What are you talking about?" asked Arlette.

The psychologist looked straight at Arlette.

"I'm talking about your affair with Coach Norman," said Louis.

Like one of those witches in *Wizard of Oz*, she was melting right there in her chair.

"Why?" Arlette asked Louis, as though she were asking why he had brought it up.

"*Why* you did it is my question."

Louis and the psychologist watched Arlette.

Arlette said, "This isn't something I was expecting to discuss today."

Louis held silence.

"Perhaps there's no need to discuss it now," said the psychologist.

"And why is that?" asked Louis. "I thought we wanted to discuss destructiveness. What could be more destructive to a marriage than adultery?"

"Prioritizing destructive behavior does little good," said the psychologist.

"I don't mind discussing it," said Arlette. She looked at the psychologist. "May I?"

"If you wish."

"Apparently Louis has done some snooping around and found out about my brief liaison. Good for him." She talked directly to the psychologist. "This is the first time in our marriage I've done this. And I have since lived with deep regret. I'll admit I didn't want Louis to know, and wouldn't have told him, because I've felt nothing but guilt and remorse over the act. What good would telling him have done? It's over, and I was ready to move on. Now, it's in the open, and I'm sorry it is because Louis may hold this against me for the rest of our lives. In fact, our marriage may crumble because of what I've done."

Louis felt as if his body were moving farther and farther from the two.

"I'm sorry Louis chose to let me know here in the safety of this office instead of facing me one-on-one," said Arlette.

"Perhaps it was for the best," the psychologist said.

Arlette looked at Louis.

He worked on zooming back in. "Adultery can destroy a marriage," he said. His voice sounded light and tinny.

"It certainly can," said the psychologist.

"Thanks for *someone* here agreeing with me," said Louis.

"Yet, perhaps Arlette was exercising her freedom to act on her own, independent of you, Louis, even as harmful as adultery can be to a marriage."

"Are you condoning what she did?"

"No."

"Then what's your point?"

"Granting marriage partners the freedom to act and think on their own, free from the overriding constraints of the other partner, goes a long way to strengthen a marriage and not harm or even destroy it. Arlette's affair might indeed be harmful to your marriage, but she may have been, in an extreme way, merely asserting herself."

"Jesus believed in absolutes, my friend," Louis said to the psychologist. "He would never have waffled on something as important as adultery."

"What do you expect to come from Arlette's admission?"

"An apology."

"She expressed regret."

"I want assurances she will never do it again," said Louis.

"Arlette?" said the psychologist.

"I have no intention of ever doing it again," she said.

Louis said, "It could destroy our marriage."

"Will you accept her apology and move on?" asked the psychologist.

Louis wasn't about to cave to their treachery. "Remains to be seen."

"What would Jesus do?" asked the psychologist. Was that a smirk forming along the edges of his mouth.

"He might destroy the temple and build it up in three days," said Louis. Reading the red was coming in handy.

"Excellent," said the psychologist. "If you were to read on, that passage meant Jesus would die and then be raised in three days. I'm happy you can see your marriage resurrected from Arlette's adultery."

Bested by a secular humanist? A Pharisee playing tricks.

"I have a plan to get out of the problems I've gotten our family into with the mob. Care to hear?"

The psychologist nodded toward Arlette, as though he needed her approval.

"Bring it on, honey," she said.

"Be advised," said the psychologist, "we have only thirty minutes left in this session. We haven't yet gotten to the most pressing issues."

"This won't take long. What I'm about to tell you could solve lots of problems."

In ten minutes Louis outlined his plan to the two of them, and by the time the session was over, neither of them had much to say.

As they were leaving, Louis commented, "Often you have to destroy something to build it up again. Right, doc?"

Arlette let him close the door. "You were full of surprises in there."

～

Louis was on a roll as he drove to his attorney's office; hadn't he just put one over on that pseudo-intellectual of a psychologist, and hadn't Arlette been receptive to his plan of dealing with the Milwaukee group? Louis appreciated Jesus and His tactics the more he thought things through. A follower of Him must sometimes be kind and humble, sometimes deceptive and destructive, sometimes sell everything and follow Him, sometimes overturn the money changers' tables in the temple, sometimes take pity on the poor and meek. And Louis was getting a special kick out of one of Jesus's actions—causing a fig tree to wither just for the hell of it. Louis took that act to be a definite example of Jesus abusing His power—not necessarily to help someone out, but just to prove a point and show off for His disciples. If Jesus could destroy, why couldn't Louis also bring down a tree or two, with a little help from his attorney?

Louis had known Adam Fontleroy since their high school days at DeSmet. They had been buddies on the debate team. Each had gone his separate ways until after Louis began acquiring properties and needed a lawyer. He'd looked up Adam and retained him as his attorney. Breaking the news to Adam wouldn't be easy, but after all it was Louis's money at stake, not his.

"You did what?" yelled Adam.

Louis hadn't expected Adam to take the news of how he had gotten himself into the mess with the Milwaukee group well. He showed Adam all the papers.

Adam was still yelling. "Why didn't you talk to me first?"

All Louis could do was respond calmly and accept total blame. Being under control actually felt pretty good.

"You're fucked," said Adam.

Louis knew that, of course.

"Those guinea greaseballs can take everything you have!"

"Does my composure surprise you?" asked Louis.

"No. Insane people are often quite composed!"

Louis let the man rant and then watched him simmer down. Finally, "This religious kick you got you and your family into must have destroyed brain cells."

"Glad you brought up my conversion." Louis testified to his recent understanding of Jesus's nature, including the part about selling everything and giving to the poor.

"Hold on, buddy boy," said Adam. "Those asswipes aren't poor. And you didn't sell them anything. They stole it from you." Adam rattled the papers in the air.

Louis didn't mind seeing Adam riled up again because, of course, Adam had a point. Remaining docile and introspective, Louis then explained what he had read in the red about Jesus's destructive side. "Care to hear my plan?"

"Can't wait," said Adam.

"I shall tear down the temple."

After a long preamble into Louis's recent troubled family life—including the church bombing, Arlette's affair with Coach Norman, Michelle's likely infatuation with an Arab Muslim, Louis's sudden resentment toward Redfern—he outlined for Adam his plan. Louis said he would indeed need to sell off his properties to make the balloon payment on the loan the group had stuck him with.

"Which leaves you essentially broke," said Adam.

Louis said he knew that.

"Sounds great so far," said Adam, his left eye twitching.

Louis explained that he would then be free and clear from the mob so that his church and family would be safe from any more retaliation from Milwaukee. That would be a load off his mind.

"You're fucking nuts, you know that."

Louis held up a hand and continued, explaining that the beautiful part of the plan was that he would deed over his part of the loan and property to Redfern College, knowing that a guy named Webster Boyd and the college president would see the deal as a tremendous gift to the college that would keep the college solvent—indeed flourishing—for years to come with all the money the new development would eventually make.

"I thought you were starting not to like that college."

Louis told Adam just to keep listening. The college would think it had died and gone to heaven by gaining the property when, really, the Milwaukee group would screw over the college just like it had him. Didn't Adam see? The group could tear down the college just like it tore Louis down. It would be Louis's revenge on the place that had fucked him over (Louis apologized for his language), hired a man who fucked his wife (again, sorry), and allowed a Muslim to date his daughter.

"I don't know what to say," said Adam, going limp and dropping his head, nearly banging it on the desk.

Louis explained to Adam—who Louis was certain hadn't read the red—that Jesus caused a fair amount of destruction in his day ...

"No details, please."

... and that in a real sense, Louis would be cleansing Redfern College by bringing it down. Withering the fig tree, as Louis put it. Tearing down the temple. Driving out the money changers.

Adam appeared to be clearing his head and lungs with long, slow, deep breaths. A good sign, Louis thought.

"Let's not continue with the theological ramifications of your master plan," said Adam, exhaling. "Stick with practical matters." Another deep breath. "Matters you apparently know nothing about."

Louis wondered how much Jesus actually considered practical matters.

"Your idea of deeding over your part of the loan to the college won't work, however sinister you might wish it to be. I assume Redfern College has lawyers?"

Louis said he was certain it did.

"Attorneys would closely examine these papers." Adam touched them lightly with a palm. "And even the stupidest attorney would never recommend doing what you so eagerly want to happen. No way."

Louis asked Adam if he was sure.

"Why the hell did you do your own deal without me? When I read about it in the *Post-Dispatch*, I thought you'd retained someone else. I never thought you'd do anything like this without legal counsel, for Christ's sake."

Louis said he couldn't defend himself on it. He guessed he had been feeling too confident.

"Or you had a fucking death wish."

Please, the language.

"I'm not sure why I'm allowing this to anger me so," said Adam. "It's your funeral."

Louis said Adam shouldn't be talking about funerals just yet. Wasn't there a way?

"A way to do what?"

Wasn't there a way to take down the college?

"And *that* would make you happy? *That* would ease the pain of going broke? The only thing being taken down is you, Louis. You want someone else to go down with you?"

"That college," Louis explained, "has ruined my marriage and maybe my daughter."

"No," said Adam. "It's not the college that ruined things." He held up the papers. "You want me to keep these, or do you want them?"

Louis quietly said Adam could keep them.

"Are you going to need help liquidating your other properties to make that ridiculous payment?"

Louis told Adam he could handle that himself.

"Yeah," said Adam. "Have a go at it."

On the way out, Louis whispered to himself, "Help me, Jesus."

⁓

"Mom, there's no need to cry."

Michelle put her phone on speaker.

"He said we're broke," her mother said.

Clovis bent awkwardly behind Michelle's chair, their heads nearly touching.

"How could we be broke?" asked Michelle.

"Some stupid mistake he tried to pull off in his latest land grab."

"Broke?"

"He's been in bed all day. Won't come out."

"I don't get it," said Michelle.

"He said we're fucked."

"Dad said *that*?"

"You don't need to know the details."

Clovis put her hand on Michelle's shoulder, and Michelle patted it gently.

"You've got to stop crying," said Michelle.

Earlier that evening, at Michelle's urging, Clovis had sat at the same dining-hall table with Abe and several tennis players. She and Clovis had arrived early, and when Clovis peeled off from the serving line to sit at her usual table, Michelle followed her.

"Aren't you going to sit with Abe and your friends?" asked Clovis.

"Sure," said Michelle.

First Abe, then, one at a time, the others joined Michelle and Clovis, no one acknowledging anything out of the ordinary. The conversation took what Michelle thought was just the correct turn after Michelle forced from Clovis the funny story about how her father had gotten his finger caught in a communion cup holder that Protestant churches attach to the back of pews beside the hymnal holders. Clovis added details Michelle hadn't heard. She ended with a flourish: "Poor Dad probably had visions of the church burning down with him dragging a pew out the door behind him."

Michelle was proud of Clovis. After dinner Abe walked the two back to Hamilton Hall where Clovis went to her room while Abe and Michelle carried on other pursuits. Later in the room, when Michelle's cell phone rang, she was telling Clovis how much the group liked her story. "You could join us every night if you want," said Michelle, before picking up and listening to her mother's crying voice.

"Why don't you pull yourself together and call me back later," said Michelle. She and Clovis listened for her mother's reply, but none came.

"Mother?"

"I'm all right," her mother finally said.

"I don't get being broke," said Michelle. "What does that mean?"

"Oh, sweetie, he made some stupid business moves ..."

"What kind of—"

"... and he says we have to sell everything we have to cover the losses."

"Moves?" asked Michelle.

"I shouldn't have called you about this, but I don't have anyone else to talk to."

"You can always talk to me."

Michelle covered the phone because Clovis was making what appeared to be a moaning sound. Clovis stumbled to her bed where she sat with legs apart, her long dress pulled tightly between her knees. She held her stomach and grimaced, baring her teeth.

"Our roles," said Michelle's mother, "are so fouled up. Now you're the mother to me."

"Let me talk to Dad," said Michelle, watching Clovis rock back and forth.

"Not the best time."

"OK then. I'll be up till around twelve I guess. Call me back."

"I've never seen your father like this. In bed all day."

"Call me back," said Michelle, and ended the call.

Clovis appeared to be holding her breath, because her face was red and she wasn't panting like she had been. When Michelle approached her bed, Clovis finally released a puff of breath.

"It's a bigger one this time," said Clovis.

"What is?"

"It's about over now."

"Did you eat something bad at dinner? Do you want to lie down?"

Michelle watched as Clovis's face returned to its normal rosy pink. Clovis stood, her feet wide apart. "Do you know how hard it's been, keeping this from you?" asked Clovis. "You're the only friend I have. My parents would kill me."

"Oh my God," said Michelle, looking at Clovis's middle, the long dress nearly reaching the floor.

"Don't worry," said Clovis. "I figure there's maybe part of another month, maybe not. I've been taking care of myself and reading about how it's done. You and I should be able to handle this."

Michelle collapsed into the chair.

"Really, all I care about is seeing its face," said Clovis. "After that, I'm not sure."

UPSETTING
THE TABLES

As far as Louis could figure, Jesus did not form many alliances—why should He?—other than with His disciples, who half the time didn't understand what He was doing anyway. Louis thought those disciples were a ragtag bunch that Jesus probably could have done without, at least for the major deals and decisions He found Himself facing. Granted, they helped carry out policy after He was gone but ... whatever. The alliance Louis had in mind to help him bury Redfern College would surely be easy to cobble together. He remembered the practical and useful axiom: When you have them by the balls, their hearts and minds will follow. Louis wanted to be certain Coach Norman understood that it was Webster Boyd who had ratted out Arlette and him.

"So how do you feel about that?" Louis asked Back Bay by phone.

"What was Boyd trying to prove by telling you?" asked Back Bay.

"All I can figure is he's got something up his sleeve for you. Are you hiding something else from the college, something he could use against you?"

That should set the coach's mind to wondering. Louis let the silence on the phone hang poignantly.

"Look, Mr. Lewis, I haven't been motivated by the most noble of intentions. I wanted to placate the stuffed shirt, money-grubbing president and curry favor to get your money for the tennis program. Practical things, like more courts, scholarships."

"You wouldn't be the first to want my money."

"To be honest, Webster Boyd and the president want the same from you. That's why we helped at the church. We went there for all the wrong reasons."

"I suspected that. As you know, I pledged lots of money to that college. And I'm going to level with you. I can't make good on that pledge. The reason? I won't go into that. Suffice it to say, I'm pretty much busted, or at least going to be."

Back Bay said, "I see."

"I'm calling because I may need your help to put Webster Boyd in his place. And the whole college for that matter." Louis needed to talk fast. "I want to …"

"What do you mean by putting Boyd in his place? And the college?"

Louis sensed some hesitation in Back Bay's voice, even fear. Which was just the spirit Louis needed. "Kind of like winning a grudge match," said Louis. "You know, when someone whips you soundly then gloats over it and you get a chance to exact a measure of revenge. As a sports-man, you know how that feels."

"Go on."

"As you're surely aware, I'm a devout Christian now. But I'm new to the game, so to speak." Sports analogies here would be just the ticket. "And I've read the rule book."

Nothing on Back Bay's end.

"The words of Jesus," said Louis. "I've read them."

"Oh?"

Louis still had him. "Jesus built things up, and He destroyed things. Did you know that?"

"All right."

Louis recalled his debating years and those exquisite moments when he was setting the trap so carefully, later to be sprung—*snap!* "Webster Boyd is a hypocrite," said Louis, "and a tattler. He found out about you and my wife, then started blabbing it. A man like that is up to no good, has blackmail on his mind. For some reason, he told me about you and Arlette but is withholding telling others until he can use the information to gain some kind of advantage on you. You needn't tell me what he's got on you. All I know is that he has something. And he'll use it, sooner or later."

Louis could virtually hear the worry wheels turning in Back Bay's head. It was probably good the coach wasn't saying anything. Let him stew. Finally, "Are you with me, Coach?"

"Where are you taking this?"

"I'm calling in my chips on you."

"What chips?"

"Because you slept with my wife, and because I've forgiven both of you without telling a soul, I'm asking a favor of you."

"But ..."

"I understand she was complicit too, and I'm also protecting her. Yet, I could have had your ass whipped—pardon the language—at Redfern over the matter. I'm banking on the fact that right now you don't like Webster Boyd or maybe even Redfern College that much. Am I right?"

"What do you have in mind?"

"Fair enough question, even though you didn't answer my question." Louis was certain he had Back Bay wriggling on the hook. "I'm forced to sell off all my assets to fix a huge mistake I foolishly got myself into. When I sell, I'll be free and clear. Then I plan to sign over to Redfern College the interest I hold in a massive development—the mistake I got into. I'll make it sound like Redfern is getting the investment endowment of a lifetime, something Webster Boyd will absolutely leap onto."

"Let me guess," said Back Bay. "The college will eventually be in the same mess you find yourself in."

"Bingo."

"And that's your revenge? Your way of destroying the college?"

"Stated simply, that's right."

"Why do you need me?"

"Because I need Webster Boyd to sign the papers on the spot on behalf of the college, without checking with attorneys. If he signs, it's only a matter of time before the college will be twisting in the wind, like I did for a couple of years. The same hammer will fall on good old Redfern that fell on me."

"Again, why use me?" asked Back Bay.

"You can cozy up to Boyd. Tell him you spoke with me. I'll even let you present the deal to him, and you can assure him that you'll let him take all the glory. Then the three of us will meet. He'll sign, and that's that."

Louis was certain the silence on the line was a result of Back Bay appreciating the beauty of the proposition.

"Exactly what am I to gain from this?" asked Back Bay. "Sounds like I have a lot to lose. The college goes down, and I'm without a job."

Louis wished he didn't have to spell things out so clearly. "With one phone call, Coach, I could have you fired within the hour. Webster Boyd holds the knowledge of your indiscretion like a cannon ready to fire. My call would be the spark. You know that. But think of the beauty of my proposal. You can endear yourself to Boyd and put yourself back on the right track with him."

"All of this doesn't say much for my future, Mr. Lewis."

"Think it over. You'll have a brighter future by carrying out my plan. Redfern will go on for two, maybe four or five years before it takes its big tumble, giving you plenty of time to shop around your sterling tennis record to other colleges. I'm sure you know your resume will play well anywhere, but not if you've been fired for sexual indiscretion. Such news travels fast, you know." Louis couldn't believe that came out so smoothly, so extemporaneously. "Don't you think it's time to move up the ladder? A major university?"

"How often do you deal in blackmail?" asked Back Bay.

"I don't see it that way."

"Appears to me that because you're bringing yourself down, you want others to take the fall with you."

Louis couldn't deny the truth of that, but he saved the best for last. "Coach, I may possibly be an instrument in God's hands used to forestall what could be a major catastrophe with my dear daughter. I'm talking about that Arab tennis player who seems to have captured at least *some* of her attention. I don't know how or why you brought him to that Christian campus, but it would behoove you to make every effort to guarantee the two do not become an item. I didn't send my daughter to Redfern to hook up with someone like him, if you know what I mean."

Long silence.

"Coach Norman?" asked Louis.

Nothing.

"Coach?"

Louis heard a long, deep sigh. "You're a tough one," said Back Bay. "'Driving a hard bargain' is the way I'd put it."

By the time he'd hung up, Louis felt the pure, crystalline glow of victory that took him back to his DeSmet days after the judges had awarded him another debate trophy. But the gleam lasted only momentarily before he felt a cloying futility that he hadn't felt in years; so long ago that he couldn't remember the occasion or why the hollowness had griped him so tightly then as it did now.

"What have I done?" he said aloud.

He heard no answers.

"Help me, Jesus."

~

After Back Bay called the switchboard operator, telling her not to put any more calls through to him, he sat motionless in his field-house office. Louis Lewis was nothing more than a fucked-up fool. Simply nuts, but smart enough to mask it and smart enough to make Back Bay's guts rumble and his eyes bleary with either fear or anger—he couldn't tell which.

Now get hold of yourself, he thought. Where was the problem here? Was it with Lewis being nuts—and, thus, nothing to worry about—or was it real enough for Back Bay to follow Lewis's plans to avoid the damned threats? He took out paper and began making a list:

1. Everything is too far-fetched. Lewis's *desperation* is making him nuts.
2. Webster Boyd wouldn't fall for my pitch. Or would he? The guy is gullible and ambitious enough to believe most anything that sounds too good to be true.
3. What if Lewis and Boyd tell the administration about Arlette and me? What would happen? Lewis is right. I'd get shit-canned. My marriage?
4. Signing papers without an attorney? No way. Even Boyd isn't that stupid. Or is he?
5. Where's Arlette in all this? Should I call her?
6. Michelle and Abe are already fucking. Nothing to be done about that. Keep under wraps. Getting blackmailed on two fronts—Michelle/Abe and Lewis.
7. Maybe now's the time to bail out of Redfern for something bigger.
8. Need to talk with Lewis more? Find out about what to tell Boyd?
9. Forget Lewis and whole deal? Let chips fall where they may? No. Play the fucking game!
10. Go home. Sleep on it.

He looked at his watch: 7:34 p.m.. He'd told his wife he'd be home for dinner at six thirty. At least she hadn't called and bugged him. He turned off his cell phone. But she couldn't because he'd told the switch-board operator not to put anyone through. He dialed the operator.

"Oh, Coach Lewis, I'm so glad you called."

He'd never heard such agitation in her voice.

"What?" he asked.

"One call right after another for you. Wouldn't give a name. Two different women by the sound of their voices. They were angry when I wouldn't put them through. I'm so glad you called me. Shall I let them through when they call again, which I know they will?"

"You don't know who they were?"

"My caller ID said unknown name and number."

Back Bay heard a beeping on her end.

"Oh, dear," she said. "Here's another one. Hold a minute."

He ran a hand over his list. Almost a full page of nothing but problems.

"Coach Lewis?" said the operator. "It's one of them again. Shall I put her through?"

"Yeah."

"Coach Norman, you've got to help. Please. Oh my God!"

The woman was hysterical. "Who is this?"

"Please help. Mom said you would!"

"Who is this?"

"Michelle Lewis. Oh my God!"

He needed to calm her down. "Why are you calling?"

"Mom told me to. She's been calling you. I'm so glad you're there."

Ah, shit. Now what?

"I called Abe," said Michelle. "He's outside the dorm. We got it all planned."

"Got what planned?"

"Meet us in the locker room. Abe will use his key. Clovis has everything ready. Please?"

"Clovis?"

"We'll be there soon. Please say you'll be there!"

"OK," he said, suddenly calm, but he sure as hell didn't know why. He hung up. Immediately the phone rang.

"This is Arlette. You've got to help Clovis with her baby. They said they're ..."

"Michelle just called—"

"... going to the locker room. Please do this, David. Michelle is panicked, and poor Clovis—"

"A baby?"

"It's a long story," said Arlette.

"Locker room?"

"Just go, please. For me."

"OK."

It would be a short walk from his office to the locker room. Why was he suddenly so calm? Maybe because some tangible event was about to happen that perhaps he could handle.

Before he left the office, he picked up the list from his desk, shook his head, and, walking to the door, tore it into tiny pieces before tossing it into the trash can.

~

Arlette thought that finally getting in touch with David Norman was as near to relief as she might find in the current situation. Just perhaps, a coach might have some rudimentary knowledge of the human body, maybe even know something about childbirth. But before calling Back Bay, try as she might, she couldn't convince Michelle or Clovis to get help. At first Michelle was working hard to persuade Clovis to go to a hospital—trying like hell, in fact. Oh, but trying to get Michelle calmed down on the phone was the first task. The girl was beside herself.

"Michelle, put Clovis on the phone. Can she talk now?"

"Here," she heard Michelle tell Clovis.

"Clovis," said Arlette, calmly, "you need to be in a hospital. Right now."

"I can't, Mrs. Lewis."

"Why not?"

"I can't let anyone know about this."

"Worry about that later. You need help with this baby."

"I've studied about it. I'm prepared. Ooohhh."

"Are you having another contraction?" asked Arlette. Clovis was breathing heavily into the phone.

"Maybe a short one," said Clovis. Her breathing gradually became more normal. "I've been timing them," said Clovis.

"Listen, Clovis, please call an ambulance," said Arlette.

"You don't understand. We have a place all picked out. Abe's helping us."

"For God's sake!" said Arlette.

"Nothing you say will change my mind," said Clovis. "That's that."

"Put Michelle back on." At least something else might help. "Listen, honey, call Coach Norman."

"What can he do?"

"Just call him. If you don't then I will."

∼

When she saw it, Michelle put a hand over her mouth to keep from screaming, since she and Clovis agreed that no one was to hear a thing.

"It's normal," said Clovis.

How could the girl be so calm? The water was all over the floor now!

"Just get a towel and wipe it up," said Clovis, far too matter-of-factly for Michelle. "My water has broken."

Michelle had laid in a supply of towels and closed and locked the bathroom she and Clovis shared with the other room. Clovis pulled up her long dress and told Michelle to put the towel on her like a diaper. "I even have large safety pins in my birth bag," said Clovis. Michelle's hands shook. She was surprised not to see blood running out as she diapered her.

"Now what?" asked Michelle, letting the dress fall back down, concealing the large towel.

"Let's go down to meet Abe," said Clovis.

"Can you walk down the stairs?"

"Just take my hand, and if we meet anyone, let go and act normal."

"It's a long way to the locker room," said Michelle.

"Everything's OK."

Michelle had the feeling Clovis was working hard to calm *her.* That wasn't right. "You'll be just fine," said Michelle. She held Clovis's hand.

"You carry the birth bag," said Clovis.

It was heavier than Michelle thought.

The walk through the hall and down the stairs was uneventful; they met no one. Besides holding her hand, Michelle leaned into the slightly bent Clovis, hoping to provide some support. By the time they reached the end of the stairs, Michelle had interlocked her arm with Clovis's, but upon entering the lobby, Clovis pushed Michelle aside, and walked with what Michelle thought looked like an overly erect and stiff gait. Michelle had been worried about the lobby, and as the two walked among the couches and soft chairs where girls chatted softly, Michelle didn't know whether to act friendly or just plod on, ignoring them. Abe was standing by the door. Neither Michelle nor Clovis spoke to him while he held the door open. Michelle glanced around the lobby before leaving, but no one seemed to notice anything. The long stairs leading from the dorm to the parking lot awaited.

"Abe, you take the birth bag," whispered Clovis. "Both of you get on each side of me. Michelle, you hold onto the rail. Abe is strong enough to support my other side."

Glancing at Abe, Michelle saw an afraid, pale face.

"Not too slow or too fast," Clovis told them.

Michelle reached for Clovis's hand, but she pulled away.

"Let me do this," Clovis said.

At last the bottom of the stairs.

"This way," said Abe.

"I know how to get there," said Clovis.

On the sidewalks through campus, couples were out for evening strolls, as usual, and as they met the three, someone might say, "Hello, Abe and Michelle." Michelle was pleased no one acknowledged Clovis.

With a clear path ahead, Clovis said, "I'm in the second stage of labor, active. The first stage lasted about six hours. The water usually doesn't break until the second stage. This could last from three to five hours. Here's another," she said, gripping Michelle's hand.

"Another what?" asked Abe.

"Contraction, stupid," said Clovis. "Ooohhh."

Clovis nodded to a stone bench ahead. "Over there."

Abe led her there where she sat, legs spread, Abe sitting beside her. "Is anyone watching?" Clovis asked.

Michelle stood in front of the two, feeling like a sentry guarding against attack. "No."

"Good," said Clovis, breathing hard. "It's calming down now. The book says active contractions last between forty-five and sixty seconds."

"Will you have the baby right here?" asked Abe.

"No. We'll go on in a minute."

"Are you scared?" asked Michelle.

"Yes," said Abe, immediately.

Michelle and Clovis smiled at each other. "I meant is *Clovis* scared," said Michelle.

"I'm OK," said Clovis. "I know what to do. Everything's in the book. In the bag."

"Let me call the hospital," said Abe.

Maybe, just maybe, Abe could talk some sense into her.

"I know what I'm doing," said Clovis. "And would everyone shut up about a hospital."

Michelle watched Clovis's pain turn into what looked like anger.

"I'm not so happy about all these people being here. I planned to have the baby by myself. Then I thought Michelle would be all right, and before I know it, *everyone's* going to be there."

Michelle watched someone approach from the left. She tried to look normal and smiled. *For God's sake, don't stop!* She walked on past.

"I'll have to have a good talk with that Coach," said Clovis. "He better not blab."

"What?" asked Abe.

Michelle realized Abe hadn't known Coach Norman was meeting them. "Mom made me call."

Abe looked at Michelle and stiffened. "He won't tell anyone."

Clovis placed both hands on the bench. "Let's go on."

"The towel still OK?" asked Michelle.

"Barely."

"What towel?" asked Abe.

"Don't worry about it," said Clovis, now standing and beginning to walk. "We've got to decide who's going to do what. With all these people, everyone ought to have a job."

Michelle and Abe looked at each other.

"It's all spelled out in the book," said Clovis. "Maybe that coach knows what he's doing."

With the field house just ahead, Michelle took some comfort in knowing Back Bay would be there. Still, she tried once more. "Please let us call an ambulance."

"Good Lord, Michelle," said Clovis, "would you just shut up?"

They trudged on.

"One question," said Abe. "What will become of the baby?"

"I had that all figured out until everyone else joined in," said Clovis.

"What did you figure?" asked Abe.

"All I wanted was to see its face."

"Then?" asked Abe.

Clovis's shoulders slumped, and she reached for both Michelle and Abe. She was crying.

∼

Back Bay hoped no one saw him standing by the back door, but it was well secluded, never any traffic there. That damned Abe still had the key.

He saw them round the corner of the building. The big girl was sure as hell walking like she was pregnant. Abe carried some kind of bag, and he was reaching into his pocket, probably for the key. When Michelle saw Back Bay, she waved excitedly.

"Coach," she said, too loudly.

He waved his arms downward. "Be quiet," he mouthed.

Michelle put her hand over her mouth, like a little kid. What the hell was he getting himself into?

Abe spoke first. "Clovis has something to tell."

"Let's get inside first," said Back Bay, herding them to the door. He put the key in the lock and rattled the handle. Back Bay forgot how it sometimes stuck.

"Let me help," said Abe.

Abe elbowed him out of the way and kicked the door gently until it flew open. The insolent little twerp! Inside, after closing and locking the door, Abe turned on the lights like he owned the joint. In a way he did, thought Back Bay.

The poor pregnant girl had a pained look on her face. "We don't need you here," she said to Back Bay, "but since you are, you've got to promise you won't tell anyone about this. Ever."

"I don't appreciate being held hostage in my own locker room," he said.

"You can leave," said Clovis.

Michelle touched his arm. "No, don't. We need you."

He looked at Abe, who nodded.

"Stay," said Clovis, "if you promise not to tell."

"Let me take you to a hospital," Back Bay said.

"It's no good," said Michelle. "We've tried."

Back Bay gave up and told Clovis he wouldn't tell.

"Give him the book out of the bag," Clovis told Abe.

It was a well-worn paperback. Several pages were marked with sticky notes.

"Page forty-two," she said. "And the next six pages. Get busy reading."

The chapter was titled "Emergency Birth Procedures." The first line read: "Please remember that this chapter is not intended to replace professional help, but in case of emergency ..."

When Back Bay looked up, Abe was walking Clovis toward the padded training table.

"No," said Clovis. "A chair is better. Three chairs. One to sit in, two more to put my feet into."

"... this simple guide will help you assess the situation and provide the person helping you ..."

"Cover all the chairs with the sheets in the bag. There's a box of latex gloves. All of you put them on."

"... until an experienced professional arrives."

Michelle's cell phone rang. "God, Mom. I'm glad you called. Yeah, Coach is here."

Back Bay thought he might be sick.

～

Louis was fully aware that to carry out a plan, one needed to assemble the necessary components; with Coach Norman firmly in place to intercede with Webster Boyd, he was almost ready to inflict upon Redfern College its just deserts. After hanging up with the coach, Louis engaged in a brief moment of prayer, asking Jesus to sanction this act of retribution, a somewhat similar act, he thought, to turning over the money changers' tables in the temple or withering a fig tree. The brief moment of prayer—as he sat in his study at the Lewis estate—turned into a much longer session of alternately thumbing through the red of his Bible and planning details of when and how to liquidate his assets in a timely enough fashion that the Milwaukee group would be appropriately appeased, and pleased. Timing would be everything.

His study had always been his sanctuary and comfort. Then the surprisingly obvious but heretofore obscured fact struck him like a blast of cold wind: his study would soon be gone along with the rest of the estate. Where would he find the energizing solace the room had always provided? And as if by divine intervention, another sudden wind-like emotion hit him, this one faint, yet tender and encouraging: Jesus will provide the way. *Sell all you have and come follow me.* Indeed.

Arlette's sudden presence by his side rattled him from whatever he'd been thinking. In an instant he had no knowledge of where his mind had been, except that now he was swiveling in his chair and facing her. She held a cell phone.

"We're flying to Indianapolis and renting a car, then driving to Towson," she said. "I've already made the reservations. Our flight leaves in two hours. I figure in four to five hours, tops, we'll be checked into the Towson Super Eight motel, where I've reserved two rooms."

She had that look Louis had sometimes seen: sheer concentration combined with such intense purpose that there was nothing he could do to detract her.

"What?" he asked.

"Long story. Very long. I'd go alone but you need to be there too. If nothing else, for me. Lots of us are in on this."

Louis wondered if she had taken some kind of drug. She showed none of her usual drunken signs.

"What are you talking about?" he asked.

"I'm going to pack our bags. I'm not sure how long we'll be there. Could be awhile."

Something about Arlette and the situation froze Louis to his chair, and he saw spots, heard ringing. Michelle had been hurt. Killed? But if so, Arlette would be a shambles.

"Is it Michelle?" he asked.

"She's fine, considering the circumstances. This isn't about Michelle." Arlette left the study.

It was that damned coach. Just when Louis thought he had him where he wanted, something bubbles up, and Arlette somehow slides into the picture. Had she gotten wind of the deal that he and the coach had worked out and now was trying to thwart it? Louis wanted to chase after Arlette and talk some sense into her. After all, this was all *his* deal with the coach, not hers. He was actually clenching his fists. And all this right after being so pleasantly in the presence of Jesus.

No, Louis would need to exercise some restraint. Take some deep breaths and slowly center himself, as he knew Jesus would want, and walk calmly from his study into the bedroom and listen to Arlette's story and plans. And after listening, maybe, just maybe, he would provide some stability to the situation. And by the end of his maneuvering, she, Michelle, and the coach would see the logic of his judgment, and they, too, would understand the wisdom of his recommendations. He was sure even Jesus had to think things out before upsetting all those money changers' tables. One shouldn't always act purely on instincts.

TOO MANY COOKS

CHAPTER 14

Louis had calmed considerably by the time they reached the airport, and Arlette felt pleasantly in control, if not still shaken at the thought of what was going on in that locker room. As Louis parked at the St. Louis Lambert Airport garage, she was on her phone to Michelle, who told her Clovis was doing well. Arlette still tried to convince Clovis to get to a hospital, but the obstinate and stupid girl would have nothing to do with it.

Louis had become silent and, Arlette hoped, resigned to the importance of their dashing to the airport. All that fuss he raised when she told him about the baby, and then his near explosion when she said Coach Norman was there assisting. Shouldn't Louis have been relieved an adult was there? And then Louis's rant about how he would use the coach to carry out those cockamamie plans of destroying the college—and themselves, for Christ's sake. What in hell did that have to do with Back Bay helping give birth? Arlette had spent as much of the last hour and a half getting Louis under control as she had trying to calm Michelle and Clovis by phone. But thank God he was now placid, if not a bit sullen.

"Park as close to the terminal as you can," she said.

She had packed quickly and, she thought, lightly until she watched Louis struggling to lift the luggage out of the trunk.

"Long term parking," he said, panting, after he closed the lid. "We'll have to wait on a shuttle."

She felt conciliatory and placed a hand on his shoulder. "Thanks, Louis. We're doing the right thing."

He nodded that odd way he did when either bemused or too distracted to focus. At least he was tranquil.

≈

"Mom and Dad are coming," Michelle told them.

Clovis was in the middle of another contraction, so she probably didn't hear what Michelle said, but it caused Coach Norman to look up sharply from his reading. He'd gone to a corner of the training room to read the book Clovis brought.

"Why?" he said.

"They've rented some rooms at the motel. For after the baby is born," Michelle said.

"Shit," is all he said before getting back to his reading.

Abe had found the chairs Clovis had requested, and she was mounted in all three, just the way she'd suggested—her butt in one, a leg in each of the others. At first Michelle was shocked, then embarrassed as Clovis hoisted her legs into the chairs with absolutely no regard for what she was exposing. Spread eagle for all the world to see. The towel/diaper was gone and lay on the floor beneath her.

After the contraction passed, Clovis said, "Might as well make yourselves comfortable for a while. This is only the second stage."

"The transition stage is next," piped up Back Bay from his corner, book in hand.

Michelle wanted her mother with them there, but probably not her dad because he'd be freaking out about now, not to mention later. Maybe the baby would hold off until her parents arrived, but even if that happened, what good would it do? Seemed to her that only the four of them were in on this. It was a cross between a camping trip and being in some kind of scary movie, not knowing what was about to happen. Yet, Michelle was surprised at how she was feeling so sheltered there—maybe like a strong ship headed into a storm. She looked around her. No one on campus knew where they were.

Abe had been sweet to Clovis, getting the chairs and patting her shoulders every now and then. He didn't seem a bit shocked at seeing Clovis exposed. Michelle wasn't sure if Back Bay even noticed. He'd been in that corner reading for the longest time.

"Maybe another two hours in this stage," Clovis said.

"Right," said Back Bay, not looking up. "Then maybe two more in transition."

That would be most of the night. What about classes tomorrow? Michelle had not missed a class yet.

"A receptacle," said Back Bay. "We need one."

Abe looked blankly at the coach.

"Something for the placenta," said Back Bay, still reading.

"Oh my God," said Michelle, putting a hand to her mouth. All of this really *was* going to happen.

Abe walked toward Coach Norman.

"Afterbirth," said Coach. "Something to put it in."

Coach didn't look up. Michelle heard Abe clattering around in another part of the room.

"I forgot about that," said Clovis, who appeared to be upset and nervous but not so much in pain, like with a contraction. Was she starting to cry? Michelle stroked her hair. She *was* crying, too.

Coach Norman finally looked up from his reading, and for the briefest of moments, stared absently at her and Clovis before coming to them. He put his arms around both of them.

"It's typical of this stage," he said. "Agitation. This is the time she needs us. We can help soothe her." He pointed to the book in his hand. "I'm a quick learner."

Michelle wanted to hug him. "I'm glad you're here."

Abe returned with what looked to Michelle like a large white bucket.

"That'll do," said Back Bay.

Back Bay had gotten a stopwatch to time both the length of each contraction and the intervals between.

"Doing fine," said Back Bay after each contraction.

Michelle wondered if he was as confident about all of this as he appeared or if he was trying to get everyone else calm. Abe and Michelle sat on one side of Clovis with Back Bay on the other. Clovis now sat on a pillow that Abe had found somewhere in the locker room. No one said much.

"No one's asked how I got pregnant," said Clovis.

Michelle was pretty sure that question had been on all their minds from the beginning; *she* certainly had thought about it. It was strange how no one responded to Clovis's question. Maybe they didn't want to own up to wondering.

Finally Back Bay said, "I think all of us understand how it happens."

They all laughed at once—a good moment, Michelle thought.

"Do you want to talk about it?" asked Back Bay.

"Might as well," said Clovis.

Michelle had the oddest thought: Clovis was like a queen on her throne, and they were her loyal subjects gathered around, listening.

"My senior year in high school," Clovis said, "I started having sex with someone. I didn't start it. Kind of fell into it. I didn't have strong feelings for him." She looked over at Michelle and Abe. "Not like you two."

Michelle wanted to take Abe's hand, but she didn't. She was holding her breath, and no one moved.

"He was a nice enough guy," Clovis said. "I guess you could say he pushed himself on me, but really I wanted to know what sex was all about, and the more we messed around with each other—exploring and all—the more I thought that learning from him might be a good enough way to start."

She moved her legs slightly, slightly scooting one of the chairs.

"You all right?" asked Back Bay, leaning toward her.

"Sure. The pillow helped. Thanks, Abe."

Michelle thought she loved him then as much as she had ever loved anyone. When would *they* have a child?

"I'm not blaming him," continued Clovis, "because I was getting into things and starting to enjoy most of it. Once or twice he made me come, which was pretty darned good."

Michelle wanted to laugh, punch Abe, or do something to counteract that bombshell coming from her roommate. She wasn't about to look at Coach.

"But it was the time right after we had sex that always messed me up. I hated him, and I hated myself, and I hated sex or any mention of it. Do you know what I mean?"

Clovis swept the room with her eyes until she'd caught each in a glance. Apparently she was expecting a reply.

"I understand," said Back Bay.

Was he referring to the times with her mother? Oh, Jesus.

"Go on," said Back Bay.

He was acting the way she'd always thought psychiatrists would.

"Well," said Clovis, "after every time, I promised myself I'd never do it again. I cried a lot in those days." She paused. "Like I'm about to now."

"You don't need to tell us any more if you don't want," said Back Bay.

Abe stood up and began rubbing her shoulders, and Michelle stroked her hair.

"I always get emotional when I think about this part," said Clovis. "It was wrong for me to have sex. God doesn't want me to have sex."

Here was a point where Michelle could comfort her; she leaned into Clovis's face and said, "Anyone would be happy to have sex with you." Clovis's eyes were red but no tears yet.

"Oh, Michelle. You don't understand. It's wrong to have sex outside of marriage. That's what I mean."

Michelle felt a surge of indignation. Like Abe and me? She should set this straight. "Abe and I love each other. You didn't love that person." She didn't think Clovis heard.

"God is making me pay for my sin."

Now she was truly crying.

"By having a baby?" asked Michelle.

"What am I going to do?" she wailed.

Michelle wondered if the crying brought on the next contraction because, in the midst of her anguish, Clovis put her hands on her large stomach, then pointed to Back Bay. He immediately pushed the button on the stopwatch.

Like so many other times in Back Bay's life after being pissed off beyond measure at something, the more the event unfolded, the less angry he became, and he actually started becoming interested. Here he was, ass deep in the mess he had gotten into—mostly by allowing himself to be blackmailed by a couple of kids—with no apparent easy way out, and, to boot, human life was at stake. He was about to witness a baby being born, reading up on the matter, and, in truth, anticipating the challenge of what was about to happen. Was it his competitive spirit?

And then that poor girl in the throes of contractions talking about how she'd sinned by fucking someone. That was the last thing she needed to have on her mind. But he couldn't get her to stop. By the time the contraction had ended, she picked right up on the same stupid theme.

"I couldn't let my parents know about it. It would have killed them, me getting pregnant and spoiling their plans to send me to Redfern. That's all they ever saved for. They're wonderful Christians."

Right, thought Back Bay. Lay guilt on their only daughter so she ends up dropping a baby in a locker room—assisted by a guy like him and watched by a couple of innocent kids who, at this point, had, no doubt, lost all respect for their once-beloved tennis coach. Not to mention his career was going further down the crapper by the minute.

"You should have told them," said Michelle.

Everyone in the damned room was naive! Michelle Lewis thinks every daughter can talk about sex with her mother like she does. Boy, they were polar opposites—a mother telling her daughter she's having an affair with the tennis coach and Clovis's mother so damned uptight she spreads shame on her daughter like nobody's business.

"No need to dwell on the past," said Back Bay. Being the moderator felt good.

"My mom and I," said Clovis, "can't talk like you and your mom do. She'd never tell me if she had an affair."

Now the pregnant twit and Michelle and Abe were looking at Back Bay. "Clovis," he said, "every parent is different. Comparisons rarely help."

He could tell by her eyes she hadn't heard.

"I had things all planned out. I would go off to Redfern, away from my parents, and have the baby by myself in the bathroom in the middle of night so no one could hear. That's what I'd planned."

"What bathroom?" asked Michelle.

"At first, I thought of the one in the dorm lobby, away from everyone. Then after I got to know you, Michelle, and how sweet you are, I thought you might help me with it in our room."

Abe and Michelle were just sitting there listening to the poor, delusional girl like they could be as taken in by those plans as she was. *All right*, thought Back Bay, *after all the hotshot plans were laid out, what the hell did she think of doing with the baby?*

"Then what?" asked Abe.

"I couldn't see any way to keep the baby," said Clovis.

What was she going to do? He had to bring this up. They were only hours away from delivering the thing. "What do you mean by 'keep the baby'?" he asked.

"Oh, don't make me say."

She'd probably start crying again. But he had to know. "You're going to have a baby," he said. "You're the mother. What becomes of it?"

"You'll help, won't you?"

Tears again. She was looking from one to another.

"Help you what?" asked Abe.

"Keep the baby?"

Why did she make it a question? Back Bay wanted to ask, *Where? At whose house? Adoption agency?* He didn't even know exactly what an adoption agency was or where to find one.

"Your baby will be fine," he finally said.

Now the three were hugging each other, Clovis in the middle, sprawled in those damned chairs. By the time they'd unclenched, Back Bay saw all three had been crying, even Abe.

Clovis got another pained look and pointed to Back Bay. He punched the button on the stopwatch.

∼

Order, or at least some *semblance* of it, was something Louis could bring to the table, and insisting Arlette not talk on her phone to Michelle so much was a good beginning. "After all," Louis said, "what can we do from here?" He thought he'd made a good enough case against the phone usage by the time they reached the ticket counter, and then by the end of the long walk through the concourse and to their gate, Arlette appeared to have understood. They still had a short wait until departure.

Instead of trying to argue with Arlette when she had insisted they leave immediately for Redfern, he had drawn within himself—out of pure fear—to let things settle and process. It was no time to bluster or put up a false front because Arlette would have seen through it, and he would have only humiliated himself again, even more than he had in the recent past. And about the recent past, he wasn't a bit proud, especially his minor flare-up when Arlette broke the baby news. The drive to the airport had been difficult, but about half way there, he reached inside himself—difficult as it was—and summoned all the strength he could find, forcing himself to talk his way through the blackness and impose his will and good sense on Arlette. Now, he noticed, while they sat at the gate, she hadn't reached into her purse for the blasted phone.

Sitting there, he sensed an unnerving separation from Arlette, and not just himself from her, but, more chilling, her from him. And it was then that a sudden realization—possibly even an epiphany—slammed him: Arlette was buckling down, getting stronger, fucking another man, controlling this baby situation, and, thus, *sliding away from him.* What was he bringing to the table these days? Even a "Help me, Jesus" seemed a paltry cry, a puny wail to put up against the blast of Arlette's strength. And then the most nightmarish thought of all: was *Jesus* pulling away? He watched people walk by, and he felt their surety, felt it even more strongly than Arlette's. Where was his certainty? Had Jesus misplaced it?

He found himself hugging Arlette right there in front of everyone, as though some electrical impulse might arc from her and imbue him with the muscle he was sure she was growing—to help regain the supremacy he once had. He guessed it wasn't supremacy he needed. That would not be Christ-like, would it? Did he need to dominate her? No. Just borrow a little of the vigor she was exuding. A smidgen right now was all he needed. He buried his head into her neck and felt her hair on his face. This woman was lovely.

Her elbow sunk into his ribs, and as he pulled away, she lightly pushed his head back. "Thanks but no thanks," she said. "I'm afraid I don't have what you need right now."

The woman was reading his mind. As he righted himself and looked around, no one had shown any evidence of seeing his crash. He supposed he was grateful for that. Sometimes small favors were all you could ask for.

"Suck it up, dear," said Arlette. "It'll only get worse." She took his hand and squeezed. "Right?" she asked. She was smiling. Her way of helping.

Small favors.

～

After landing in Indianapolis, getting the rental car went smoothly— Arlette had left it up to Louis, about which he felt entirely adequate, even skillful—and the drive to Towson was uneventful, thank goodness, with Arlette talking on the phone only briefly to Michelle, Clovis, and Back Bay.

"Things are holding steady," she said. "Coach Norman read the book."

"What book?"

"Clovis brought a book on emergency childbirth procedures. Coach is in charge. Sounds like he knows his stuff."

With a good fifty miles left to drive, Louis felt his ship listing, taking on water. He was floundering while too many folks seemed to know their stuff: Arlette had gotten strong, Coach Norman was showing his mettle in front of Michelle, and even the Arab was there, who had absolutely no right to be. Louis could envision Abe and Michelle going through some kind of perverted bonding by witnessing the birth, giving them ideas of their own. Trying to right the ship was Louis's only option.

"Too many cooks spoil the broth," he said.

"What are you talking about?" asked Arlette.

"It occurs to me, and far too late, that Michelle and Abe have no business being there."

"They're there, and that's that," said Arlette. "And of course they should be there. Clovis said she's grateful for them. They're helping."

Louis had visions of Arlette and him walking into that locker room with Clovis still in labor, and Louis rationally convincing all involved of getting a real doctor. He would call around and overpay some local physician to visit the locker room and deliver the baby. Louis had pulled off much bigger and better deals in his life.

"Things change," he told Arlette. "When we get to the locker room, we'll convince them to get a real doctor."

"Oh, you think *we're* going to witness that birth?"

"Why not?"

"Have you thought about complications, Louis? About all that can go wrong? Do you want to be there when the baby dies or when that poor girl dies because no one knew what the hell to do?"

Louis hadn't considered that.

"And then all the legal ramifications? Michelle's a minor, nothing can happen to her. Abe, who knows? The blessed coach is in charge. I mean, after all, he's read the fucking book, hasn't he? One thing goes wrong, and that man's ass is grass."

Arlette certainly had a point.

"We're here on a contingency basis," Arlette said. "If the mother and baby make it through—and I mean *if*—we've got a temporary place in that motel until somebody figures things out from there."

Louis was glad he was driving because Arlette's power in that moment was so strong that at least he had control of something—the car.

"And don't even consider trying to work your magic on this thing," said Arlette. "Haven't you done enough already?"

In moments like these, Louis knew what to do. Let her talk. The woman was sounding more like his mother all the time.

"What becomes of that baby?" Arlette asked. "The girl was going to have it on her own and probably drop it in a dumpster somewhere. Stupid! Then Michelle comes along and finds herself trapped into this whole thing, along with Abe. Why do you think I got Coach Norman involved? He can take all the heat, not that Michelle and Abe won't either if anything goes wrong. And, by God, things will go wrong, my fine friend."

Louis stared at the road.

"The best we can hope for is that the baby and mother are safe and delivered to the Super Eight without anyone knowing. What happens next is anyone's guess."

"Are you all right?" he asked.

"Oh, sure," she finally said.

"Everything you said made perfect sense."

"It did?"

"Yes." He supposed he might as well say it. "You've got things under control. The only one around here who does."

"Listen, Louis. It's about time you understood that nothing's under control."

He could only wait, sensing another salvo was on its way.

"Not since," she said, head in hands, "you brought Jesus into our lives."

How dare she say that!

"But perhaps that's normal," she said. "When we think we have things figured out, all hell breaks loose."

He certainly didn't agree with that, but saying something now wouldn't be prudent. He relaxed his hands on the wheel. How long had he been gripping it so tightly?

MOVE THIS THING ALONG

CHAPTER 15

It took everything Arlette had not to rush immediately to that field house after they arrived at the Super Eight. She had to hold firm on that. Louis had stopped nagging her about being on the cell phone, so at least that was a consolation. Michelle was keeping her apprised by phone, and occasionally Back Bay would say something. The coach was being kind and accommodating, making her almost sorry for hanging him out to dry like she had. Actually, maybe nothing would go wrong, and the whole mess would turn out right.

"They're in the transition stage now," she told Louis.

He was sprawled on the bed watching television.

"The contractions are lasting about seventy seconds now. She's getting tired."

"I would think so," said Louis.

It was always impossible to tell what he was thinking when he got into one of his moods, but one thing was certain now—if he didn't want to talk, that was fine with her. She did, however, let him know about the plans after the baby was born: She and Louis would dash to the locker room and then drive to a hospital emergency room in Southward, a larger town just twenty miles away, and have mother and child checked out. After that, they'd bring them back to the motel room, at which time ... well who knew what? So much depended on Clovis.

Arlette was pleased with having worked out the plans and even more pleased that everyone involved was amenable. Louis hadn't said much about it. He had thrown himself into the silent state he occasionally put himself in over the past month or so. At first, she'd been troubled by the sullenness—so unlike him before his conversion—but lately she'd come to see the value. It shut him up. He had been in it since arriving at the motel.

Sometimes on the phone, she could hear Clovis weathering another contraction, which always caused Arlette's stomach to curl. But after each one, when she talked to Back Bay, he said things were all right. She assumed he knew what he was doing, but still ...

~

Back Bay should have been checking how dilated her cervix was. The book said three centimeters at the early stage, seven centimeters in active, and ten centimeters in transition. No way he'd do that. He'd just have to judge what stage she was in by the length of the contractions. As far as he could tell, this stage was somewhere between transition and pushing/birth (contractions that were forty-five to ninety seconds apart).

Oh my God! Was that the crown of the head he was seeing? The little thing had lots of hair. His hands were shaking as he double-checked the book. Pushing time. Pushing/birth could take anywhere from twenty minutes to two hours.

"You've got to push now," he said.

At thirty minutes, he caught a breath. He had memorized these parts of the book: *"When the head is almost completely out, wipe it with a towel, especially the mouth and nose, to clear away any mucus and blood."*

"A towel," he said. One arrived in his hands.

He wiped the crying head. OK so far.

"Guide the head downward to bring out the top shoulder ..."

OK.

"... *and to deliver the bottom shoulder, lift its body upward.*"

Check.

"*With the shoulders delivered, the rest of the body should come quickly.*"

How quickly?

"*The baby will be very slippery. Be careful.*"

He put both arms beneath the head and shoulders, forming a basket. And pop! He was holding a squalling, bloody baby. No need to induce breathing. The thing was obviously getting air.

"*Dry off the baby then place it skin-to-skin on the mother's stomach.*"

OK. That was done.

"The string," he said.

Someone handed it to him, and he tied a hard knot onto the umbilical cord. The book had said to use a clamp. Clovis had brought a strong nylon string for it.

"Scissors," he said. *Snip.*

"*The placenta will be delivered from five to twenty minutes after the birth.*"

He sensed the three of them (now four) were huddled together before him, but he didn't look up.

"Oh, shit," he said. "The bucket."

Abe handed it to him.

When the placenta came rolling out and was safely in the bucket, he felt the room going dim.

~

Michelle and Abe had been so occupied with Clovis and the baby that she didn't notice Back Bay on the floor until she was about to ask him a question. "Abe," she shouted and pointed to the coach.

"I'm OK," she heard Back Bay say, and out of the corner of her eye saw Abe helping him to his feet.

The baby was crying like crazy. All Michelle remembered telling her mother on the phone was that they should get there *now*. Clovis was crying—Michelle didn't know whether out of pain, relief, or joy—and cradling the baby.

"Now what?" Michelle said to no one in particular.

Back Bay was squatting beneath Clovis with a towel.

"Dammit," she yelled over the baby's squalls. "What now?"

"Try her breast," Back Bay said.

Clovis was still wearing her dress. Michelle took the scissors Back Bay had used and began cutting the dress from the top of Clovis. "Help, Abe," she said.

By the time Michelle had exposed a breast, Abe was trying to work the baby's mouth to it. Abe finally took the child from Clovis's arms then readjusted the baby so it could find the nipple. Almost immediately the crying stopped.

"Good," Michelle heard Back Bay say. He was saying something about breastfeeding helping postpartum bleeding.

Had she called her mother? She couldn't remember. Once Abe had the breast and baby under control, she called.

"What's wrong?" he mother said.

Then she remembered she had already called.

"Nothing's wrong."

"I don't hear the baby crying," said her mother.

"Are you on the way?"

"Yes. What's wrong with the baby?"

"Nothing," said Michelle.

"Why did you call? Why isn't it crying?"

"It's breastfeeding."

She heard her mother tell her father.

"Let me talk to the coach," her mother said.

Back Bay was standing and staring at the baby, now wrapped in towels. She handed him the phone. As far as Michelle could tell, the baby was getting food. But how could you tell?

Now Back Bay was smiling.

"What?" Michelle asked.

"Your mother wants to know if it's a boy or girl."

She snapped her head toward Clovis and the baby. She hadn't noticed. "Boy or girl?" she asked.

They looked at each other blankly, but no one knew. Now they were all smiling, even Clovis, who held her nursing baby.

~

"How could they not know if it was a boy or girl?" Louis asked.

Apparently Arlette was telling him, but with the combination of trying to drive—don't get in a rush and cause someone to suspect something—and wondering what in the hell they would do next, Louis didn't really care to know the gender. A minor detail at best. Too many other things to worry about. Things like if they were breaking some law. (Well, of course they were, but Louis didn't have the time or the inclination to think that over.) At the hospital emergency room, would things go well? Would they be questioned? Back at the motel, who would be staying in that other room they'd rented? Probably the mother and child, and knowing Arlette, she'd be there too, leaving him alone in the room—or would Back Bay be there with him. Abe? Michelle? No, Back Bay lived in Towson, and the kids had dorm rooms. Would the motel people suspect mischief, hanky-panky—small town and all—with the comings and goings? How long would they stay there? When could he draw the coach aside and get the deal working with Webster Boyd? Maybe with all this drama, it wouldn't be the right time. But since Louis was in Towson, now was the time to set that in motion.

Arlette was still talking. When he looked at her, she was on the phone. Good. Leave him out of this as much as possible. But he needed to get his bearings. Probably another ten minutes. Where to park? Would people see them going in the field house? Arlette had said something about a back door. She'd know about that. Just home in on the college, then listen to Arlette later.

Louis wanted to keep his mind on practical matters, logistics—the kinds of things he had manipulated so well all his life. Sure, he had let this baby situation ride past his direction, but, after all, didn't women know more about childbirth? Yet so much had been slipping away lately. Soon, though, when they got back to the motel, and after he'd finalized plans with Back Bay, then he'd be back in the saddle—hands-on, sensible.

But he had frightened himself since all this started—how he'd actually hoped the baby would die and how all they had to do was whisk it away and be done with the whole fiasco. If that happened, surely Clovis would be all right, since she hadn't planned to keep the kid anyway—at least that's what Arlette said that Michelle said—and Michelle would get over things, knowing how his girl could bounce back from tough times, like being down two sets and coming back to win the match.

Troubling thoughts. And then there was the worst of all his hoped-for scenarios: the baby *and* mother would die, which would wipe out all future complications and get things back to where they were only a few short weeks ago. With that happening, Michelle would experience a true object lesson (don't get pregnant), and he would be able to talk sense to her about the dangers of cavorting with foreign men; then Abe would be out of the picture. He imagined that the trauma of two deaths would somehow right things, bring back some balance and order to situations that were spinning *way* out of control. But how would they deal with Clovis's body? They wouldn't. They'd bring things out in the open—none of this secrecy stuff—and Michelle, Abe, and Back Bay would be disciplined, and in a short while, all would be forgotten. Who could blame Michelle for wanting to help with the baby?

On the heels of those thoughts, Louis segued straight into how death itself was the ultimate way to resolve most matters: get rid of problems by destroying them, wipe them out. Kill the problems yourself, or at least have them destroyed. Simple, simple. The Milwaukee group operated that way. Which immediately shot him to that part of his life, one he could handle—and *would* handle—once he was back in St. Louis. Sell off, make the balloon payment, sic Back Bay onto Webster Boyd, and Louis's once-problems would be solidly Redfern's. All he had to do now was …

"Louis, Louis." It was Arlette talking. "Have you heard a word I said?"

"Sure."

"Park over there." Arlette was pointing to a near-empty lot. "Coach said to wait until we don't see anyone then walk around the building. He'd leave the door unlocked."

Should be simple enough, he guessed. "Who's coming with us?" he asked.

"Just Clovis and the baby."

He turned off the ignition, and they waited.

"I don't see anyone around," said Arlette.

"Oh," said Louis. "Was it a boy or girl?"

Arlette gave him one of her looks. "You didn't hear a word I said, did you?"

Might as well fess up. "Not everything."

"I think we should go now," said Arlette, opening her door slowly.

Louis opened his and was careful to close it as quietly as he could. It didn't matter, though, because the Lexus doors, Louis realized, were engineered so well they hardly made a sound. He let Arlette lead the way since she had surely gotten the directions, but caught up to her and took her hand. He thought he felt her try to pull away, but she left her hand in his.

"By the way," she said. It's a girl."

Louis decided to become a better listener.

~

He thought the place looked like a slaughter house. Bloody towels everywhere, and then when he looked into that bucket. *Help me, Jesus!*

He had truly appreciated Michelle's long hug when he and Arlette walked into that awful place, and, he had to admit, was mostly touched by Abe's firm handshake and his "Thank you, Mr. Lewis; thank you, Mr. Lewis" while he pumped Louis's hand. Louis was pretty sure he wasn't yet ready for a hug from the tall kid.

It was Louis's survey of the place while Arlette and the others were hugging and talking that made him want to leave immediately. And that bucket. Then, my Lord, they had the baby sucking on the breast right out in the open like that, and look at how they acted so proud of the little thing (the baby, not the breast). Already they were like some joyful family. This, for Pete's sake, wasn't the time for such glee; they needed to clear out, and Louis should impress upon everyone the need to make haste. Come on, folks! Yet, how could he insinuate himself into that group, all that oohing and aahing? It was like a baby being born in the midst of a war zone. They needed to become refugees and flee the devastation just as soon as the adorations ceased. Louis shouldn't enter the circle. After all, someone had to be in charge. And look at Coach Norman, the dried blood on his arms. The guy should probably jump in a shower—this was a locker room, after all—and rid himself of the deed.

Without warning, just like that, the wrongness of it all consumed Louis, and he realized how solitary and even forsaken he was, standing off by himself looking in. Had he isolated himself or was this a natural result of—dare he say it?—trying to follow Jesus? Louis would need to explore that more.

Where did that shiver come from?

Perhaps he should test the waters, stroll into the group and venture a gaze, join the rubberneckers, see why such jubilation and exaltation could come from something so wrong. In five steps he was there, and his arms encased the shoulders of Coach Norman and Arlette, both not reacting to his being there (was he really just an apparition?). He watched the pale, exhausted mother touching the child's cheek and making tiny circles there. Louis remembered Michelle in Arlette's arms like that only a few years ago, and before Louis could cover the scene with the net of rationality, he caught himself actually smiling, the most natural and complete reaction he thought he'd had in weeks. He couldn't stop. He tuned out what everyone was saying. He wanted to stay there just a bit longer before he had to do what he knew he should: move this thing along.

It didn't take much, really. "Let's get them to the hospital" was all Louis had to say, and everyone seemed to pull together.

"Can she walk?" Abe said.

"I think she can," said Arlette.

Abe appeared actually to be lifting Clovis from her slumped position within those chairs and into more of a normal sitting orientation, although Louis wondered how in the world *anyone* could lift that girl.

"Be careful," said Michelle, hand over her mouth.

Louis had watched Michelle in the last several minutes attending to Clovis like a doting, worried parent.

"Someone take the baby," said Back Bay.

The coach must have performed expertly before Louis arrived. Back Bay held himself with such poise, maybe the sign of the true athlete under pressure. Louis had seen Michelle react with such composure on the tennis court, such unflappability. Louis's stomach rolled, seeing Back Bay take charge of such an important maneuver. Was Arlette as equally impressed? She was caressing Clovis's forehead, not noticing Back Bay's aplomb. Now the coach was lifting the baby from Clovis's wide stomach and pendulous breast. His smile had gone, and the coach appeared to Louis like a surgeon finishing a long procedure with grace and care. He handed the baby to Arlette who nuzzled it to her chin.

With Back Bay on one side and Michelle and Abe on the other, they helped Clovis rise from the chair—still covered with bloody towels—and try to stand and maintain equilibrium. She stood for several seconds with the others still at her side and began walking toward Louis. What should he do? Go to the door and hold it open.

As he turned and walked, thinking of the Lexus and how Clovis would fit in the back seat, he was shocked to see that he and Arlette had left the door open. He would stand at the opening and act like he was doing something important as they passed slowly by. Then there'd be the long walk to the car ...

"What's going on here?"

Louis's shoulders twitched at the sound of the voice, then a tremor pulled at his throat followed by an all-out spasm in his gut. A uniformed man stood facing Louis.

"What is this?" said the man.

When Louis spun to look back into the room, Back Bay, walking slowly beside Clovis, was looking at the man.

"Aw, shit," said Back Bay, mouth gaping.

"What's going on in here?" said the man again.

Now everyone had stopped walking.

"Coach Norman?" asked the man.

"Look, Ben," said Back Bay, "we've got some things to get done here before we can talk. OK?"

"I don't think so," said the man.

But Back Bay grabbed Clovis's arm again and began ushering her along.

"Move over," said Louis to the man.

"You're not getting out until I find out what happened here," the man said sternly to Back Bay.

"You've got my promise we'll talk, Ben. Just let us get this woman to a car."

"I'm following you," said the man.

"I'm sure you will," said Back Bay.

Louis watched the man survey the room. "Oh my God," he said.

"Don't you campus cops have anything better to do?" asked Back Bay, leaving with the others.

The spasm in Louis's gut had turned into a shudder that he could now feel all the way to his toes.

I GUESS WE CAN BE FRIENDS

CHAPTER 16

Coach Norman had said he would take care of things, but Michelle, alone in her room without Clovis, had time to think things through and was pretty sure things would *not* turn out well. How could he take care of things when that guard wasn't about to budge from wanting to take them right to the college president? Then Michelle's father stepped in and, in his usual way—puffing up a little and making himself look mean—told the guard that they had to take Clovis and the baby to a hospital.

"Why didn't you do that in the first place?" asked the guard.

"We had our reasons," said her father, acting like suddenly *he* was the one who delivered the baby.

Michelle could tell her mother was pissed at her dad. Later, Michelle knew, her mom would probably lay into him. Maybe not, though. Her mom was totally preoccupied with the baby but not so much with Clovis. Funny, but Michelle wanted Clovis to be all right more than she did the baby. Perhaps her mom would forget about her dad being an ass in front of everyone. She and her mom were used to ignoring him.

The guard wasn't too happy about her parents leaving, but with both Coach Norman and her dad bullying their way through the situation, the poor guard didn't do much. Her dad handed the guy his business card and said they would be back the next day "to settle things up," and the guard must have taken it to mean that everything would be swept under the carpet because he shot back, "You won't be settling a darn thing with me. It'll be the president or maybe even the town police, depending on what I find here." Clovis started crying about then.

Michelle's parents, Clovis, Abe, and the baby had disappeared into the dark and turned the corner of the building, and Michelle was left with Coach and the guard. That was when Coach Norman must have decided you can catch more flies with honey than vinegar, and he started cozying up to the guard.

"Let's step back inside," Coach Norman said.

They'd been just outside the open door with enough light coming through to see.

"Don't think you're going to weasel out of this, Coach," said the guard.

Coach had that smile on his face Michelle recognized from when he had been recruiting her, especially when he'd sat in their family room with her parents.

"Ben, you've got to see this thing from several angles," said Coach Norman.

"I got one angle. You people was up to no good."

"Would the president want word of this to spread around? A girl having a baby in the locker room?"

"No idea what the president wants," said the guard.

Michelle watched the coach put a hand on the guard's shoulder. "And what about your job?" asked the coach.

"What about my job?"

"In a way, *you* let this happen? On your watch."

"I'm not taking no blame for this."

Michelle saw where the coach was headed.

"You and I can end this right here, Ben. No mess, no questions."

The guard looked down at Michelle's dad's business card. "Who is this guy, Coach?"

"Influential donor to the college. Big money."

The guard kept staring at the card, thinking. She wondered if the coach knew her dad was broke, at least according to her mother.

"What's he got to do with all this?"

"Let's just say," said Back Bay, "he's a guy who wouldn't want this spread around."

How long would it take for this to sink into the guy's skull? Michelle was rooting for the coach. Kind of like match point. Lots of tension.

"Well ..."

Michelle pictured the guy's house and wife, probably some kids to feed. Couldn't he use the money?

"This isn't right at all," he finally said. "I'm locking this place up and spending the rest of the night right there." He pointed outside the door. "I got a report to file. I got people to answer to." He looked at his watch. "I'm parking myself right out there."

Game, set, match—to the guard. Why had she stayed there to watch all this? Abe appeared at the door.

"I know who you are," the guard said to Abe. "But you," pointing to Michelle, "I don't figure how you got in this."

She looked to Coach Norman, who shook his head slightly.

"Oh, well," said the guard. "It'll all come out in the wash. Sometime tomorrow morning I'd judge." He swept his hand toward the door, where Abe still stood. "All out."

Michelle walked quickly to Abe, and he engulfed her in his arms. Never had a hug felt so good.

She sat so long in her room recalling what happened (barely being aware of the sun coming up) that she hadn't thought of calling her mother. Then she remembered she had classes that morning, not sure she could force herself to go. Already she missed Clovis—how even in the short time they'd lived together they had settled into morning routines before heading off to class. Those habits had established for Michelle a devotion and loyalty to Clovis that she'd never considered until she was forced to be without her. Michelle began tracing their relationship's evolution: first encounter (Michelle saw her as oddly disgusting and mildly entertaining); dinner with her parents (polite, yet socially inept); evenings in the room (warm, sad, talkative); dining hall (shy, jealous, hurt); labor and giving birth (forthright, courageous). Clovis was so much unlike Michelle's friends from Ursuline Academy that she was momentarily embarrassed to admit such true emotion for her. But perhaps she was closer to Clovis than she had been to anyone.

Michelle wondered why she wasn't crying, how she could feel such an outpouring of love for the girl and remain so strong and tranquil. Maybe it was Abe's presence in the mix. How he'd performed through it all, almost like he had been trained for it. And Coach Norman had flown into action like a real champ; the way he caught the baby and knew what to do—*caught* was a funny word for it, but the baby slid right into his outstretched arms. Before she knew it, she was picturing Coach Norman as her father, walking around the house fixing things and making her mother laugh. The three of them would take long vacations to Europe, watching and playing tennis on the famous clay courts. Then she and Abe would marry, perhaps live in Algeria, where Back Bay and her mother would come to visit two or three times a year, maybe even meeting up on the Italian Rivera, just a step across the Mediterranean. She and Abe would produce such beautiful children. The proud grandparents would ..."

Her cell phone rang.

"Hi, honey. Did I wake you?" It was her father.

"No."

"Your mom and I have news. Clovis and her baby are fine. Everything checked out. We're on our way to the Super Eight."

Her Dad's voice was wimpy, not like Back Bay's.

"Good," she said.

"Your mother wanted me to call. She remembered about a car seat. I'm driving. Clovis is in the back resting."

Michelle could picture her back there, droopy eyelids, legs spread apart. What would she be wearing?

"Can I talk to Mom?"

"She's pretty wrapped up with the baby."

She heard her mother saying something in the background then a general commotion.

"Your dad dropped the phone," said her mother.

Michelle could picture it. "Everything all right?"

"The baby is precious, Michelle. And healthy."

"How's Clovis?"

"In the back," her mother whispered. "Sleeping."

"Is she OK?"

"Just fine. An amazing experience. This baby girl is such a gift."

"But Clovis is fine?"

"Yes."

"Clovis was very strong the whole time during labor and birth."

"I'm sure she was."

Her mother and father hadn't been there to hear Clovis tell her story about keeping everything so secret. About how no one was to know. How Clovis's parents would have reacted. Michelle wanted her mother to know, to love Clovis as she should. But no, all her mother could do was talk about that baby. "Has Clovis talked much?"

Her mother was whispering again. "She clammed up in the emergency room. Wouldn't say a thing."

"There's a reason for that," said Michelle.

"So we had to say she was our daughter, to keep matters on the up-and-up."

"What?"

"Our daughter. That's the only way we could get in and out of there."

The cell phone went heavy in Michelle's hand. She thought she heard her mother cooing into the phone. "This little thing is sooo darling."

"Hand the phone to Dad."

"He's not comfortable driving and talking on the phone."

"Oh, that's right," said Michelle. "Never was much of a multitasker."

~

Arlette said that, at least for the first night, she wanted to stay in the room with Clovis and the baby. "You'll get lots more rest by yourself," Arlette told Louis.

It was daylight so who could rest anyway? Sure, Louis had been up all night, but day time was for getting things done. After that hospital episode, he needed to check lots of items off his list, not the least of which was to forget the huge lie they had perpetrated on that rinky-dink hospital: Clovis was his daughter and the baby was their grand-child. He guessed Jesus Himself might have lied a time or two—he didn't remember reading about that, however.

After safely tucking the lie away, Louis could focus on trying to stomp out a fire that would surely be blazing any minute. He had already been planning his strategy for when all of them met with that campus guard and whoever else—surely the Redfern president. Louis's guess was that everyone would best be served by covering the whole thing up, and he would press that upon the president. After that was settled, then there was the matter of Coach Norman helping him with his plan. The poor coach had been through quite a trial by fire with delivering that baby, so Louis wasn't at all certain when to get that ball rolling. But roll it must.

Back Bay would assuredly call Arlette to keep them apprised. However, this thing might drag out all day before any action happened. Maybe Louis should first visit the president himself. A preemptive strike. That way, Louis could not only resolve the Clovis situation, but also deal directly with the president on the property deal and bypass Webster Boyd altogether.

Louis stood in his room, stretched his arms to the ceiling and decided he was ready to take things into his own hands for a change. Arlette could deal with the postpartum mother and baby in the other room.

Louis was always at his best with the first appointments of the day, and he assumed that was also true of other executives. Something about the mind being fresh and not worn down by all the daily minu-tiae that constantly assault your average exec. The meeting would be a challenge; he would need to hone all his skills to come out the winner. Doing this with no sleep the night before didn't exactly work in Louis's favor, but a good, quick shower and shave would help considerably.

And it did. When he reached the office, he decided to play it formally. He handed the receptionist his business card. "I'm wondering if the president is available for a brief chat."

The secretary looked at the card—rather uneasily, Louis thought.

"Louis Lewis," said Louis. "From St. Louis."

"Oh, yes," said the young lady, still looking at the card. "I'm told he had a busy night."

That didn't bode well. "I'm certain a president's days are replete with events and whatnot," said Louis.

"Yes. Events."

Still, she hadn't looked up.

"Just have a seat, Mr. Lewis. The president should be in shortly."

He turned his back to find a seat—pretty plush office—and took a corner chair.

"Coffee, Mr. Lewis?"

"That would be lovely."

"I'll just make some."

She looked relieved to have at last found something to do. Weren't receptionists supposed to be calm and convivial? This one was far too skittish, even mousy. Or was Louis causing this? Was it his obvious power and importance? The events of last night?

The coffee was strong. Three sips and he was righting himself, feeling the energy to soldier on through this. The door opened. Louis hadn't met the president, but without question that was him. A tall man, on the spindly side, pointed nose, dark suit, tasseled loafers. Even lawyerly. Not a good sign. Louis had seen this type.

Louis felt isolated and hidden, as though he'd been cast on a dung heap. Where had he run across that phrase? His stomach jumped. The young thing at the desk met the president's eyes, then handed him Louis's card. Neither person said a thing. She tossed her head to Louis's corner. The president made a rather protracted show of placing the card into a side pocket of his jacket before he leisurely turned toward Louis. And there came the ingratiating smile, the executive amble toward Louis with the hand barely extended, waiting for Louis to reach for it on the president's terms, on the president's turf. This was most definitely his first appointment of the day. Mr. President would be at his sharpest. Maybe coming here wasn't the best idea after all.

"So nice to finally meet you," said the president.

Louis shook his hand and could barely return the greeting.

No, this definitely wasn't a good idea.

~

All Back Bay told his wife was that he had an early appointment. Nothing about meeting with the president and most certainly nothing about the baby incident, although explaining why he was out all night sure as hell wasn't the easiest thing he'd ever lied to her about. She bought it well enough: lots of around-the-world recruiting calls from the office on the college's dime ("you have to talk during the daylight hours in Europe, you know") and he eventually just fell asleep on the couch in his office.

He couldn't say he took great pleasure in putting shit over on his wife, but the night's doings especially needed to be quashed. And he wasn't finished quashing. The damned early morning meeting with the president and the high-and-mighty Ben—what a prick for such a low-level college employee!

He'd hoped to have cleaned up the locker room, but asshole Ben stood good on his promise to camp out in front of the back door, and, to boot, the dickhead had phoned the president. That's when Back Bay decided to go home and get a couple of hours' sleep before the inevitable. The president called at 6:30 a.m., no doubt from his home, away from secretaries and the college switchboard. He informed Back Bay that he had inspected the locker room with Ben and expected some answers about what exactly had gone on in there; thus, the 8 a.m. meeting with the president and then, later in the day, meeting with all the Lewises, Abe, and Clovis.

The only consolation? Back Bay knew the president wouldn't want all this to become public. A tarnish to the president's fucking Christian campus—and fundraising.

As Back Bay contemplated all the political machinations that might possibly ensue as the group sat in council with the president, he was surprised to realize that he did not fear presidential upbraiding or whatever skirmishes might take place between the pompous Louis Lewis and the president. Being in the moral right reinforced Back Bay on this one, a position in which he hadn't often found himself. After all, he had come to the aid of another human, a child was born, and, as far as he knew, both mother and child were fine. His thoughts went to Clovis, that sad girl who told the doleful story of her family and her obvious uncertain plight. What would happen to that baby and mother? And who had the courage to help them?

Arlette had the courage, but the more he thought about her and that pitiful husband of hers, the more angry—and frightened—Back Bay became. Stupid people often caused the most damage, and something about the possibility of Louis Lewis's actions harming Arlette sent Back Bay into fight mode. If Lewis wanted to destroy himself, Back Bay supposed he had the right, but bringing down Arlette, Clovis, and the baby with him—now that Back Bay had developed this fatherly affection for the mother and child—wasn't something he was likely to tolerate. Screw the college. Back Bay's allegiances suddenly lay elsewhere. What a startling turn of events.

He left his house at 7:15 a.m. The president had assured him it would be only the two of them before later meeting with the others.

～

"Go right on in," said the receptionist. "They're waiting."

They?

Louis Lewis was perched on the leather couch smiling like a shit-eating monkey.

"I hope you don't mind Mr. Lewis being here," said the president, "in view of the fact I previously said it would just be the two of us."

Back Bay minded a lot.

"I don't mind at all," said Back Bay.

"Mr. Lewis thought it prudent to meet with me first thing this morning, now that the event is still fresh in his mind."

The coach's and the president's relationship had turned on a mutual tolerance they each shared for the other's power at the college. Back Bay had brokered power in certain college quarters, leaving the president interestingly deferential to him. He guessed he and the president had a relationship based on respect. And then there was all the fundraising crap the president had foisted on him, trying to slip into the Lewis's wealth. Now, each was likely to parlay whatever capital he had gained to his own advantage.

"Mr. Lewis and I," said the president, "were just discussing the tragic explosion of his church home, in St. Louis."

"Not the birth in the locker room?" asked Back Bay, pissed already.

"We hadn't gotten to that yet," said Lewis.

Hang Back Bay out to dry. Not really unexpected.

"Perhaps now's the time to discuss that," said the president.

"That's why we're here," said Back Bay.

The president let roll everything he'd heard from Ben the guard about what he'd found and then everything Mr. President himself had seen when Ben took him there. Surprisingly, it was all accurate, no one trying to alter the facts. Lewis was sitting there on his leather throne punctuating the president's remarks with an occasional "Right, Right," as though the bastard had been there the whole time.

"I've had Mr. Ben Kramer, the guard," said the president, "seal the locker room, and even as we speak, I have instructed him to clean it thoroughly and dispose of all things used there last night."

"Then what?" asked Back Bay.

The president looked first to Back Bay then to Louis. "Then we forget this happened."

Back Bay was expecting this but not so immediately, so perfunctorily.

The president continued. "I'm certain Mr. Lewis here, with his philanthropic interest in helping Redfern, wouldn't want prospective donors—of whom he knows many—shying away from aiding Christian higher education because of some ill-publicized event such as this." He turned to Back Bay. "Nor, I'm sure, would Coach Norman wish prospective athletes having to factor such an event into their decisions to attend Redfern."

Back Bay guessed Louis had softened up the president on the land deal scheme. And apparently the president had bought it.

"So you're saying," said Back Bay, "that while we forget the birth ever happened, we should also forget what becomes of that baby and her mother? The mother, you know, is a student here."

"The young lady made some very unfortunate and wrong decisions. And it's my understanding she is loath to make this public."

Where did he learn that?

"Isn't that right, Mr. Lewis?" asked the president.

"That's the way I understand things," said Louis.

Why in the hell would Louis tell him that? Perhaps to shelter Clovis. Keep her safe.

"What do you see happening to Clovis Ginch and her baby?" asked Back Bay, wanting to jump across the bastard's desk.

"Because of her poor decisions, it's out of our hands. Of course, we wish the best for her and her child and will most definitely keep them in our prayers."

"That's it?"

"I think we can all agree that …"

"You're not even going to visit your wrath upon us? Excommunicate this whole sordid group?"

Back Bay wondered what it would be like to flatten that pointed nose.

"I'm not saying I condone what went on," said the president. "I certainly intend to meet with Ms. Ginch, Mr. al-Fiasa, and Ms. Lewis to discuss the inappropriate nature of their actions."

"Certainly," said Louis, wagging his head.

"And to silence them," said Back Bay.

Back Bay noticed the man squirming presidentially in his chair.

"That will not be my major intent, Mr. Norman."

"And," said Back Bay, "what kind of threat will you hold over their heads?"

Back Bay wondered about the source of all his anger. Pent up over the years? Spur-of-the-moment indignation? Wanting to defend Clovis Ginch in some small way?

Mr. President's spiky nose reddened, and his lips moved nearly imperceptibly, silently. Could the man be cursing under his breath?

"Perhaps," said Louis, waving a hand, "we've already settled this issue without carrying it any further. Agreed?"

Louis clapped eyes on Back Bay.

"I'm done talking here," said Back Bay, extending a hand to Louis in a mock high five. "Sometimes it's best to know when to walk away. Too much emotion is often counterproductive. I—a coach of all people—should know that."

He leveled an aching smile at the president and wondered if his lips were quivering. At least the president hadn't fired him or booted the kids out of college. But maybe even *that* would have been the best. A ticket out of this place.

"I'm happy you're seeing this our way," said the president.

Our?

"I expected," said Back Bay, "to be called in here for a reprimand or worse, and I ended up shooting off steam because I wasn't. How's that for interesting psychology?"

Not bad in covering his ass by mollifying a president with a touch of self-deprecation. Back Bay had to admit, though, that Louis Lewis worked the session well.

Neither Louis nor Back Bay said a word walking past the receptionist's desk, nor did they speak while leaving the building. They had parked in the same lot. Back Bay said, "Were you working him?"

"Like a charm, I hope."

"I suppose you're softening him up to help pull off your scheme?"

"I can deal with him now and forget Webster Boyd."

"Good plan, since that leaves me out of the picture to help with Boyd."

Louis leaned on his car—as if to show he was settling in for a longer discussion than Back Bay hoped—and affected a knowing, assured look.

"I'm afraid," said Louis, "you're in the picture now more than ever.

Your status with this college is tenuous at best, given the way you acted in front of the big man. He wasn't a bit pleased with you."

"I caught that."

"And instead of *merely* sleeping with my wife, you're now an accomplice to what is probably some crime. The president could fire you at any time over that. And don't forget I hold the trump card with Mr. President. Should he learn of you and Arlette, you're doubly screwed."

"Hollow threats. You don't have squat. The only capital you've got with that man is your past reputation, which, as far as I can tell, is crumbling. Gone."

Things were getting down to the nut-cutting.

"I guess you didn't really see what was going on in there," said Louis. "I saved your ass and probably all the others' too—Arlette, Clovis, the baby, and Michelle. That man would have tied all of us in knots. He wanted blood. More intent on getting my money than acting on principle. I called his bluff. He's a weasel."

"That's old news."

"What's the new news?"

Back Bay had just talked himself into a corner. The new news was that he had helped a human in a moment of crisis and was feeling some kind of unfaltering loyalty to both the damned mother and child, but how could he tell Louis *that*?

"I'm still thinking about what went on in that locker room," said Back Bay. He eased out a smile. "Post-traumatic stress syndrome I guess. Feels like it might stay with me awhile."

"I understand," said Louis. "I'm still shaking over getting caught and figuring out how to cover our asses."

"Well, I—"

"I haven't yet learned to think morally," said Louis. "I've got lots to learn about that. Seems like that was your first reaction. To do the right thing."

Back Bay watched the earlier composure slowly drain from Louis. As they leaned on the Lexus, Back Bay agreed with Louis: yes, he *had* acted morally. He'd done what he'd had to do at the moment, and it turned out to be the right thing.

"You were selfless," said Louis, finally.

How do you take such a compliment from a guy like Louis Lewis? Was he joking? Louis put his arm on Back Bay's shoulder.

"I'd like to think I could've acted like you in that locker room. Truth is, I froze and hadn't a clue what to do. I left everything in Arlette's hands. She's a good woman and can handle things."

Back Bay didn't know what to say.

"Are you going to sleep with her anymore?" asked Louis.

The man asked a straight, practical question, not full of any emotion. A simple yes or no.

"No," said Back Bay.

"Good," said Louis. "Then I guess we can be friends."

"I suppose so," said Back Bay.

"Because," said Louis, "I've got work to do. A college to bring down. You can stand by and watch or make yourself available."

A coldness returned to Louis's face.

"Is that the moral thing to do?" asked Back Bay.

"Try reading the Bible, sir. Jesus destroyed quite a bit in His day. And for all the right reasons." Back Bay would need to think that over.

THERE'S BEEN LOTS OF THAT LATELY

If Arlette were standing outside of herself, she'd likely be embarrassed by what she saw: a maudlin woman reduced to baby talk interspersed with only an occasional cogent adult comment. Clovis's baby had returned Arlette to a time when tiny Michelle occupied all her waking moments, forcing the outside world to shrink into a nebulous existence about which she had only passing interest. Arlette remembered she had quit reading newspapers or watching television back then. Even shopping for household items or clothes held scant interest unless it had directly to do with Michelle. Caring for Clovis's baby was doing the same.

When Louis surprisingly said, after meeting with Back Bay and the president, that he had to fly back to St. Louis, she wasn't particularly distressed by his typical rash decision. "I'll hire someone to stay in the motel while I'm gone," he said.

She knew she'd need someone's help because Clovis had sunk into a funk. Neither Arlette nor Michelle could bring her out of it. Clovis seemed to be only pretending an affection for her child. And she refused to pick a name. She would occasionally hold the child and say things like "baby, baby," then tell Arlette she was tired and go to sleep.

During Clovis's waking hours, usually when the baby was asleep, she couldn't stop talking about how she had to stay at Redfern and not let her parents know. Often the more she talked, the more she appeared to hold her future brightly before her—with a sense of relief that the baby was finally born and she wouldn't need to worry about that secret anymore—and then she might hug Arlette, thanking her for what she did, before her thoughts meandered back to her parents and how they would react to the news.

"They'd kill me," she said. "Kill me."

"Not literally," Arlette said.

"No, not literally."

"Then what?"

"They've saved up money to send me here. God sent me here."

"Did God or your parents send you?"

"Oh, Mrs. Lewis, don't try to trip me up."

And then Clovis would usually launch into a discussion of God's will, sounding like Louis, managing to sidestep facts and reality. Poor God would be blamed for all things great and small, ugly and good, evil and blessed. Somehow Arlette could bear such talk more calmly with Clovis than Louis. Still, it irked her.

"What name has God laid upon your heart to call this little girl?"

Clovis was a good sport about it; she smiled then didn't say anything.

"Well, you've got to choose a name," said Arlette. It was Baby Doe on the hospital records, and Clovis became Clovis Lewis—Louis and Arlette's daughter. "She can't be Baby Doe all her life."

"God will provide a name," Clovis finally said.

"I wouldn't trust God for that," said Arlette. "Might choose something like Jezebel. How would you like that?"

"Oh, Mrs. Lewis."

"God works in mysterious ways, you know."

"Sometimes you remind me of Michelle. Always having fun."

"That's us all right."

The irony flew past Clovis, and while Arlette didn't intend to bruise her with sarcasm, she still enjoyed firing salvos at such naiveté. Perhaps Clovis was a prime fit as Louis's daughter.

A sitter for Arlette and Clovis arrived—a simple, thirty-something woman who said she had been working in the Redfern dining hall when Coach Norman (obviously Louis had conned him into finding someone) had told her he'd heard of a family at the Super Eight who needed help for a few days with a baby and would she want to make some extra money? When Coach Norman told her how much she'd make, she said she'd quit the dining-hall job in a minute because she didn't like working there in the first place, but it was steady money, and after this little stay at the motel was over she could go out and get a better job. How could she turn down such good money? And she *did* like babies. She had two children of her own, but her ex had custody. Oh, my, what a cute little child! What's the precious thing's name?

The sitter allowed Arlette some time alone in the other motel room to sleep—and think.

∿

Abe suggested Michelle skip her classes and get some sleep after being up all night. He said Arlette had things under control at the motel and, most importantly, Clovis and the baby were all right. She didn't want to leave Abe, although she didn't tell him that exactly. She wanted to curl up with him in a bed with one of his long legs flopped over her and with her arm resting on his chest as they slept the day and night away. Strange, she thought, how they had fucked but never slept together. Wouldn't sleeping together be as intimate, or more so? Two people wrapped up with each other for hours? Waking briefly and patting the other softly? Is that what married couples did every night?

"I'd better go to classes," she told Abe. "Besides, I want to tell Clovis's professors that she's sick and will probably be out for two or three days."

But when she got to her room, she felt her body wilt. Then came the call from her mother telling her that Coach Norman had received a call from the president's office asking him to contact Michelle and Abe: the president wanted to speak with them and would be expecting them in his office.

"Would you call Abe?" her mother asked.

"I'm scared," Michelle said.

"Just tell the truth," her mother said.

"Did the president ask for Clovis?"

"She's not able to come just yet."

Michelle held Abe's hand as they walked into the president's office. She had seen the president at the first campus convocation and heard him speak. But in his office, he seemed taller than she thought, almost as tall as Abe, but skinnier.

Would they want sodas? They said they would, and while the secretary was getting them, he smiled and asked how the beginning of the semester had been, what they were majoring in—those kinds of things. He asked Abe about the tennis team and hoped he did as well or better as last year, and did Abe get back home to Algeria much? The president seemed to rely on Abe to carry the conversation, which suited Michelle fine, even though the thought crossed her mind that, later, the president might detect her fear and shyness and try to catch her by causing her to say something that would contradict what Coach Norman or her dad had told him. She had to pee but thought she could hold it. The soda tasted good but burned the back of her throat. She drank half the glass in one swallow. Abe didn't touch his.

The president was sure they knew why he wanted to speak with them. They said they knew. He was also certain they knew that they had endangered the lives of the mother and baby and that the unfortunate incident could have caused deaths. Michelle and Abe didn't respond. He told them those deaths could have brought serious consequences to them and Coach Norman. The president was talking about criminal charges. Had they considered that when they entered into the proceedings? This time he waited for them to say something. Michelle looked to Abe. Abe said that Clovis was going to give birth by herself and that their helping her may have saved her and the baby's lives. Abe wondered if the president had thought of *that*. Michelle wished Abe hadn't said that because the president appeared to be clenching his jaw, but Abe probably knew what he was doing. The president said either situation was enough to have caused great damage; didn't they agree with that? Again, he waited for them to say something. Abe said that Clovis had prepared herself well for the birth and that Coach Norman read from a book on how to deliver a baby and that the coach did an excellent job. Abe said they all tried to convince Clovis to go to a hospital, but she kept refusing, so there wasn't anything else for them to do but help her. What would the president have done in a case like that? Michelle thought Abe overstepped his bounds with the president, and she fidgeted in her chair, wondering if the president noticed her reaction. He must have noticed because he looked at her and addressed her as *young lady* before asking what she had to say. Did she intend for Mr. al-Fiasa to do all the talking?

She knew she should say something quickly, but nothing came to mind. Finally, she said that she was happy for Clovis and that Clovis was a sweet girl who had a hard life and that Michelle wished the president wouldn't let Clovis's parents know. Michelle said he could do anything to them but hoped he wouldn't punish Clovis in any way.

The president said he could decide to punish them in any way he saw fit. He looked at Abe and called many of his comments *impudent* and said how disappointed he was in the young man. If it weren't for the fact that the president didn't want the incident spread around, didn't they know he had the right to expel them immediately? He paused.

Michelle and Abe said nothing.

He leaned back into his swivel chair and said he would make a deal with them—while looking directly at Michelle. He wouldn't speak with or punish Clovis for her actions if the two of them promised they would uphold the good, Christian name of the college by not relating what went on. To anyone. He said they could scratch each other's back on that one, couldn't they? He smiled while waiting for an answer. Michelle looked at Abe and Abe back at her. She told the president they had a deal. Abe nodded to the president. The president asked if the nod meant yes. Abe said it did.

∼

Back Bay parked in the back of the Super Eight motel—not wanting
to be noticed—and found the room numbers Arlette had given him.
He knocked on one door, and a woman answered. He heard a crying
baby within the room.

"Is Arlette Lewis here?"

She pointed a thumb to the right. "In that room."

He knocked several times and rattled the door knob. Arlette appeared, apparently freshly awakened, a bedspread wrapped around her.
"Oh, David. Hold on a minute."

He remembered telling Louis he wouldn't sleep with Arlette anymore. He heard the baby crying in the next room.

Wearing a robe Arlette opened the door. He walked in and looked
around the room. "Where's Louis?"

"Gone to St. Louis to work his deals."

Why had he asked about Louis's whereabouts first? It really wasn't
the first thing on his mind. "Who was that woman in the other room?"

"A sitter for Clovis and the baby. I needed some rest."

"Sorry to have disturbed you."

Arlette crossed her arms, seemingly to wrap the robe more tightly
around her. "Have a seat," she said.

"How are Clovis and the baby?"

"Fine."

She appeared to be shivering. "Are you cold?" asked Back Bay.

"David, I'm keeping that baby."

Back Bay wasn't entirely surprised. "What about Louis?"

"He'll get over it."

What an odd reaction.

"Does he know?" asked Back Bay.

"Not yet."

He could picture Louis's reaction. Either rage or a far-off stare
followed by a wimpy acceptance.

"Does Clovis know?" he asked.

"Not yet."

"Did she ask you to take it?"

"In so many words, no."

Coming to the motel was probably a mistake. He was driven by an unsettling unease about Clovis and the baby, and if he were honest with himself, a fatherly interest compelled him even more strongly. He couldn't shake that baby's helpless look and Clovis's despairing tales about her parents. What exactly had he hoped to find at the motel, and what did he think was his role? Seeing Arlette transformed from her unruffled self into this robe-clutching thing weakened him in some unexplainable way. What rights did he have to visit the child? He didn't even have the balls to tell his wife about what had happened.

He said, "You can't take the baby from Clovis."

"No one is suggesting that. She'll agree. She's got no other choice."

Why had Louis gone off on his insane, hopeless mission and left this struggling woman behind? Left *all* his women behind? What a dick.

"Look, Arlette, all Louis can do now is watch your wealth go down the crapper. And he thinks he's going to pull off the noble task of taking the college down with him. All in the name of Jesus. The man's nuts."

She stood. Maybe she'd get some fire back. But she didn't say anything.

"And," Back Bay said, "the president has written Louis off, just as he has me and probably Michelle and Abe. He'd just as soon see us gone. But in an odd sort of way, we've got his hands tied just as he has ours. The damndest thing I've ever seen."

She sat back down, arms dangling at her side. "All that's left is that poor baby," she said. "Maybe that's why I was brought into the whole affair—for her sake."

"Are you happy about all this?" asked Back Bay.

"I just might be." She rose again. "But I don't have much time to think about that. I need to clean up and get back to the other room."

He recognized his invitation to leave. "I'd like to see Clovis and her baby."

"Of course," she said, walking into the bathroom. "Maybe you can come up with a name. The mother appears to be open for suggestions."

When he knocked on the other door, the woman opened it softly. "Shh," she said. "The baby's finally asleep."

"I'm David Norman, the one who delivered the baby."

"Oh, yes. Clovis has been talking about you."

"May I come in?'

"I don't know why not."

He tiptoed through the darkened room. There on one bed slept Clovis and her baby. He couldn't help himself. Maybe the woman wouldn't notice.

"It's OK," she said.

He felt her hand on his back.

"It's fine to cry," she whispered. "There's been lots of that lately."

∼

One thing was certain: Arlette was not the same woman he had once fucked. And maybe he wasn't the same person either, which set him to wondering why he had leaped into the whole sordid affair with her in the first place. He never considered himself unhappily married; in fact, the last several years with his wife had been nearly problem-free. Financially secure, a calm life in Towson, plenty of respect and notoriety with his career. His wife had no reason to complain either—she had hit her stride as an elementary teacher and received nothing but acclaim from the community. But stupidly he had always left his sexual urges unbridled, and when they hit, he always let them trot right on unchecked. And others seemed to want him and didn't check theirs either.

And then there was the childless thing. Even though he and his wife had certainly considered children, they enjoyed and appreciated their lives too much to be interrupted. Until he delivered that child, he never knew that the gravitational pull from a baby's force field could be so strong. Then standing there watching that baby sleep had nearly caused his knees to crumple. The birth itself had been one of those tasks he'd performed under pressure, not understanding the significance at the time. Yet, in some small way, Back Bay knew the child was partially his, and standing there watching it, he sensed his attachment, his claim to the small life.

He would need to let things be. Who could buck Arlette's steely will? The woman was a force of nature.

Driving from the motel and back home, he fought off the most curious urge: to tell his wife everything—about fucking Arlette, about the baby. Why should the clouds have parted so suddenly to make him want to tell her? Was it the right thing?

Hell no, it wasn't the right thing! Christ, man. Come to your senses. Walk away from the mess you've stirred up and let the rest of those people go their way. You've got tennis to coach. A wife to live with. Let this be the one true and last big lesson.

Then he remembered the president. Back Bay had most definitely shot his wad with *that* man. Even the smallest slip down the line on Back Bay's part could force the president to ax him. The whole incident had gone into Back Bay's permanent record, and the son of a bitch might eventually, if the political time were right, let the incident out into the rumor mill, causing more pain down the road. That's the way college presidents did things.

Coming clean with his wife might be the best. But what a stupid move *that* could turn out to be!

Too much had happened in too short of a time. He had lots to think over, that was for damned sure.

QUITCLAIM DEEDS
CHAPTER 18

After meeting with the president, Louis had bluffed his way through the conversation with Back Bay, but on the plane back to St. Louis, all that strength had melted and left him a simpering scaredy-cat, afraid to face what he knew lay ahead: watching his empire crumble. For all the bravado he'd mustered in front of the president and Back Bay, Louis—in his isolation on the plane with nothing to read—thought of how he hadn't fooled the president one iota, and probably not Back Bay either. How could Louis have felt so emboldened and formidable at one moment and so craven and impotent the next? And where, by the way, was Jesus in all this? Where was His backing? Did Jesus back people at one moment, then abandon them the next? Convince them to destroy in His name, then convince them all was lost? And the most frightening thought of all: was Jesus playing Louis for a fool?

Surely it must have been the rarefied altitude in that plane that had caused Louis's brain and will to soften, because once on the ground, and after a good night's sleep in his own bed, he was imbued with the Jesus-renewed spirit again. It felt good to drive to Adam Fontleroy's office. The cold, practical counsel of an attorney would be just the ticket. Maybe like sparring with the Pharisees. Jesus always won those dogfights.

~

"Again, I tell you," said Adam Fontleroy, "you're out of your mind. Even when we were at DeSmet, Louis, I always took you for a smart guy, if not a bit gullible. Smarten up, my man. You wouldn't fool anyone at that damned college. Even if they're whimpering idiots, they'd check out, in detail, all the ramifications of what you're trying to play off as a bonanza to them. If it sounds too good to be true, then ... well you know the rest."

Louis's stomach began flipping again.

"And with that stupid-assed deal you made with that criminal outfit in Milwaukee, you fucked yourself up the ass. You've got zippo against them. You're going down, and I advise you to settle up immediately, or from what you've told me, they could do some real damage to your *family*, Louis. Hear me? Your family!"

Help me, Jesus.

Adam rocked back in his chair, and the red left his face. Good sign, thought Louis.

Finally, Adam said, "Quitclaim deeds."

"What?"

"That might be your only salvation right now. Sign over all your properties to them in quitclaim deeds."

Why hadn't Louis thought of that? Sure, the president would jump on the quitclaim deed bandwagon, and, bam, before he knew what hit him, the college would have possession of all Louis's property.

"That's brilliant," said Louis. "The college would absolutely lap that up."

Adam's head fell into his chest. "Holy shit, Louis."

"What?"

"I'm talking about signing quitclaim deeds over to that *Milwaukee group*. Get it in your melon that you've got nothing with that college anymore. All your ill-conceived plans to destroy that place are completely ridiculous. I'm talking about trying to save your family's lives here. To get the criminals off your back now. You don't have time to negotiate deals with them. Divest yourself of all your holdings quickly, and you divest yourself of any problems with that outfit. Understand? I'm talking to you as a friend, Louis. Listen to me."

There it was again. Louis was on top of the world one minute—in the shitter the next. "No other angles, Adam?"

Adam blew out a breath and walked around his desk. "I'm having an associate lawyer right now pull all your files and start preparing the papers. I'll even contact the group myself on your behalf and see that all is taken care of. It'll be a pleasure to speak with their slime-bucket lawyers in Milwaukee. I'm certain they're gentle, friendly folks. Don't you imagine?"

Louis sat alone in the office and watched black spots dance around the room. The blood must have been leaving his head. He put his head between his knees and then, in a few seconds, looked up again. No spots anymore. Louis took that as a good sign.

He arrived at the Kirkwood nursing home, with KFC, just before he knew his mother would be wheeled to lunch in the dining hall. Betty, the chief administrator, was not in, but when Sarah, second-in-charge, saw him in her doorway, she sprang from behind her desk. After the usual pleasantries, she assured Louis that he and his mother could most certainly have the north lounge for lunch. She said she was sure his mother would appreciate the KFC he brought, and she wished all the family members that visited residents were as kind and considerate as he was. He shook her hand, leaving the usual fifty dollars in her palm.

His mother appeared to be happy to see him, but wondered why in the hell he couldn't call before coming instead of surprising her all the time.

"Did you have a previous engagement?" Often that kind of humor worked with her.

"I was set to have my usual morning sex with the old fart across the hall, Louis. Now he's going to be disappointed."

Louis looked carefully to detect humor or disgust. He decided it was disgust.

"Sorry," he said.

"What did you bring?" she asked.

"The usual. But this time I got baked beans and macaroni salad instead of coleslaw and potato salad."

"Well, aren't you the clever one?"

Two nurse's assistants arrived, and Louis left the room—his usual routine—while they lifted her out of bed and into the wheelchair. He could never bear the thought of watching them wrangle the helpless woman out of bed. He often wondered if it was worse with her having a shot body and intact mind rather than a shot mind and intact body. This way, with the good mind, at least he could talk with her, which, in some way, was a good thing—he reckoned he deserved and needed most of the abuse she lobbed at him.

"She's ready, Mr. Lewis," one of the aides said, wheeling her into the hallway. "Doesn't she look pretty today? She likes the pink dressing gown she's wearing. Looks so good in it."

"A vision of loveliness," he said, trying for either humor or the truth, whichever might work for the moment.

"Which lounge?" asked his mother.

He took his position behind the wheelchair and handed the two aides their money, after which they fawned awhile then marched back down the hall. As he began pushing, he delivered his usual line, "Do you want a fast or slow ride? If fast, keep a lookout for radar." She liked it the first few times, but he was certain he'd worn it out over time.

"Just get me there, Louis."

This wasn't the appropriate mood for what he had to tell her this time.

"I got a mix of Extra Crispy and Original Recipe," he said. "So you can have your choice."

"Dandy and swell," she said.

This would take some effort.

The table in the lounge was littered with pieces of some board game, and by the time he'd cleared it, an aide had come trotting in apologizing about the mess, assuring them the table would be spic and span the next time.

"Thanks, dearie," his mother said.

The aide told them again she was sorry.

"We know," said his mother. "You're sorry."

The aide confirmed once again how sorry she was and stood in the doorway. Louis wasn't about to cross her palm, this time for nothing, so he began setting up their plates and food. When he looked up, she was gone.

"They're such toadies," his mother said.

"They take good care of you."

"Money talks."

The time was ripe—he thought he would tell her while they ate.

"Did you bring plenty of napkins?" she asked.

Damn. He popped up and walked down the hall to the dining hall. When he returned, her hands and mouth were already smeared with grease and most of the macaroni salad had fallen onto the large bib he had tied to her front.

"Go ahead and clean me up," she said. "I think I've had my fill."

She talked while he cleaned and continued talking as he began eating. She told him she knew why he had come and had been expecting the news ever since he had told her about his problems. She wondered what he had in mind for her to do now that he had no money. That, he said, is what he wanted to talk about. "Then talk," she said. "This should be interesting."

He lied about all he could for what must have been a good fifteen minutes. Talked about how the Milwaukee group had relented and about how he had engineered a settlement through his and their attorneys. It was a complicated business transaction, he told her, but in time, things would be even better than before.

When he finished his hopeful story, he had eaten the rest of the chicken and all the macaroni salad and baked beans. All the napkins lay in a messy heap before him.

"You never could lie worth a damn," she finally said.

"What do you mean?"

"Louis, just wheel me back to my cell. I've heard enough."

As he pushed her back down the hall, he wished the "fast or slow ride" line was fresh again. But some things could never be revived.

After she had been lifted back into her bed, she asked what else had happened in his life because it was clear to her something was weighing heavily on his mind and that, by the way, she didn't appreciate being lied to, and why did he think he could fool her with that claptrap?

Louis thought that maybe telling her the truth about all the unpleasantness surrounding Clovis's birth would balance out—and even negate—all his earlier lies. Use the truth to supplant the lies. Seemed a logical tactic. He told her all of the story about Clovis in exquisite detail and with such verve that he seemed to have been transported back to that time and place, feeling that he wasn't even in his mother's room, had been unaware of her presence. By the time he finished, he felt cleansed of something. The truth shall set you free!

He looked at his mother, who had been so quietly listening to his story. But as he looked more closely in the dim light, he noticed her eyes were closed. Then he heard the soft snores that, no doubt, had been covered up by his long and truthful story.

∽

The psychologist hadn't exactly seemed eager to arrange a spur-of-the-moment session, but Louis imagined the fear and futility in his voice must have convinced him to meet. Kind of like an emergency-room visit. Why shouldn't a psychologist's office offer the same services?

In the elevator, traveling to the twenty-eighth floor, Louis wondered if this might be a mistake, going there without Arlette, who, after all, had suggested they see this guy. But then, in truth, every session had been largely about Louis and *his* problems rather than *their* problems. Why not go solo once, especially at this point, when Louis had actually entertained some pretty troubling thoughts.

∽

"Suicidal ideation," corrected the psychologist.

Louis had just said "harming myself." Now he seemed to have the guy's full attention.

"How long have you had those thoughts?" asked the psychologist.

"About an hour and a half."

Louis told him about the visit with his mother.

"And why does she make you feel that way?"

"I'm beginning to think she always has."

"So is this the first time you've had suicidal thoughts after talking with her?"

"Yes."

"And tell me specifically what might have triggered it this time."

"She fell asleep when I told her about Clovis's baby and all that."

"All of what?"

"How much time do we have?" asked Louis, knowing the full story would last awhile.

"However long it takes."

Louis could feel the gurglings deep within but knew he could staunch them, could stem the tidal wave. If he broke down, the chance might never present itself again.

After telling the complete story about Clovis and the baby, the psychologist said, "And your mother?"

"My mother?"

"Why did your mother falling asleep during the story cause you to think of suicide?"

"That's a good question."

"Has she ever not listened to you at other times?"

"Many times."

"What was so special about this time?"

Louis was surprised at how blank his mind went. He tried his best to think. Nothing.

"Remember the theme of our earlier sessions with you and Arlette?"

"Tell me," said Louis. "My mind's empty."

"Destructive behavior."

That again. "I remember."

"Those behavioral patterns from you and Arlette were largely operating on a subconscious level—probably have been for years. And in your case, many years, stemming, probably, from your relationship with your mother."

Louis was working hard to understand.

"Making any connections?" asked the psychologist.

"I'm trying."

"For some reason, your destructive behavior simmered up from your unconscious to your conscious mind today. You thought of destroying yourself."

For the briefest of moments, Louis wanted to accuse the man of using stupid psychobabble. Then Louis shivered. Destroying himself?

"You're the doctor," said Louis. "Why did I want to destroy myself?"

"The answer lies within you."

"But Jesus has given me a new hope to live."

"Something broke that hope down when your mother didn't listen to your story."

Louis had to admit he had a point.

"You wanted your mother to be as interested as you were in the story about that girl's birth and baby."

"But I'm not that interested."

Now the psychologist was staring harder than ever, as if to say that Louis *was* interested.

"Why would I be so interested?" asked Louis.

"Maybe because the opposite of destruction came into your life. Birth. A new life."

"But the baby didn't come into my life. She's Clovis's baby."

"What does Arlette say about it?"

"About what?"

"About whose baby it is."

Louis didn't appreciate the implication behind that.

"All I'm asking is for you to think about something," said the psychologist. "Your mother once again ignored what you said, but this time, when the news was about the blessed event of a new life into your world, your mother destroyed a new source of hope. Maybe you weren't aware that was going on in your head. You've been so accustomed to blindly banking on your mother's opinions—and secretly resenting them—that when she destroyed hope, instead of facing her squarely, which you apparently rarely have, you turned to the ultimate destructive behavior—destroying yourself."

Far too much to contemplate.

"Do you think what I said has any credence?" asked the psychologist.

"I certainly hope not."

Louis must have been sitting silently for a long time, because the next thing he knew, the psychologist was asking if he wanted to say anything at all.

"I don't know," said Louis.

"That's fine." The psychologist moved slightly in his chair. "Now, we always like to end a session with a goal, a plan of action, or an insight gained. Anything to say along those lines?"

Louis said he couldn't think of anything.

"What do you plan to do?" asked the psychologist.

Louis realized his options had shrunk considerably in the last few hours. "Go back to Redfern," he said. "See what's up there."

"Good plan. When you get there, you might be surprised."

Louis was sure that would be true.

NAME THIS CHILD

Michelle needed to talk sense into someone, but whether to start with Clovis or her mother was the question. Clovis usually stared off into space and generally acted weird regardless of who was around; her mother thought the world was full of lollipops and roses and couldn't talk about anything but the baby, who, by the way, still didn't have a name.

Michelle felt like a mother to both Clovis and her mother—on top of going to classes, Michelle appeared to be the only one worrying about what might happen next. The whole situation wouldn't resolve itself by people just sitting around in motel rooms. If her father were in town, he at least would make a decision, even if the wrong one. And she hadn't even seen Coach Norman. It seemed to Michelle he had a big old stake in the matter.

But it was Abe she could turn to, and for the next days, when not in classes or at the motel, they were somewhere alone talking. There was so much to talk about. And so far they hadn't missed sex at all (now that their perfect hangout was spoiled). So, they talked about what to do, with Michelle listening and marveling at Abe's insights. He sure was a good thinker!

He thought the president knew that Coach Norman and Michelle's mom were having an affair and that Abe was Muslim. Michelle asked him why the president didn't bring it up, and Abe said the president didn't want to show all his cards, to hold something back to use later if needed. Michelle asked when he might need to use that. Abe wasn't sure. Maybe if one of them (including Michelle's parents, Coach Norman, or even Clovis) told what happened. Then the president would be able to come back with something and force Abe and Coach Norman to leave the college.

Michelle wanted to follow Abe's logic about that, but wasn't certain she could. If the president kicked out Abe and Coach Norman, Michelle asked, couldn't the two of them then just say what happened without any fear of being hurt? Abe thought for a long time. He said Michelle was right. It didn't make much sense. Then what was the president afraid of besides not wanting people to know that a student had a baby in the locker room? What was the big deal? Maybe that was enough, said Abe. Somehow it didn't seem to be enough, but what did Michelle know about such things?

Finally Michelle slapped herself on the forehead, "It's my dad. The president wants his money."

Abe agreed that Michelle's dad was the bargaining chip. Was that a good thing? Neither one could say. But her mother had told her all the money was gone. Could that be true?

Michelle held Abe's hand for a long time as they sat on a bench close to Hamilton Hall. She thought about how her father always seemed to put himself into the center of everything, making her and her mother's worlds revolve around his. It just wasn't fair; especially this time, when Coach Norman was in the middle of everything and did such a wonderful job with the birth. Why was her father suddenly pulling strings as always? On top of that, Clovis was Michelle's roommate and friend. If anyone was to pull strings, it should be one of them.

She snuggled closer to Abe and felt his hand creep gently up her leg, right there on the bench, in full view. He stopped, then retreated. She wondered if he were starting to pulse, as she was. But where could they go? No locker room this time. God, she wanted to kiss him. She reached into her backpack, pulling out her phone.

"Mom, we've got to talk."

"Fine."

"Can you pick up Abe and me?"

"But the baby," said her mom.

Michelle shook her head hopelessly. "Clovis and that other woman are there. Come pick us up in front of Hamilton Hall."

"OK. Give me a few minutes."

"Abe and I need some time alone."

"What do you mean?"

"In the motel room." Had Michelle ever been so bold with her mother? "Look," said Michelle. "We're all adults here."

Her mother wasn't saying a thing.

"Besides," continued Michelle, "later today, all of us need to talk. Including Coach Norman. He needs to be there with us. Without Dad. He's not back yet, is he?"

"No."

"We've got to make some decisions."

Michelle reached for Abe's hand. "No one's doing anything, Mom, and it's time things started to move."

"What do you have in mind?"

"We just need to talk without Dad."

"He's flying in tomorrow."

Her stomach jumped at the thought of her dad, his power and control.

"Please pick us up."

Nothing.

"Mom?"

"OK, honey."

Was her mother crying? Either that or taking a long drink.

"Mom, are you drinking?"

"I haven't had a drink since this baby was born."

Abe called Coach Norman at his office and told him he should meet with everyone at the motel that evening. Michelle was amazed at the sway Abe seemed to hold over that man. The conversation was short.

"He'll be there," said Abe.

They walked slowly to the front of Hamilton Hall and sat on the steps waiting for Michelle's mom.

Michelle's mom was fine with letting her and Abe have the other motel room to themselves for a while. It felt a little creepy with her mother right next door, but Michelle soon forgot as Abe engulfed her. She found herself relaxing and enjoying the sheer tenderness of his movements, the way he controlled the love making so effortlessly. After her first orgasm (he hadn't come yet; was this the way most men proceeded?) and when she had regained a bit of clarity, she wondered about Abe's sexual experiences. Why not ask?

"Anyone at Redfern?" she asked.

"Three," he said so matter-of-factly that she nearly laughed from the jolt of it before feeling a mix of anger and sadness. "But we've kept it secret from everyone."

"Who?" she asked.

When he told her, she didn't feel so bad because she had met them and knew he couldn't come close to loving them the way he did her. She wanted to talk more about them, but soon he was doing his business full force again. After, she made him tell her more, and they both laughed about his escapades. She felt so grown up with Abe. Later, showering with him was especially delightful. Their first time.

She and Abe were holding hands as they walked into her mother's room, and there sat Coach Norman with the baby in his arms. He looked tense and frozen, but he was smiling. Clovis lay on the bed, eyes closed, and Michelle's mother was hovering over Back Bay. She was smiling, too, and when she placed her hand on Back Bay's shoulder, Michelle wondered if the two were in love. They could have been a couple with their first child.

"Where's that woman?" asked Michelle.

"Sent her away for today."

"Good."

Michelle went to Clovis, pushed at her playfully, then watched a faint smile creep onto her face; she hadn't been asleep at all. Everyone in the room was smiling, except for the baby, but to Michelle she looked happy. Abe sat on the bed beside Michelle and reached over and stroked Clovis's hair. What a gentle man.

"We must name the child," said Abe.

Clovis's smile left, but she regarded Abe intently as he removed his hand from her head and stood upright. Michelle shivered as Abe's power swept the room.

"My tradition says the child should bear the father's name. I am Abdul al-Fiasa, which means *Of Fiasa*, my father. Abdul is *my* name."

"There is no father," said Clovis.

Michelle wondered if everyone in the room understood what Clovis was saying.

"You must choose a father," said Abe.

Abe was rigid, no longer gentle, and Michelle was frightened. Clovis still gazed earnestly at him. "No father," she said.

"But you must name her," said Abe.

"Abigail," said Clovis, finally.

Abe looked at Back Bay holding the baby. Now all of them were looking.

"Lewis," said Clovis. "Abigail Lewis."

Michelle was the first to cry.

~

That sealed it for Arlette. For two days she had imagined her and Louis keeping the baby, and through Abe's prompting, Clovis had confirmed it. The child was theirs—at least for the time being. Clovis had shown no interest in the child. Had she bequeathed Abigail to them? Forever? There was no way of knowing and no sense pursuing it any further because Abe had taken charge and was talking about practical matters. It was good someone was because Arlette had no interest in anything beyond the room.

Yet, Back Bay had, in a way, nudged her out of the single-mindedness the baby had plunged her into. When he walked into the room, she knew she didn't want much more to do with him. And when she put her hand on his shoulder—to test her emotions to be certain—she felt only the shoulder of a man she had once fucked but did not care to love. Louis was enough. It was easy to love a man with Louis's obvious faults and transparent emotions. Not a lot of work involved in that any more.

The others were discussing what to do next. She should pay attention.

"He made me very angry," Abe was telling Back Bay.

Arlette wondered who. Back Bay still held the baby, who was falling asleep. He rocked gently.

"What makes you think he wants to get rid of us?" asked Back Bay.

Were they referring to Louis?

"He knows I'm Muslim and that you had sex with Mrs. Lewis."

Of course Louis knows, she thought.

"Well," said Back Bay, "he can fire my ass if he wants. And what's he going to do about you with one year left?"

Arlette guessed they were actually talking about the president of Redfern.

Abe was standing rigidly by the bed. "I don't like waiting on a man like that," said Abe. "I want to leave."

Arlette watched Michelle lurch slightly where she was sitting on the bed. "Abe?" Michelle said.

"To leave this place with Michelle."

Michelle put her hand to her mouth then looked at Arlette.

"All of us should leave," he said.

Exactly, Arlette thought. What were they doing there in the first place? Louis and his precious desires had always sent them scampering to wherever the hell he wanted. Maybe, just maybe, Louis had made his last fucked-up decision. And now this tall, Muslim man was talking sense. This was too rich!

"All of us pack up and leave Redfern?" asked Back Bay, as he swept his arm around the room. His eyes landed on Clovis in the bed. Arlette had never seen her so focused.

Clovis lifted her hand, as though she were in a classroom asking to be heard. "I stay. Abigail goes."

Arlette held her breath, as Clovis looked directly at her.

"You and Mr. Lewis will give her a Christian home."

Now there was a novel notion. Raise this girl to be a little Louis-Christian. But what Arlette thought might be a smirky little laugh traveling up her throat turned out to be a full-out sob. She imagined she was telling Clovis that she and Louis would most certainly raise Abigail, when, really, all that erupted was a gush of tears and a shudder. The tremors wouldn't stop.

~

The thought of Arlette and Back Bay going off with the baby and starting a new life had certainly crossed his mind, especially as he sat in the motel room holding the child. But Back Bay had learned long ago not to give much leash to his overactive imagination: Arlette would be too much of a handful, even if he could pry her away from Louis. And then how could he possibly negotiate leaving his wife and all the shit that would ensue? But this baby, this Abigail was indeed incredible! When Arlette started her slobbering after Clovis gave the baby away to her, he was biting his lower lip and imagining starting over with Arlette and Abigail anew. The kid in his arms had turned him into mush.

Arlette was still crying, which had caused the whole room to erupt in emotion, including Clovis in the bed, bellowing like a cow. He and Abe were the only ones containing themselves, and Back Bay wasn't sure he could keep munching down on his lip any longer without tearing it apart.

Abe had certainly opened a can of worms with his crack about all of them leaving Redfern. Just great. No one in the room had set down roots like Back Bay had, and here was a kid suggesting he pack up and leave his coaching career and home. Just march off because some overweight, repressed, freshman girl dropped a baby in his hands. But, my God, now the shit was hitting several fans. And there was the wild-assed Louis with the possibility of doing all manner of damage to several people. Yet, Abe was no doubt right: the only reason the president hadn't shit-canned them was because he still thought Louis was good for lots of money. And the truth was that soon Louis wouldn't have a dime.

Clovis had stopped her bawling, and the other two women their crying. They were all standing in the middle of the room hugging—with help Clovis had lumbered out of bed—and telling each other how much they loved one another. Abigail didn't stir in his arms during all the commotion.

And the most amazing sentiment swept Back Bay as he watched the love fest continue. He was not biting his lip any longer. All the unpleasant events he'd recently been plunged into had transfigured themselves into something of a placid resignation. *What the hell?* he thought. Just what was the problem? Maybe there wasn't one at all. Look at those people; and here he was sitting holding a baby. Perhaps he would tell his wife about the baby and his meeting with the president (of course there'd be no need to tell her about fucking Arlette) and be done with it. Why couldn't he pursue other jobs? After all, Abe seemed to be willing to call the shots himself rather than letting the president make the first move. Why shouldn't he and his wife do the same? Dropping one set doesn't mean the match is lost. Fight his way out of this. Maybe even move to St. Louis, inquire into a coaching job at St. Louis University or do private coaching until something better came along. Lots of options, really. Take control of the game. Rush the net, by God!

Things were simmering down, all of them back to a semblance of composure, and there he remained with the sleeping Abigail. Clovis sat on the edge of the bed with her legs spread while Arlette, Michelle, and Abe huddled like lost lovers.

"So what's the program?" he asked no one in particular.

"We're so happy for Abigail," said Clovis, apropos of nothing.

"I mean, what are you going to do now?" he asked.

He wasn't sure the others heard him. He didn't intend to have a conversation with Clovis. "I'm going to stay," she said. "And do God's work here at Redfern."

You stupid thing, thought Back Bay. If God's work involves fucking someone, make sure God supplies the condoms. "Good idea," said Back Bay. "Stay in school."

"I've been praying about it," said Clovis. "It's God's will."

That takes care of one of them.

"How about the rest of you?" he shouted at the others. Abigail jumped like she'd been goosed.

Arlette wheeled. "David, you've frightened the baby."

Abigail twisted her mouth then let out a mini squall followed by a bona fide cry. Arlette took the baby. "Poor little Abigail. Did the mean coach make you cry?"

There was no way to win. Another try. "So what are the rest of you going to do?"

Michelle and Abe were looking over Arlette's shoulder as she rocked and comforted Abigail. "Packing up and leaving," said Michelle, looking to Abe for what appeared to be some kind of confirmation.

"Abe?" asked Back Bay.

"Maybe Algeria," he said.

Michelle nuzzled close to him.

With the baby in someone else's arms, Back Bay saw no need to stay longer. He walked past Arlette toward the door.

"David," said Arlette. "Please be here when Louis arrives."

"Why's that?" he asked, hand on the doorknob.

"We're all in this together."

She had a point. Still standing there, he dreaded the idea of being in Louis's presence again. But the thing that gripped him the tightest as he went out the door was whether Abe really meant what he just said about leaving with Michelle.

CLOSING THE DOOR
CHAPTER 20

Louis worked a pretty sweet deal getting the Milwaukee group to rent him a unit in an apartment complex he had deeded over. And the sons of bitches didn't pull *all* the strings by any means because he negotiated tough: guaranteed himself the largest unit in the complex at half its rent. Oh, sure they didn't cotton to the plan at first—the crafty shysters—but Louis stood pat, and they saw it his way. He and Arlette could move in two weeks. Their little grins and leers didn't fool him; they knew they'd been bested on that one. (Of course he didn't tell them that he was quaking in his depths with having his family holed up in a Super Eight until he could find a place to live.)

He had to admit, they had shown no mercy as they opened the proceedings with the kind of not-so-subtle threats that would make Tony Soprano shiver. He'd never been so scared in his life, and he couldn't wait to get right to the quitclaim deed news. Man, did they jump at that. It was like they had come loaded for bear and found out they wouldn't even need a pop gun. He'd outmaneuvered them. At least that was the way he looked at it.

And my, oh my, did he cover his ass on the move by spreading the word to everyone that he and Arlette were merely *transitioning* from one place to another. He couldn't count how many people wanted to know why he would move from the magnificent Lewis estate way out to west St. Louis County in one of his apartment complexes, notwithstanding its obvious class and location. He said he'd gotten an amazing offer on the estate that he couldn't bear to turn down, and so why not just take advantage of things immediately and bivouac for a while out in the boonies until something else opened up? People always laughed at the boonies part because obviously that part of West County was *not* the boonies.

"Well, you've got a good landlord," one of them quipped.

"Did you have to pay a big damage deposit?" another said.

"Think you'll get evicted?"

In a way, it was great fun, pulling the wool.

He took solace in the fact that he'd done all he could in a messed-up situation about which he was controlling almost nothing. But finding a place to live showed he still had something going for him—even if Arlette and the rest of them had completely taken leave of their senses. Gone nuts!

All Louis ever wanted was the best for his family—and, of course, he also wanted to exact a measure of revenge from the Christian college he had once trusted implicitly; he was having trouble even saying the name Redfern. *Odious* was the word for that place and certain people connected with it. Back Bay Norman came to mind. Louis realized he had wrongly and naively forgiven the man for sleeping with his wife, because recently Louis heard straight from the coach's mouth he never had any intention of buttering up Webster Boyd so Louis could carry out his plan of destroying the college, never mind that the plan wouldn't have worked anyway. Louis had bargained in good faith with Back Bay to help broker the college's downfall by forgiving Back Bay his adultery with Arlette. A little quid pro quo, if you will. But no. After the coach learned Louis's holdings and wealth were kaput and Louis had no bargaining chip, Back Bay just came out and told Louis right there in the Super Eight in front of Clovis, the baby, Arlette, Michelle, and Abe that he had never had any notion of helping out. Louis guessed all Back Bay really cared about was his own skin and told him so. Back Bay just laughed. And did the others come to Louis's rescue? No!

"You mean to say," he asked Arlette and Michelle, "that you're going to let him talk to me that way?"

Michelle wouldn't look at him, and Arlette, of course, was occupied with that damned child. Abe's eyes were boring into him, and Clovis perked up.

"Mr. Lewis," the blimp in the bed said, "some of us don't appreciate that you wanted to harm Redfern."

Louis exploded. "You," he pointed to Back Bay, "had sex with my wife, and you," he pointed to Abe, "are a Christian-hating Muslim who has designs on my daughter. In a nutshell, Clovis, that's what your blessed Redfern has done for me."

Louis thought she might take flight from the bed and crush him, but instead it sent her into another round of crying, the likes of which he had seen several times since his return to Towson.

"Great," he said, waving his arms. "Just great."

Louis proudly announced his apartment procurement, effective in two weeks. Arlette said Michelle and Abe would stay in the apartment. Louis's mouth dropped.

That's when Abe dropped the bomb. "Michelle and I will be with you only for a brief time in the new apartment."

"What are you saying?" Louis asked Abe.

Abe looked to Michelle. "Abe and I are traveling to Algeria to meet his parents."

Louis was struck immediately and revoltingly with his sudden lack of money. "Exactly how are you getting there? Tramp steamer?"

"We may stay there. Settle down," Michelle said. "Abe says it's a good country."

Arlette was still fiddling with the baby, so there was no ally to be found. "Will you marry him?" he asked Michelle, trying to swallow a gasp.

"We love each other," they both said, as if rehearsed.

He couldn't tell if the hand on his shoulders was Michelle's or Arlette's. When he finally looked up, Abe himself was there, lightly massaging. Louis had to admit it was comforting. Then from somewhere within him fizzed up a bit of mockery that both shocked and delighted him.

"I suppose you're going to tell me next Back Bay Norman will be our house guest, too."

"Only if he wishes," said Arlette, who apparently had been listening all along while Abigail fussed in her arms. "He and his wife are welcome to visit anytime."

"Very magnanimous of you," Louis said.

"Don't mention it," said Arlette. "David and I are history."

"Coach?" said Louis. "What will you do?"

"Keep the president and Webster Boyd happy until I can plot an exit strategy—with my wife."

Louis's and Arlette's eyes met, and they grinned at one another for the first time in a while. Louis thought it might be the right time for his own bomb-dropping, now that everyone else had made plans behind his back. "Guess what loyal son can't afford nursing home fees anymore?"

Arlette's quick glance was the most spontaneous reaction he'd seen in her since arriving. "What are you saying?" asked Arlette.

"There are three bedrooms in the apartment," he said. "Enough for mother to have her own room."

"God help us all," said Arlette, making the sign of the cross. Then she countered with her own bomb by telling Louis they were keeping Abigail, which nearly sent Louis into apoplexy; Abe held Louis firmly in the chair to keep him from toppling over. When he had righted himself, with Abe's help, he searched the others' faces, hoping maybe it was only a cruel joke at his expense.

"Sounds like," said Arlette, "it'll be you, me, Abigail, your mother, Michelle, and Abe in a cozy apartment."

"You're serious?"

"A new start," she said.

He had to admit she was right about that.

"Dad, Abe and I won't be there long," Michelle said. "Then it'll be just Grandma, you, Mom, and Abigail."

"But ..."

"Go back to St. Louis," Arlette said, "and get things ready. Let us know when we should show up."

That baby had obviously poisoned the woman's mind. "But ..."

"I've already thought some things through," Arlette said. "We can make things all legal. Clovis can sign some papers, and we'll eventually have Abigail as our own. No one will be breaking any laws, and Clovis can stay in school, then visit us any time she wants. Right, Clovis?"

"That's right, Mrs. Lewis."

"But ..." So many things were swirling that Louis couldn't find a place to start.

"Dad," said Michelle. "This would make everyone happy."

How in God's name could anyone be happy? "My whole world has come crashing down."

"Suck it up," said Back Bay.

Louis had forgotten he was there.

"Everyone else is moving on," continued Back Bay. "Maybe you should, too."

Louis wondered if he should be taking this—the man had no right to speak to him that way in front of the others. But nothing would come out of Louis's mouth.

"Save just enough from our estate to fill the apartment," said Arlette. "You decide. I'll shop for baby furniture when I get there."

"This is so exciting," said Michelle, her head on Abe's shoulder.

"It's not exciting worth a damn!" Louis blurted, immediately sorry he'd said it. But no one seemed to have heard.

It was nearly impossible to take stock of everything he'd just been subjected to, but as he watched all of them pool together as if he weren't there—leaving him secluded in the small room with nothing more to do than think things through—he gathered the details of what had been foisted upon him: Arlette had become engrossed with that child to the point of obsession and, heaven help them all, talked about adoption, which Louis would do all he could to block; Michelle was walking away from a college tennis program to marry an Arab Muslim with the distinct likelihood of converting and raising dark, towel-headed children; Coach Norman said he would eventually leave a prestigious coaching job, with the consolation prize to Louis of returning Arlette. The only one coming close to doing the right thing was Clovis Ginch, who would stay at Redfern—although the circumstances she'd set in motion were tangled up in everything else. But even the God-fearing Clovis was halfway off her nut!

Was Louis the only sane person left standing?

~

While the notion of formal confession was definitely a Catholic premise and one Louis was pretty sure contradicted biblical teachings, the potential value of such an act became more and more enticing as he made his way back to St. Louis. Since there was no way he could possibly reconcile Arlette's, Michelle's, and Abe's proposed actions with everything that was good and decent, getting Pastor Ummell's take might relieve some of the heart-heaviness he was carrying and even provide a solution or two. Louis might even admit to the cause of the bombing, if he gauged Pastor's receptiveness. Play it by ear.

"Prayer changes things," said Pastor, after Louis told him he needed some helpful advice concerning his family.

On the plane coming back, Louis had offered up some prayers— mostly out of sheer fear and trembling. Being closer to God, up that high, Louis reasoned, might even add a dimension not afforded on the ground, although he was sure that in a more lucid state, he might not have resorted to such a simple thought. After all, the pastor had once told the congregation in a sermon that the Holy Spirit abided with people always. Besides, Louis was pretty certain God didn't live high up above the clouds. Exactly where He was, though, troubled Louis from time to time.

"They seemed secure in what they said they were going to do," Louis replied to Pastor's admonition.

"Never, never doubt what God can do."

When Louis had called asking for a counseling session with Pastor Ummell, he had apparently cleared his appointment book, because the next day after he arrived, Louis was in the wood-paneled office with a cup of coffee. Something in Louis's mind feared Pastor's intentions; the man still wanted his money.

Louis began by saying Arlette wanted to adopt a newborn child. Telling more than that wouldn't be prudent.

"Praise God," said the pastor. "A noble act."

"I'm not at all certain I want a child," said Louis.

"Have you and Arlette prayed about it?"

"No."

"God's will is not discernable except through prayer."

Louis wondered if Arlette had prayed about it. Likely not. Then he remembered Clovis.

"I'm sure Clovis has."

"And who is that?"

"The child's mother. A fine Christian woman."

Louis felt he was wearing heavy boots that were slowly sinking into mud.

"You've met the mother?"

"Yes."

"I see. Through an adoption agency?"

The boots were making a sucking sound as he tried to lift them.

"Yes. An adoption agency."

Pastor's fingers on his right hand tapped the desk. "In St. Louis?"

"Actually," said Louis, "in Towson, Indiana."

"There's an adoption agency there?"

"Yes." If Louis didn't reach down and begin yanking at the boots, he'd be mired there for good. "Not many people know about it. A fine place."

"A state or private agency?"

"That's a good question. Arlette has handled all the details."

Now both of Pastor's hands were on the table, his fingers beating out a menacing rhythm.

"I see," said the pastor. More finger drumming.

Jump in and rescue this, thought Louis. "The place came highly recommended. Arlette says it's top-notch."

"Agencies don't usually allow prospective adoptive parents to see the birth parents before adoption. That would be highly irregular."

"In our case they made an exception."

"Have you seen the child?"

"Oh, she's a fine, healthy child. Cute, too."

"So you've seen it?"

"Yes."

The fingers stopped moving, and Louis saw no way to pull out of the mud. He was up to his knees.

"I'm troubled by what I'm hearing," said Pastor Ummell.

"And so am I. That's why I'm here."

"Louis, as a member of the clergy, I'm duty-bound to hold as confidential all that transpires in a session such as this."

"I understand."

"You may tell me the truth of what is actually troubling you."

Truth was truth, thought Louis. Ignore the details and cut to the essentials. "I don't think we should adopt that child."

"Louis, you have forced me to read between the lines. I must ask you a question that I see embedded in your answers."

Louis had sunk to his armpits in mud. But his hands were still free. "What's your question, Pastor?"

"Is the child you speak of Michelle's baby? Did she go off to Towson, Indiana to have it? To hide from this congregation and the larger community?"

Now the man was speaking foolishness. "Of course not. How could you ever think that?"

"I'm growing increasingly impatient with what you're telling me. For me to help you, you must speak honestly."

But how could Louis do that now, after he'd already mired himself in the quicksand? To retreat now and fess up would destroy everything he'd built up with the pastor and Crestview Temple.

Then Louis felt his mind running at time-warp speed, the speed of light, just like in the old days when he was debating at DeSmet. *The man's caught me in lies that would be ridiculous to wriggle out of. He wants my money, money I don't have. The man might just be acting out of selfish motives rather than honestly wanting to help me. Look at him sitting there like a Pharisee! Since my world is crashing down anyway, why did I think coming here would help what is inevitably and inexorably happening around me? What was I thinking?*

"You know what, Pastor?"

Pastor's hands were folded sedately on the desk. He nodded.

Look at the son of a bitch. He's so smug that he doesn't even need to say anything!

"I made a mistake coming here," said Louis. "I should have known all along I didn't need your advice. Arlette and I will handle this adoption on our own terms."

Was that a twinkle in the man's eyes?

"I'm sorry," said Pastor, "that you feel you have to fabricate excuses for what has happened to Michelle."

Jumping across the desk and knocking the holy shit out of the man would feel plenty good. "I haven't given you excuses, Pastor."

Still that smug silence. Louis placed his hands on the arms of the wingback chair and rose slowly, thinking of how to exit gracefully. If Pastor could make a silent statement, why couldn't Louis? As he turned the doorknob to leave, he wondered if Pastor might give him a parting shot, a guilt-ridden admonition.

"Just leave the door open," said Pastor. "I have another appointment in five minutes."

All Louis could think to say was, "OK."

But it felt good to close the door behind him.

⁓

He wasn't completely destitute; he still had a couple of checking accounts and certificates of deposit he could draw from for expenses. Then there were two mutual funds he could cash in. When those ran dry, it was anyone's guess. He'd worry about that after everything and everyone had been safely packed into the apartment.

If nothing else, he was finally in complete control of something. He drove to the estate and made a run of the house, and within fifteen minutes had mentally cataloged everything he thought would fit into the new apartment, and in another fifteen minutes had rented a storage unit for the remainder. Then he called a moving company and scheduled to have everything moved either to the apartment or storage unit. This should work, he told himself.

He spent a few nights in the estate by himself. Most nights he dreamed of being lost in a vacant high-rise building, screaming for custodians or night watchmen to help him find his way out because, somewhere in his mind, he had an inkling the building was scheduled for demolition the next day. And what if he couldn't get out?

CLEAN SWEEP

CHAPTER 21

"No need to come back here," said Arlette, from the Super Eight in Towson. "As I said, all's well."

Louis hadn't yet told her of his recent success in furnishing the apartment. He didn't mind—saving the good news for last would make things even sweeter. He hadn't heard her so happy in weeks, her voice fairly dripping with contentment and calm. "Have you been drinking much?" he asked. "No," she said, "not a drop. Have to stay on top of my game for Abigail."

But why wouldn't she have also needed to stay on top of her game for him and Michelle all those years? That's what Louis wanted to know, but he knew better than ask. As she went on and on, he listened patiently, knowing later he'd tell her all about the move.

"Abigail has learned to nurse so well and gets plenty of milk."

"That's good," said Louis. With boobs the size of Clovis's, who wouldn't?

Then Arlette started in on all the baby things she had bought at Walmart, naming and describing each item in such tender and doting detail that Louis found himself shutting it out and spinning a pencil on the coffee table before him. He scanned the room. The way he'd arranged the furniture wasn't bad, really.

"How's Clovis?" he asked at a break in the litany.

"Sweet and happy. Oh course, she has her little down times—you know, postpartum depression, I'm sure—but she knows Abigail will have a caring home. And she'll get to see her child whenever she wants. Right, Clovis?"

Louis heard a shout, "I love you, Mr. Lewis." Clovis had yelled so clearly that she might have been on the phone herself.

What was he supposed to say to that? "Tell Clovis," said Louis, "that Abigail will have a fine home." Louis clamped his jaw at the thought of keeping the little nipper.

"And a Christian home," shouted Clovis.

"Certainly," Louis replied. That is, if Arlette didn't stand in the way.

"How's Michelle?" Louis asked. About Abe, he wasn't so interested.

"They're occupying the room next door."

They're? For a nanosecond the full impact of the situation hadn't accosted him. When it did, he slammed his fist on the coffee table, sending the pencil flying. "They're staying together in the same room? Sleeping there?"

"Now, Louis," said Arlette. "Calm down. They're acting like real adults."

"But they're not adults," he shouted.

"Things here are going so smoothly that ..."

"Those two kids are having illicit sex with your approval!"

The young folks would have a rude and sudden awakening when they found their little cohabitation plans shot all to hell in Louis's apartment, the place he'd worked so hard to establish. But wait. Three bedrooms. His mom in one, he and Arlette in the other. He hadn't fully considered Michelle and Abe. Things would just have to get worked out. No teenage fornication in *his* house—that is, apartment.

"That will surely stop once they're here," he said.

"Whatever," said Arlette.

Louis may have heard something crashing, falling into splinters. He stopped for a moment. It was his life he heard tumbling and clanking to the ground, and he knew it—as sure as he knew Michelle and Abe would share the bedroom in his apartment and end up going to Algeria; as sure as he knew Abigail would intrude into the rest of his life; as sure as he knew Arlette would devote the next considerable years to raising a child not their own. The bitterness of it all rose to the back of his throat like bile, and he could not speak with Arlette further.

When he hung up, she was saying something about Back Bay Norman. Louis didn't catch all of it, but her tone was amiable, good humored. Something about Back Bay being with his wife and working on their marriage.

His dear Arlette had reconciled the current events into her life effortlessly and harmoniously. It was actually a pleasure listening to the richness of her voice and demeanor, contrasting so sharply with his despondency and hopelessness. Hanging up was probably the wrong thing to do; but he did, and was alone on the couch by the coffee table.

He'd call her back later and say they must have gotten cut off by some unfortunate phone disconnection. *Disconnection* was, of course, the correct word. There was too much disconnection going on in his life while others were finding new and thrilling connections.

He thought he'd continue sitting on the couch until either Arlette called him back or until his mother, in her new bedroom—complete with the hospital bed and all the other equipment he outfitted her with—called for him. He could have paid the next few months' fees at the nursing home, but why not make a clean sweep and just move her in now? Not postpone the inevitable. He had set her up in the master bedroom, the one with its own bathroom. Why did he do that? She couldn't use the bathroom anyway, staying diapered all day as she was. (Changing her diaper wasn't as bad as he thought it might be.) Surely a little altercation would arise with Arlette when she arrived. Or maybe the kids would cabbage onto the bedroom, of course with Arlette's approval. Still, that was what he had done, and things would stay the same for a little while.

The apartment was pleasantly quiet. Yet, *he* was anything but quiet. *Scared shitless* is the way he would once have described his state. But he couldn't say exactly what he was so frightened of, except that he *was*.

Now that he'd finished setting up the apartment, there was nothing left to do but wait. Maybe he wouldn't tell the others about the apartment, let them hang out in the Super Eight for days—possibly even abandon them forever. But doing that would scare him more than anything, especially having to deal with his mother alone.

He decided he needed some control—that was it, pure and simple. Regain the upper hand. Just like in the old days. Just a modicum of control would suffice with the people in his life. A teeny bit.

His mother was still silent, probably sleeping or just staring off as she usually did. Going into check would not do a thing. She might start in on him, and he was savoring the quiet too much.

Think about things some more, Louis told himself. Analyze. Plan your next move. But the more he thought about next moves, the more desperate he became—forlorn, defeatist.

Then the most remarkable—even stupefying—realization overcame him, almost like a fleeting interlude from all that had been assailing him: Possibly, just possibly, people can't control life. Only give in to it. Hum. Submit, Louis, submit. But then that might be one of the most naive and trite thoughts he'd ever had. Submit to what exactly?

He rose from the couch and made his way toward his mother's room. Did Jesus ever say anything about submitting? It's possible. Maybe about giving to others ... going the extra mile.

"Louis," he heard his mother faintly say.

He walked down the hallway. "I'm coming." As he went into the master bedroom, she was staring straight at him. "What do you need?" he asked.

Her face was blank.

"You called for me," he said.

"Yes, I know."

"So what is it?"

"I seem to have forgotten."

"Thank God for small favors," he said.

"What?"

Louis walked from the room. "Small favors," he repeated.

Back in the living room he sat on the couch and stared at the coffee table, noticing the pencil had fallen to the floor. Would he be happy with small favors? Would Arlette?

Only vaguely realizing he had picked up the pencil, he set it in motion and watched it spin on the table. When it stopped, he spun it again ... again ... again. Finally allowing it to stop, he felt no duty or obligation whatsoever to keep it spinning. The more he might spin it, the more it would stop, and then he'd have to keep it up. What a silly compulsion! Just let things be what they are.

The couch was soft, the apartment still, no more spinning. He thought he might take a little nap, maybe just a short unplanned one in the middle of the day. What could it hurt? Seemed the rest of his life was pretty much planned out for him anyway. He stretched his legs out the full length of the couch, then flipped his shoes off and sent them, one by one, flying across the room. This was his place and people weren't intruding. And even when they eventually would, he wondered if such small favors like taking a nap in his own apartment might continue to grant him the same measure of contentment that was slowly washing over him. A silent apartment, comfortable couch, old and harmless mother, the prospect of a short nap with his shoes off. He might even take his socks off, too. All pleasures worth savoring for the moment.

The rest of his life would just have to wait.